ACCLAIM FOR JEREMY BATES

"Will remind readers what chattering teeth sound like."
—*Kirkus Reviews*

"Voracious readers of horror will delightfully consume the contents of Bates's World's Scariest Places books."
—*Publishers Weekly*

"Creatively creepy and sure to scare." —*The Japan Times*

"Jeremy Bates writes like a deviant angel I'm glad doesn't live on my shoulder."
—Christian Galacar, author of GILCHRIST

"Thriller fans and readers of Stephen King, Joe Lansdale, and other masters of the art will find much to love."
—*Midwest Book Review*

"An ice-cold thriller full of mystery, suspense, fear."
—David Moody, author of HATER and AUTUMN

"A page-turner in the true sense of the word."
—*HorrorAddicts*

"Will make your skin crawl." —*Scream Magazine*

"Told with an authoritative voice full of heart and insight."
—Richard Thomas, Bram Stoker nominated author

"Grabs and doesn't let go until the end." —*Writer's Digest*

BY JEREMY BATES

Suicide Forest ♦ The Catacombs ♦ Helltown ♦ Island of the
Dolls ♦ Mountain of the Dead ♦ Hotel Chelsea ♦ Mosquito
Man ♦ The Sleep Experiment ♦ The Man from Taured ♦
Merfolk ♦ The Dancing Plague 1 & 2 ♦ White Lies ♦ The
Taste of Fear ♦ Black Canyon ♦ Run ♦ Rewind ♦ Neighbors
♦ Six Bullets ♦ Box of Bones ♦ The Mailman ♦ Re-Roll ♦
New America: Utopia Calling ♦ Dark Hearts ♦ Bad People

FREE BOOK

For a limited time, visit www.jeremybatesbooks.com
to receive a free copy of the critically acclaimed
short novel *Black Canyon*, winner of Crime Writers
of Canada The Lou Allin Memorial Award.

The Sleep Experiment

World's Scariest Legends 2

Jeremy Bates

"There's something in us that is very much attracted to madness. Everyone who looks off the edge of a tall building has felt at least a faint, morbid urge to jump. And anyone who has ever put a loaded pistol up to his head... All right, my point is this: even the most well-adjusted person is holding onto his or her sanity by a greased rope. I really believe that. The rationality circuits are shoddily built into the human animal."
—Stephen King

The Sleep Experiment

PROLOGUE

Flanked by his defense team, Dr. Roy Wallis exited the San Francisco Hall of Justice minutes after a jury had acquitted him of all the charges filed against him in his nearly month-long trial. Hundreds of boisterous demonstrators, cordoned off behind police tape, filled Bryant Street outside the austere building. Many held homemade signs proclaiming dire end-of-time warnings such as: "The RAPTURE is upon us!" and "Judgment Day is coming!" and "REPENT now for the END is near!"

Dr. Wallis stopped before a phalanx of television cameras for an impromptu and celebratory press conference. When the throng of journalists and reporters quieted down, he said into the two-dozen or so microphones thrust at him, "Walt Whitman once wrote that 'the fear of hell is little or nothing to me.' But he was Walt Whitman, so he can write whatever he damn well pleased." Wallis stroked his beard, reveling in the knowledge the world would be hanging onto his every word. "I'm guessing," he continued, "Walt most likely never believed that hell existed in the first place, hence his cavalier attitude." He shook a finger as if to scorn the father of free verse. "But I, my lovely friends, I now know hell exists, and let me tell you—it scares the utter shit out of me."

Resounding silence except for the *cluck-cluck-cluck* of photographs being snapped.

Then everyone began shouting questions at once.

LAST DAY OF INSTRUCTION
SIX MONTHS EARLIER

"**W**hy do we sleep?" Dr. Roy Wallis said, his eyes roaming the darkened auditorium inside UC Berkeley's School of Public Health, Education, and Psychology. Five hundred or so students filled the tiered gallery that fanned around him, though the stage spotlights washed most of them in black. "It seems like a silly question, doesn't it? Sleep is sleep. It's an essential part of our survival. Sleep, food, water. The Big Three you can't do without. Nevertheless, while the benefits of food and water are quite evident to us, the actual benefits of sleep have always been masked in a shroud of mystery."

He depressed the forward button of the presentation clicker in his right hand and turned slightly to confirm the image on the projection screen behind him. It depicted a sleeping person with several question marks above her head.

"The truth," Dr. Wallis continued, "is that nobody really knows why we sleep, even though the subject has fascinated humans for more than two millennia. The Rishis of India agonized over our states of waking consciousness and dreaming. The ancient Egyptians built temples for the goddess Isis, where devotees met with priests to engage in early forms of hypnosis and dream interpretation. The Greeks and Romans had sleep deities such as Hypnos, Somnus, and Morpheus. The Chinese philosopher, Lao Tzu, compared sleep to death. William Shakespeare characterized sleep as 'nature's soft nurse' due to its restorative nature. However, in terms of scientific understanding, the exact mechanisms of sleep remained largely mysterious until the mid-twentieth century. Researchers have since shown that neural networks grown in lab dishes exhibit stages of activity and inactivity that resemble waking and sleeping, which could mean sleep arises naturally when single neurons work together with other neurons. Indeed, this explains why even the simplest organisms show sleep-like behaviors."

Dr. Wallis clicked on the next image. A photograph of an alien-looking worm on a black background appeared behind him. "Cute, isn't he? That's Caenorhabditis elegans—a tiny worm with only three hundred and two neurons. Yet even it cycles through quiet, lethargic periods that you could argue might be sleep. Admittedly, it's not sleep as we think of the term, but that's because we have larger and more complex brains, which require deeper neural networks. More neurons joining with other neurons equals a greater period of inactivity—such as the seven or eight hours of shuteye we experience each night."

Wallis paced across the stage, stroked his beard.

"Nevertheless, even if this theory is true—neurons drive our stages of wakefulness and sleep—it still doesn't explain *why* we sleep, or what exactly is *going on* during sleep. And a lot is going on, my friends. Our bodies don't simply shut down when Mr. Sandman comes a-knocking. On the one hand, it seems our brains use this period of inactivity to take out the trash, so to speak. The brain is a huge consumer of energy, which means all those waste chemicals that are produced as part of a cell's natural activity have to get flushed out sometime. Moreover, it seems the brain also uses this downtime to reorganize and prioritize the information it has gathered during the daytime, as well as to consolidate our short-term memories into long-term ones. This explains why when you lose sleep, you tend to have problems with your attention span, working out problems, recalling certain memories, even regulating your emotions.

Everything's a little out of whack."

Dr. Wallis scanned the dark veil before him. The few spectral students he could make out in the first couple of rows were watching him intently.

"Having said all of this, the human brain is an incredibly complex and powerful organ. It has more than enough computing power to get its housekeeping done while we're awake. So why shut down the entire body each night and leave us as defenseless as newborns? Is there something else going on during sleep that we don't know about? Maybe." He shrugged. "Or maybe not."

Click. A moody Neolithic scene appeared on the projection screen in which a band of fur-clad prehistoric humans hunkered inside the mouth of a cave as the setting sun bloodied the evening sky. Each burly figure gripped a stone weapon. Each set of large eyes appeared weary and watchful of the lurking dangers that night called forth.

"For our poor stone-age ancestors, it made sense for them to search for resources during the daytime when they could see best, and to hide during the nighttime when predator activity was at its peak. Yet...what do you do while hiding? If any of you have played Hide-and-Seek with an obtuse friend or sibling, you know that hiding becomes boring fast, because you're not doing much of anything. Imagine hiding in the same spot from dusk until dawn. Every night. Three-hundred-sixty-five days a year. It'd be worse than listening to a tape of Fran Drescher and Gilbert Gottfried arguing on an eternal loop. So to pass the time—and as a bonus, to conserve energy—their bodies shut down until it was time to get up and go look for food again. Such a solution applies not only to humans but pretty much every lifeform on the planet. Hell, even machines similarly 'sleep,' not to stave off boredom, of course, but to conserve energy."

Dr. Wallis paced, stroked his beard, paced some more.

"So back to my initial question of why we sleep...? Well, if you want my opinion, I believe the answer to be pathetically pedestrian. We sleep, my young friends, to pass the time and to conserve energy. All that other jazz I mentioned that goes on when the lights are out—your brain flushing waste chemicals, categorizing learning and memories—that's all ancillary, accomplished during sleep because sleep offers a convenient, not necessary, time to do so."

Click. Gone were the prehistoric humans on the projection screen, replaced by a gleaming city of glass and steel. He gestured toward the image.

"London, England. A far cry from the untamed plains and forests of ancient Eurasia, isn't it? No cave lions or bears are going to get you there. Food's not a problem either. Enter any supermarket to access aisle upon aisle of every type of food imaginable, all of which is restocked daily. Thus safety from predators and conserving our energy are no longer problems for contemporary humans. The majority of the population has evolved beyond such basic needs. So allow me to now ask you a *new* question, my inquisitive friends." He paused dramatically, acquiescing to the showman inside him. "In this enlightened day and age, do humans even *need* sleep?"

△△△

"I won't beat around the bush," Dr. Wallis said. "My answer is simple. No, I don't think humans need sleep. I think the entire human race is sleeping solely due to habit."

Chatter and uncertain laughter filled the auditorium.

Wallis waited it out for a few seconds before holding up his hands, palms forward, to command attention once more.

The mutiny died down.

Wallis depressed the forward button on the presentation clicker. The new image showed a businessman in a suit and tie seated behind a desk in a cluttered cubicle. His eyes were bloodshot, his face lined with exhaustion. A steaming cup of coffee stood next to his keyboard. "Yes, I know what you're thinking. If we don't need sleep, why do we look like this guy after an all-nighter? I'll tell you why. Because while you were out partying, your body was building up what biologists refer to as sleep pressure. That's right, that's what they call it —sleep pressure. What exactly is this sleep pressure, you ask? Well, those same biologists don't know. They've simply named something they don't yet understand. Think dark matter. We know it exists, we just don't know why. So...sleep pressure," he repeated as if tasting the word. "Sleep pressure. Indeed, it's like a Tolkien riddle game, isn't it? What accumulates during wakefulness and disperses during sleep? What is this metaphorical tally of hours, locked in some chamber of the brain, waiting to be wiped clean every night? And imagine... what if we could *access* it? What if we could *reprogram* it?" He smiled. "What if, my beautiful friends, we could *delete* it? Yes, delete sleep pressure. Remove forever tiredness and sleep—that colossal waste of time when we fall unconscious every night, that evolutionary anachronism that has no practical benefits for contemporary humans. Imagine if you had an extra seven or eight hours every day just how many more selfies you could post to Instagram?"

Some chuckles, though not many. The air in the auditorium sizzled with expectation.

Dr. Wallis went to the podium in the center of the stage. He played his fingers down the lapels of his tailored suit jacket. When he was sure every set of eyes in the audience were upon him, he said, "Let us consider what happened in January of 1964, my friends. A high school student in San Diego named Randy Gardner went eleven days—that is, two hundred and sixty-four hours—without sleep. Most interesting of all, near the end of the eleven days, he was not shuffling around like a zombie. On the contrary, he, among many other fascinating feats, was able to beat the experiment's researcher in pinball. He also presided over a press conference in which he spoke clearly and articulately. Overall, he proved to be in excellent health."

"How long did he crash for?" a male voice in the darkness called out.

"Thank you for the segue," Wallis said. "How long did he sleep for after the eleven days? Not for as long as you would expect. A mere fourteen hours—twice the number of hours the average person sleeps today. When he woke, he was not groggy at all. He was completely refreshed. That boy is now an old man. He is still alive today, to the best of my knowledge, and time has revealed no long-term physical or psychological side-effects at all."

Silence—but not the bored kind found too often in lecture halls across academia. Rather, this silence was wound tight as catgut, ready to be plucked with a deafening revelation.

Dr. Wallis did not plan to disappoint. He said, "As amazing as Randy Gardner's eleven days of wakefulness is, it pales in comparison to several other cases of people who have defied sleep. During the First World War, a Hungarian soldier named Paul Kern was shot in the head. After recovering from the frontal lobe injury, he was no longer able to fall asleep or become drowsy. Despite doctors telling him he would not live long, he survived without sleep for another forty years, when he died from natural causes in 1955. More recently, in 2006, a few months into a new laboratory job, a man named John Alan Jordan spilled industrial-strength detergent on his skin, which contaminated his cerebral spinal fluid. Soon after, he stopped sleeping and has not been able to sleep a wink since. Likewise, a man named Al Herpin developed a similarly rare case of insomnia, though for unknown reasons. When medical professionals inspected his house, they found no bed or other sleep-related furniture, only a single rocking chair in which Herpin said he read the newspaper when he wanted to rest. To this day he remains in perfect health and doesn't seem to suffer any discomfort from his remarkable condition. There are other cases too: a woman named Ines Fernandez who hasn't slept for decades despite consulting dozens of doctors and taking thousands of different narcotics and sedatives; a Vietnamese gentleman named Thái Ngọc who hasn't slept since suffering a fever in 1973. And so on. What's most amazing is that in every case the subjects remain perfectly healthy. Ines Fernandez is still alive and kicking. Same with Thái Ngọc, who boasts of carrying two one-hundred-plus pound sacks of rice more than two miles to his house every day."

Dr. Wallis retrieved his glass of water, beaded with condensation, from the podium. He took a sip. The warm water soothed his throat.

He set it back down and said, "Call these folks evolutionary freaks, if you want, call them anything you like, if that will help you accept their extraordinary stories. But one thing they make perfectly clear is that humans don't *need* sleep to survive. We sleep because we have always slept. Because of that mysterious thing inside us all called sleep pressure...sleep pressure that perhaps one day we will be able to isolate and negate..." In the distance the sixty-one-bell carillon in Sather Tower began to chime. Wallis glanced at his wristwatch: the class was finished. "Good luck on your exams everybody!" he said over the clamor of students packing their bags and making a general exodus toward the doors. Then, cheekily: "Don't stay up too late cramming!"

ΔΔΔ

When Dr. Roy Wallis finished transferring his notes from the podium to his leather messenger bag, he discovered he was not alone in the auditorium. A woman remained seated in the front row of seats. With almond eyes, high cheekbones, a prominent jawline, and straight and glossy black hair, she was beautiful in a classical Asian sense. Her brown eyes sparkled when they met his. She smiled, her cheeks dimpling.

She clapped her hands lightly. "Great lecture, professor," she said. "I really enjoyed it." She stood and ascended the stairs to the stage. She was dressed cute-tomboyish in an oversized plaid shirt, loose blue jean overalls rolled up at the cuffs, and powder-blue sneakers. She stopped on the other side of the podium. "But I think you might have overlooked something."

Dr. Wallis zipped his messenger bag closed. "Oh?" he said. Penny Park was one of his brightest students. She was also one of two researchers he'd selected to assist him with the Sleep Experiment in ten days time. She was from a low-income family in South Korea and was currently receiving a full academic scholarship. Despite having only lived in the States for three years, her English was impressively fluent. Her accent, however, needed some work, especially her pronunciation of Rs and Ls, which she consistently mixed up.

"Predators," Penny said. "You mentioned prehistoric humans needed to hide from predators during the night, and sleep resulted from hiding, something to pass the time."

"I did say that, Penny. I'm glad you were paying attention."

"Don't patronize me, professor. You know I *always* listen when you're speaking. But I was saying…okay, our ancestors, they had to hide during the night. But what about *predators*? The ones at the top of the food chain? They just hunt. They don't need to hide. So they don't need to pass the time and, according to you, they don't need to sleep. But they *do* sleep. So what you say doesn't make total sense. Why don't they just hunt all the time? Never go hungry?"

"You raise an excellent point, Penny," Dr. Wallis told her, impressed with her astuteness. "Predators do indeed also experience sleep pressure. Why is this? I believe for the same reason prey animals experience it. Boredom."

"Boredom?"

"They evolved to do one thing: hunt. But hunting 24/7 would grow tiresome, for lack of a better word. Sleep provides a break from this routine. Keeps them…sane, I suppose you might say. Anyway," he added, motioning Penny toward the exit doors and falling into step beside her, "perhaps the Sleep Experiment will shed some much-needed light on the subject?"

"I'm so excited to be participating in the experiment. I think about it all the time."

"Me too, Penny. Me too."

She pushed through one of the double doors. Wallis flicked

off the stage lights, then gave a final, nostalgic glance around the empty lecture hall, knowing he would not be back until the new fall semester in September.

"Professor?" Penny was holding one door open for him.

"Coming," he said and joined her.

DAY 1

MONDAY, MAY 28, 2018

*I*t's like a ghost town, Dr. Roy Wallis thought as he stood at his office window, looking out onto Shattuck Avenue. Across the street, the alehouse and Thai restaurant, which were usually crowded with professors and students alike, appeared closed. The street was deserted. There were still some people around the historic campus, of course, many of them international and migrant students studying language courses, but for the most part it was...like a ghost town. Gone was the rambunctious noise of the shuffling mobs, the optimistic energy that embodied the next generation of young Americans. In its place the nearly thirteen hundred acres were unfamiliar yet beautifully peaceful—allowing Wallis to see it almost as he had all those years ago when he was a bright-eyed tenure-track professor.

Clouds drifted in front of the sun, and Wallis caught his reflection in the glass of the window. With his slicked-back undercut and his long, groomed beard, he had been compared to everyone from a lumberjack to a circus ringmaster to a hot Abe Lincoln. The latter was from a female graduate student. Admittedly, he had a lot of admirers amongst his female students. He was both embarrassed and flattered by this, given he had recently turned forty-one. Still, he wasn't trying to be some sort of "hipster professor" with the haircut and the beard. Both simply suited his face. He'd worn medium-length hair and stubble for a while, and whilst he'd liked the subtle sophistication of the stubble, he'd eventually decided a real beard had to be thick and strong and, well, manly. Consequently, he'd grown the stubble out five years back, kept his beard in meticulous condition with regular visits to his barber and daily moisturizing and oiling, and he hadn't looked back since.

Wallis turned away from the window. All tenured professors had their own offices to decorate as they wanted. Given he was now the psychology department head, he not only had his own office, but a spacious one to boot. Although not technically allowed, he'd had the institutional white walls repainted Wedgewood blue and the gray carpet replaced with a high-pile black one three years ago. The furniture was all campus surplus stuff, but he'd brought the abstract acrylic artwork—as well as a watercolor of an intense-looking Sigmund Freud smoking a cigar—and other miscellaneous items from his home. Some of his colleagues praised the personal touches; some became so inspired they spruced up their offices with their own lamps and area rugs; some never commented at all; and some openly told him they were gaudy and unacademic. Wallis didn't care what any of them thought. The space, for him, was welcoming and comforting, maximizing his productivity.

Dr. Wallis went to the mini-fridge and retrieved a bottle of water. He contemplated a beer from the six-pack of Coors Light he kept in there but decided it was too early in the day for that. Hanging on the wall above the fridge were his medical degree from the University of Arizona and his Ph.D. summa cum laude from UCLA; a few awards he'd received in recognition of his research into circadian rhythms and narcolepsy; and two framed photographs. The first was of him posing with the great and late father of sleep medicine, Dr. William C. Dement. The second was of him and a colleague one hundred and fifty feet underground in Mammoth Cave, Kentucky, where they'd spent two days charting their fluctuations in wakefulness and body temperature when freed from the regulating influence of sunlight and daily schedules—

A knock at the door startled him. Wallis frowned. Classes and exams had finished the previous week. Who would even know he was in his office?

He opened the door. "Penny?" he said. She was wearing a pair of heavy black-framed eyeglasses today that sat precariously on her button nose. A long, loose purple sweater reached farther down her thighs than her shorts. Her long hair was woven into a single braid that hung forward over her shoulder. "Didn't we agree to meet at Tolman Hall?"

"I know," she said, her cheeks dimpling beneath the glasses, "but I got here early, so I thought I would walk over with you?" She pointed to one of the psychology-related cartoons taped to the door. "I like this one best. So funny." The comic depicted Goldilocks reclining on a psychiatrist's couch and telling him: "Alice is in Wonderland, Dorothy is somewhere over the rainbow, but I get trapped in a cabin with bears."

"She has it easy compared to Rapunzel."

"The girl with the long hair?"

He nodded. "I like your hair. I don't think you've worn it like that before?"

"Because when I pull it back from my face like this it makes my head look too big. Many Koreans have too large heads, did you know that?"

"No, I didn't."

"Anyway, in Korean society, a single braid means a single lady." She held up her left hand and wiggled her ring finger. "And I'm single! Thought I'd try a braid for luck."

"Well, good luck," he said. "Give me a sec and we'll head off." He collected his blazer and messenger bag from his desk, then locked up the office behind them. They took the stairs to the ground floor and exited through the main doors. The day was humid yet overcast, with dark clouds in the distance threatening rain.

Penny Park was smiling. "Do you remember the quote you began your Sleep and Dreams course this year with, professor?" she asked.

He thought back. "No, not off the top of my head."

"'Do one thing every day that scares you,'" she said proudly.

He nodded. "Right—Eleanor Roosevelt. Thinking about getting those words of wisdom tattooed on your forehead?"

Penny laughed. "No! I was thinking about the experiment today."

"Ah," he said.

"Are you scared at all, professor?"

"There's nothing to be scared of, Penny."

"You're not even a teeny tiny bit nervous?"

Wallis hesitated. Then shrugged. "Maybe a teeny tiny bit."

ΔΔΔ

Dr. Roy Wallis wasn't sure how well the Penny Park situation was going to work out.

Last month, when Wallis made the general announcement to his senior Sleep and Dreams class that he wanted to hire two students to assist him with a sleep experiment for three weeks during the summer break, ten students applied. During the first round of informal interviews he remained coy about what the experiment entailed, explaining little more than the successful applicants would need to be available eight hours a day on a rotational schedule to provide 24/7 shift coverage. This dissuaded half the students, who promptly withdrew their names from consideration. Wallis re-interviewed the remaining five applicants, explaining in more detail what their roles would involve, namely observing and recording the actions of two subjects under the influence of a stimulant gas. Two more applicants bowed out. The remaining three included Penny Park, another international student from India named Guru Rampal, and a member of the school's rowing team named Trevor Upton. Trevor was intelligent, focused, and sociable, and he would have been Wallis' first choice had his class attendance last semester been better. Two necessary qualities Wallis required of his assistants were punctuality and reliability. Which left Penny Park and Guru Rampal as the last candidates standing.

Dr. Wallis had been confident they would both perform exceptionally, and he still believed it. The problem with Penny Park was that she was revealing herself to be a flirt. Over the last two years she'd visited during office hours a handful of times, and though she'd always demonstrated a sharp, sardonic sense of humor—you might almost call it *teasing*—he'd thought nothing of it until three weeks ago. After selecting Penny and Guru as his assistants, he'd taken them across the street from the psychology building to the alehouse for pizza and beers. Guru, it turned out, didn't eat pizza or drink alcohol and insisted he was fine sipping a glass of Coca-Cola. Penny, on the other hand, finished off most of the pitcher of regular-strength beer Wallis ordered. There are two types of drinkers. People who can handle their booze well enough it would be difficult to tell whether they were drunk or not, and people who cannot. Penny most definitely fell into the latter category. At first her compliments were flattering: "You're actually one of the only professors that dress *well!*" and "I know how this sounds, but you work out, right? You must work out?" But then came the blasé touches. Eventually Wallis excused himself under the pretense of using the restroom so he could sit on the other side of the table from Penny when he returned. Guru was not blind to Penny's advances and wore a big, goofy smile on his face for the next twenty minutes or so until Wallis—ignoring Penny's appeals for another pitcher of beer—requested the bill from the wait staff.

Since then Wallis had communicated with Penny via phone and email about the experiment a few times, but he'd only seen her face-to-face on the last day of classes when she'd remained after his lecture in the auditorium.

She had seemed like the old Penny Park then, as she did today...but the problem was, Wallis had had a peek behind the curtain. He knew how she felt about him. And that made him uncomfortable—and concerned.

Wallis wasn't averse to professor-student romances.

Although frowned upon by some amongst academia's establishment, dating a student above the age of consent was legal and permitted in most universities. Wallis was in an off-and-on-again relationship with a former student right now.

No, what concerned him with Penny's solicitous behavior was how it might affect the Sleep Experiment. They would be working together closely on it for the next three weeks, and he would need her attention focused on the experiment, not him.

I'll play it by ear, he decided. *After all, I'm probably blowing what happened at the alehouse out of proportion. She was drunk, having a bit of fun. Nothing more to it than that.*

ΔΔΔ

To say Penny Park had a crush on Dr. Wallis was a gross understatement. She was in total freaking love. And who could blame her? He was sexy, in shape, and fashionable. And not only all of this, but he was also her *professor* which, in a kinky kind of way, made him even sexier.

If asked, Penny would probably say it had been a case of love at first sight. She often sat in the front row of her classes because then you didn't have to deal with all the goofing around from the jocks, stoners, and "cool girls." And this was where she was sitting on the first day of Dr. Wallis' first-year psychology course. For the duration of the fifty minutes she could barely look away from him, smiling pleasantly whenever he made brief eye contact with her.

Later that week, she stopped by his office during his office hours to ask him about some of the homework questions he'd assigned. She remembered how nervous she'd been to be alone in his presence, which was odd for her. She was an extrovert and a pretty one at that. She'd learned from an early age that she could get together with any of the boys in her grade simply by singling one out and showing him a little bit of interest. By the age of sixteen, she'd probably had close to two dozen boyfriends, most of whom she'd bored of after a week or two. She'd simply never found herself attracted to any of them in the first place.

Not like she was attracted to older men.

She'd learned why she had this fetish a year earlier from, ironically, Dr. Wallis himself. In his Developmental Psychology course, he explained that when financial and social status gains were ruled out, a young woman's interest in a mature man often came down to her relationship with her father while she'd advanced through puberty. According to Dr. Wallis, when a father is unable to deal with his daughter's burgeoning sexuality because it makes him feel uncomfortable or unsafe, he avoids her the best he can, and when this is not possible, he derides her for wearing makeup or promiscuous outfits. Unable to win his benign attention during this important stage of her development, she is forced to look elsewhere for that attention.

Indeed, this scenario described Penny Park's rocky relationship with her father to a tee. And in her case, during her teenage years, the only adults she knew well aside from her parents were her teachers—which might explain what happened in her senior year.

One evening after school, Penny had stayed late at the library to study for an upcoming test. While leaving the building, she passed her biology classroom and saw her teacher, Mr. Cho, seated at his desk, marking papers. She'd been having erotic dreams about him for nearly a year at that point, and when she'd met his wife at a school festival the week before, she found herself instantly jealous of the woman. The hag was old —older than Mr. Cho, by the looks of it—but she'd been all prim and proper with perfectly coiffed auburn-dyed hair, big doll eyes (double eyelid surgery anyone?), two-inch pumps, and an immaculate Louis Vuitton handbag. The perfect little housewife who shopped all day and whose only responsibilities in life were limited to tidying up the house and cooking for her husband.

Ever since that encounter, Penny had fantasized about stealing Mr. Cho from the woman, and so that evening while she was leaving the high school, she spontaneously and recklessly entered her teacher's classroom under the pretense of asking about the upcoming exam—all the while flaunting her sexuality, which, by eighteen years of age, had become second nature to her. When she crossed her legs and saw Mr. Cho's eyes going to the excessive amount of thigh showing beneath her short plaid skirt, she took the plunge, saying in an offhand manner, "I'm going to be in Itaewon around seven o'clock this evening. There's this little bar that's *so* fun. It's called The Railway Club, in Haebangchon. Maybe if you're nearby, you might meet me for a drink?"

Penny, of course, knew Mr. Cho would be nowhere nearby. The high school was in Jungnang-gu in the eastern suburbs of Seoul. He likely lived somewhere close by. Itaewon, on the other hand, was smack-dab in the center of the city and popular with tourists and foreign workers. This was exactly why she'd chosen the location: it was a discreet place where two people could meet and not run into anyone else they knew.

Mr. Cho considered her offer for a long moment, and Penny was just about to blurt she'd only been kidding around, when he said, "You're too young to drink, Penny."

"I'm almost nineteen." She shrugged and smiled. "Besides, they know me at the bar. They always serve me." Which was partly true. She'd been there once after watching a live band at a nearby venue, and she hadn't had any problems ordering a drink.

"Seven o'clock, you say?" Mr. Cho said.

Penny nodded, still smiling.

"You will be with your friends?"

"No, just me."

"I might be in the area."

Penny arrived at The Railway Club fifteen minutes late and found Mr. Cho seated at a booth with a nearly empty pint of beer in front of him. When she sat down, they ordered snacks and two more beers. Penny was not a seasoned drinker, and Mr. Cho took advantage of this, plying her with beer after beer, which she happily imbibed. After an hour or so, she moved to his side of the booth so they were brushing up against each other. She rubbed his crotch through his pants, while his hand explored beneath her skirt. When she tried kissing him, he suggested they go somewhere else. He paid the bill and took her to a bawdily decorated love hotel. The only room available was dubbed "The Ramen Room," and the queen bed was actually inside a giant replica of a Styrofoam instant-ramen container.

Despite the dozen or so boys Penny had previously made out with, she'd never had intercourse before. She didn't tell Mr. Cho this, he didn't ask, and she enjoyed the experience tremendously. After he left—he told her they should walk to the train station separately—she stayed behind in the room, pleasuring herself in the two-person bathtub with an assortment of sex toys that had been stored on a shelf above the flat-screen television.

She and Mr. Cho met up on six more occasions before she graduated later that year and moved to California to begin her studies at UC Berkeley.

Despite this experience with an older man, Penny had been unable to work up the courage to proposition Dr. Wallis that first day she'd visited his office in the autumn of 2015. She'd only been in the United States for a single month then, everything was still new and a little bit frightening, and she wasn't as confident in her skin as she'd been in South Korea. Moreover, Dr. Wallis was not a high school teacher; he was a professor at one of the most esteemed universities in the country. He had a presence and swagger that Mr. Cho could never match which, combined with his rugged good looks, likely afforded him no shortage of beautiful women.

Undaunted, however, Penny continued to visit him during his office hours most weeks over the following three years, each time telling herself this would be the day she asked him out, but she never made any headway. Being a very popular professor, he almost always had a colleague hanging out with him in his office, or a line of students at his door waiting to see him...and on those two or three occasions she'd caught him alone? Well, the moment had just never seemed right.

Then last month Dr. Wallis announced in his Sleep and Dream class that he was looking for two students to assist him over the summer hiatus with an experiment that would take place on the campus grounds. Penny immediately applied for the position and, to her exhilaration, was selected. She could recite Dr. Wallis' phone call verbatim, with him concluding, "So if this sounds like something you'd be interested in, Penny, I'd love to have you on board."

The next day Dr. Wallis invited Penny and a nerdy Indian named Guru Rampal out for pizza and beers, so they could all get to know each other better. Penny did her best to remain professional with the professor despite her running-hot libido, knowing it wasn't the right time or place to cozy up to him. Yet after a few beers this restraint went out the window—and her flirting didn't exactly go well. She was far too forward, and Dr. Wallis showed little if any interest in her advances. When she woke up the next morning, she was sure he was going to call to say he was replacing her on the experiment. But he never did.

And here I am today, she thought. *Just the two of us, walking together to Tolman Hall.*

Nevertheless, Penny wasn't going to make the same mistake twice. No more in-your-face wasted girl. She would allow her relationship with Dr. Wallis to develop organically over the next three weeks until she was confident she had won him over.

And win him over she would.

∆∆∆

Nearly one hundred and fifty years old, the campus of the University of California Berkeley was a mosaic of classical and contemporary buildings that lined symmetrical avenues and winding pathways alike.

Tolman Hall, it could be argued, was the ugly duckling of the brood.

Constructed during the middle of the last century at the height of the Brutalist style, its exposed concrete and stark, geometric design had drawn a mixed bag of praise and criticism from the public over the decades. The Psychology Department had called it home since 1963 before moving into Berkeley Way West this year. Tolman Hall had since been deemed seismically unfit, slated for demolition, and shuttered up.

Which made it the perfect spot on campus to conduct the Sleep Experiment.

"There she is," Dr. Wallis said, looking up at the doomed building.

Penny said, "You know, after they announced they were going to knock it down, it went viral on Instagram."

"Vial?" he teased.

"*Viral*. Sorry I don't speak so perfect English like you, professor."

Wallis nodded. "I can imagine she's gone viral. You either love her or hate her. Personally, I have mixed feelings. She served our department well for over fifty years. But the nature of our work has changed significantly, and she's no longer state-of-the-art, is she?"

"Spooky even. Especially now, with all the doors and windows gone. Like a monster, wanting to eat us up."

"You certainly have a vivid imagination, Penny. Ah, there's Guru."

△△△

Guru Rampal was leaning against a nearby tree, ankles crossed, thumbing something into his phone. He had thinning black hair which he wore in a Teddy Boys-inspired pompadour (presumably to mask the bald patch on top); dark, sleepy eyes (now covered by a pair of sunglasses); and light mocha skin. He was slim despite an incongruous belly, which his too-tight Pac-Man tee-shirt did little to hide. His beige khaki shorts were neatly pressed, his white sneakers glaringly spotless.

He had been born in a small village on the outskirts of Delhi, India, and like Penny Park, he had only been in the United States for a handful of years. He too was one of the lucky international students receiving a full-ride academic scholarship. Unlike Penny, however, he remained uninitiated to the ways of the West. Yet what he lacked in street smarts, he made up for in book smarts. He was one of the most promising students Dr. Wallis had ever had the pleasure of teaching, and he no doubt had a bright future ahead of him in whatever area of psychology he pursued, whether that be academia, industry, healthcare, or policy.

"Guru!" Penny called. She always pronounced his name *Gulu*, like the city in Uganda.

Guru glanced up from his phone. "Hi, guys!"

Dr. Wallis and Penny joined him at the tree.

"Like your shades," Penny said.

"Thanks, babe." He took them off and hooked them to his collar.

"Uh, don't call me babe, please."

"Really?"

"Really!"

Guru shrugged. "I bought them for ten dollars at Target," he said in his syllable-timed accent. "I think they give me more cool factor. Do you guys agree?"

Wallis slapped him on the shoulder. "You get any cooler, Guru, we're going to start calling you Iceman."

"Iceman," he said. "I like that. You can start calling me that right now."

Penny pointed. "Hey, are those our professional lab rats?"

Guru said, "Or in the words of George Bernard Shaw, 'human guinea pigs.'"

"That's them." Wallis checked his wristwatch. "And right on time."

ΔΔΔ

The three scientists watched the Australian backpackers approach Tolman Hall, smiling and waving. They both sported deeply tanned bodies and beachy blonde hair. The woman, Sharon Nash, was dressed in a white singlet over a bikini top and cut-off jean shorts; the man, Chad Carter, wore a Billabong tee-shirt and board shorts. They walked at a leisurely pace in grungy flip-flops, as though enjoying a stroll through a park.

Whoever said stereotypes aren't true? Wallis mused. *Especially in the case of twenty-something Australians who come to California for the surf.*

In May, Wallis had placed an advertisement in the San Francisco *Chronicle* for two test subjects to participate in what he'd described as an in-patient sleep study. He was surprised by the avalanche of replies. He emailed each potential recruit a tailor-made screening test with inclusion and exclusion criteria. He settled on the two Australians for a myriad of reasons. Their BMIs were within the ideal range. They were non-smokers. Neither was taking medications, and neither had any history of pre-existing medical conditions, allergic predispositions, or anaphylactic reactions. Moreover, their answers to several questions he'd posed indicated they were Type B personalities. People in this camp tended to be more relaxed than Type A personalities, more tolerant of others and more reflective, while also displaying lower levels of anxiety and higher levels of imagination and creativity. As a bonus, the Australians were friends but were not romantically involved.

In short, Wallis couldn't have asked for two better test subjects in an experiment that required them to be cooped up in a room together for three weeks.

Dr. Wallis greeted Chad and Sharon with firm handshakes, then introduced them to Penny and Guru.

"Mate, love the sunnies," Chad told Guru. "You moonlight as

an Elvis impersonator or something?"

Guru beamed. "See, I told you guys. They *do* give me more cool factor."

Penny was eyeing Sharon's bikini top. "Were you two just at the beach?"

"Had a quick dip this morning," Sharon replied. "We were told clothing was going to be provided for us, so we didn't bother to change."

"Or bring any," Chad added.

"Or bring any," Sharon agreed.

"Clothing is most assuredly provided," Wallis told them. "Clothing and much more. You will be perfectly comfortable for the next three weeks. Come, follow me."

△△△

Berkeley Property Management had already stripped the interior of Tolman Hall bare, salvaging all the furniture, light fixtures, flooring, and cabinetry. What remained was a hollowed-out concrete block fitting its condemned status. Tearing down the skeletal structure would have already begun had Dr. Wallis not negotiated with the property manager to postpone work until the following month, after the Sleep Experiment had concluded.

Wallis led Penny, Guru, and the two Australians into Tolman Hall's west wing and down a flight of stairs to the basement. The building still had power, and he flicked a master light switch. The old fluorescent lamps in the ceiling clunked on one after the other, bathing the windowless space in light.

"Oooh, this place is so creepy with nobody around," Penny said.

"Like an insane asylum from a movie," Guru said.

"Enough, you two," Wallis quipped, annoyed they were going to give the Australians the jitters.

"No worries," Chad said. "Shaz and I don't scare easily. As long as there's no derro living down here, we're all good."

"Derro?" Penny said.

"Derelict. You know, vagabond, bum, trash pirate, gutter rat, broke dick—"

"Yes, I understand now, thank you."

Wallis led the way among the maze of hallways. The design was rumored to have been inspired by the maze-rat experiments performed by the building's namesake, behavioral psychologist Edward Chance Tolman.

Wallis stopped next to a room with the door still intact and, next to it, a large red X spray-painted on the wall.

"X marks the spot!" Penny chirped.

"I made that," Wallis explained, "so the demolition contractors remembered not to remove anything from the room." He opened the door, stepped inside the dark cavity, and turned on the lights, which revealed a small antechamber. Ten feet in, a fabricated wall stretched from one side of the room to the other. It featured a long rectangular viewing window and another door that led to the space where the Australians would be living for the next twenty-one days. In front of the window was a table on which sat a touch panel controller the size of an iPad and a silver laptop computer.

Wallis sat down in the room's only chair. "Excited for the reveal?" he asked.

"Busting," Chad said.

"I cannot see anything," Guru complained, cupping his hands against the viewing window.

"That's because the lights aren't on, genius," Penny said.

"I am a genius, you know? My IQ is—"

"Tell someone who cares."

"Children, enough," Wallis said. To the Australians, he added, "This space used to be one of the building's largest conference rooms. I had that wall constructed for the experiment to separate this observation room from...let's call it...the sleep laboratory."

"But we won't be asleep, mate," Chad said. "So that doesn't

really make sense."

"Yes, but given the nature of the experiment—it's called the Sleep Experiment, after all—I think—"

"That doesn't make sense either. Shouldn't it be called the Sleep*less* Experiment?"

Penny giggled.

Wallis smiled politely. "That doesn't exactly have the same ring to it, does it?" he remarked.

"Nah," Sharon said, somewhat nasally. "I'm with Chad on this one. Sleep lab? Nah, doesn't make sense, mate."

"You two are free to call it whatever you wish," Wallis said tersely. "But why don't we have a look?" He powered on the touch panel controller, then pressed a button on the side of it to display a lighting control page. He tapped five buttons in quick succession, which in turn powered on the five LED ceiling lights in the sleep laboratory.

"Oh em gee!" Penny said. "How cool!"

"Sweet," Chad said.

"Sweeeeet," Sharon parroted.

"That is bigger than my family home in India," Guru said, impressed. "And I have four brothers."

Dr. Wallis was glad they all approved. He had spent months applying for state and federal grants, but after consecutive rejections—citing the ethical concerns related to the experiment —he'd decided to fund everything himself. "The room is fully contained, of course," he said. "You have a library with an eclectic mix of authors from Bronte and Atwood to Poe and King. A home theater's right next to it. There are over eighty available channels, I believe, as well as Netflix. There's also a DVD player and a good collection of movies. A small gym—"

"And a basketball court!" Penny said. "Holy moly."

Wallis nodded. It wasn't technically a court, as there were no defined sides or line markers, just enough space in front of a basketball net on a pole to shoot some hoops or have a game of one-on-one. "Kitchen's there," he continued, pointing. "The refrigerator is fully stocked. Same with the pantry. You both stated you have no food allergies. But if you want anything specific, please let me know, and I can get that for you too."

"Why're there beds?" Chad asked. "We're not supposed to be sleeping."

"You won't be sleeping." He indicated the large tank at the far end of the antechamber. It was about the size and shape of a home's natural gas heating system. "That contains the gas-based stimulant. It's already being vented into the sleep laboratory. After you've breathed it in for a few minutes, you won't be able to fall asleep no matter how much you might want to. The beds are there for…personal space, I suppose you could say. You're going to have a lot of time on your hands. Even if you can't sleep, you might want a place to lie down and relax."

Sharon kept gazing at the tank. "The gas is…safe, right?"

"Of course," Wallis said. "It's been thoroughly tested."

"What's in it? I mean, what's it made up of?"

"The formula, I'm afraid, is a trade secret."

"If he told you," Penny said, "he'd have to kill you."

"What if we want to leave the room?" Chad asked. "The door's not going to be locked or anything, is it?"

"Locked? No. However, leaving the sleep laboratory is discouraged. This is a controlled experiment. All factors must be held constant except for one: the independent variable. In this case, that is both of you. If either of you were to leave that room, you would be breathing regular air, thereby introducing a second independent variable into the experiment that may affect the ultimate results of the experiment."

"To be precise, professor," Guru said, "with any human testing there are *inherent* uncontrolled variables such as age, gender, and genetic dispositions. So in the strictest sense, this is not a controlled exper—"

"Those inherent uncontrolled variables would be filtered out in further experiments, Guru," Wallis said.

"But the bottom line," Chad said, "is that we're stuck in that room for twenty-one days?"

"Correct. Which was in the Subject Information and Consent

Forms you both signed," Wallis said, growing impatient. "If you are having cold feet, I need to know right now as I have an entire list of other—"

"Nah, mate," Chad said. "No cold feet." He looked at Sharon.

"I don't want to back out," she said. "We can keep traveling for another six months with the money we make."

"You heard her," Chad said. "We're not backing out. But..." He shrugged. "Say something happens? Like one of us feels sick? You'll let us leave?"

"Of course," Wallis said. "You are not prisoners. You are free to terminate the experiment at any point you wish."

"But we won't get our bonuses?"

"You get bonuses?" Penny said, surprised.

"For completing the twenty-one days," Wallis explained.

"I'm not getting a bonus. Are you, Guru?"

"No, no bonus for me," he said. "At least not that I know of."

Wallis sighed. "You two aren't the ones going twenty-one days without sleep."

Penny cocked an eyebrow at Chad. "How much is your bonus? In fact, how much are you getting paid?"

"Penny!" Wallis snapped. Seeing her startled expression, he bit back his frustration. "Penny," he said more reasonably. "This experiment is not about money. It's about science. I chose you because I thought you understood this. However, if you feel you are being unfairly compensated, I suppose we could discuss—"

"No, professor," she said, looking bashful. "You're right. This isn't about money. I'm sorry. I really don't care about...I was just..."

Wallis stood and squeezed her forearm reassuringly, which brightened her up. To the Australians, he said, "You will find a bathroom with a small shower at the very back of the sleep laboratory. It's the only section of the room we won't be able to visually observe you. Nevertheless, we'll still be able to monitor you with these." He produced two smart wristwatches from his messenger bag and handed them over. "They'll track your heart rates, stress levels, and movement. You'll find wireless chargers next to the TV. When the watch batteries are low, please charge them."

"How do we talk to you?" Sharon asked. "I mean, if we have questions about anything later on?"

"The intercom system," Wallis said. "There are six microphones installed in the ceiling, as well as a loudspeaker system. You don't need to do anything; we'll be able to hear anything you say via this tablet here. If you have a question, just ask away. One last matter. Did either of you bring your phones with you?"

"You told us not to," Chad said.

"So you didn't?"

He shook his head. "Left it with my mate."

Sharon, looking guilty, slid hers out of her pocket. "I didn't know if you were serious or not."

Wallis held out his hand. "Unfortunately, there's to be no contact with the outside world. Can't have you live streaming the experiment on Facebook—"

"I wouldn't!"

"I'm sorry, Sharon, but I made it clear that—"

"I know. Fine." She handed him her phone. "Don't lose it."

"I'll keep it locked away in my office and return it to you the moment the experiment is completed. Now, any further questions?"

The Australians looked at each other. They exchanged hopeful smiles, which did little to mask the uncertainty wading beneath.

"All right then," Wallis said. "Let's get started."

△△△

Dr. Roy Wallis had scheduled himself to work all the shifts between two p.m. and ten p.m. He bid farewell to Penny Park and Guru Rampal, opened the laptop's word processor, then lit up a cigarette. To hell with the campus' indoor smoking bans;

Tolman Hall was going to be nothing but a pile of memories and rubble in a month. What could a little smoke hurt?

The Australian test subjects spent their first hour in the sleep laboratory examining every corner of the room, reminding Wallis of a pair of hamsters sniffing out their new cage. Curiosity sated, they both sat down on the sofa and turned on the TV. Sharon took control of the remote but acquiesced to the home renovation program Chad wanted to watch. During a commercial she got up and fiddled around with the exercise machines. She then approached the viewing window, stopping when she came within a few feet of it. Her side was mirrored, so she would be seeing her reflection, not Dr. Wallis.

She pushed an errant blonde bang behind her left ear. The action was hesitant, almost shy, though up until this point her personality had been far from shy. Her thick-lashed eyes swept from one side of the mirror to the other, as if seeking a spot in it she could see through. They were a light blue with a hint of spring green—the color, Wallis thought, of a tropical lagoon. Her bare lips pursed as if she were about to say something. Instead, she waved.

Wallis tapped the Talk button on the touch panel controller and said, "Two-way mirror."

Sharon looked up at the ceiling, where his voice had come through the amplified speakers.

Chad looked up too, then returned his attention to the television.

"Now I really do feel like a test subject," Sharon said. Her voice, transmitted through the speakers in the touch panel controller, was tinny but clear. She tapped the two-way glass. The sound was sharper than it would have been if she had tapped a regular window because there wasn't any framing or other support behind the glass. Wallis doubted she knew this. She had tapped for the sake of tapping it, nothing more. "Twenty-one days," she added. "No sleep. Wow."

"No sleep," Dr. Wallis agreed.

"What are Chad and me gonna do?"

"Catch up on your reading?" he suggested.

"I guess."

"The complete collection of H.P. Lovecraft is on the bookshelf. I brought it from my home library."

"He writes horror, right?"

"Horror, fantasy, science-fiction. The collection is 1600 pages, so it should eat away some of your hours."

Sharon shook her head. "Scary stuff puts me on edge. As a kid I used to get nightmares a lot…and I guess I still do."

"That's not unusual," Wallis said. "One out of every two adults experiences nightmares on occasion."

She smiled crookedly. "Right. I forgot you were a sleep doctor. Is that what I should call you? Doctor? Or doc?"

"You can call me Roy."

She appeared to think it over. "Nah, that just doesn't seem right. I like doc."

"Doc's fine then."

"So…doc…why *do* we have nightmares?"

"They're often spontaneous," Wallis told her, lighting up a fresh cigarette. "Even so, they can be caused by a variety of factors. For instance, some are caused by late-night snacks. Food increases your metabolism, signaling your brain to become more active. Some are caused by different medications, especially antidepressants and narcotics, which act on chemicals in the brain." He tapped ash into his empty paper coffee cup. "There are psychological triggers as well, such as anxiety or depression, as well as certain sleep disorders."

"What kind of sleep disorders?" she asked.

"Insomnia and sleep apnea would be the more common ones. Restless legs syndrome would be another—"

Sharon cut him off with a brisk laugh. "That sounds like something a dog looking for a hydrant might have."

Wallis smiled. "It manifests itself in a strong urge to move, which naturally makes it difficult, if not impossible, to fall into a deep, peaceful sleep."

"I feel pretty restless right now."

"You're in a new, unfamiliar environment. Try to relax. Soon this place will feel like home. Humans have a remarkable capacity to adapt."

"Because we have big brains, right?"

"Social brains," he amended. "We're hardwired to create, share, and pass on knowledge. This is what allows us to adjust to new situations so easily, and what differentiates us from our early ancestors, and our early ancestors from primates. But we're getting off-topic, aren't we?" Dr. Wallis crushed his cigarette on the floor and made a mental note to bring an ashtray during his next shift. He tossed the butt into the coffee cup with the three others he had smoked. "Nightmares, Sharon," he finished, "are a perfectly normal part of dreaming that release pent-up emotions. I wouldn't worry too much about having them now and again. They're vital for mental health. Chad, how're you doing?"

Chad stuck a thumb in the air without looking away from the TV. "All good, mate."

"Thanks for the talk, doc," Sharon said, pushing the same errant lock of blonde hair as before back behind her ear, from where it had slipped loose. "I don't feel as lonely anymore. I think I might be chatting a lot with you over the next three weeks...if that's all right?"

"Perfectly."

"I just wish I could see you. Talking to my reflection is a trip."

Before Wallis could think of a suitable reply, Sharon wandered to the bookshelf, where she began sorting through the one hundred or so books he'd borrowed from Berkeley's Doe Library.

Wallis watched her for a little longer, then stood, stretched, and went to the bathroom down the hallway by the decommissioned elevator. All the fixtures had been removed save for, at his request, a toilet, urinal, and sink. He used the urinal, washed his hands—making another mental note to bring some toilet paper, soap, and hand towels next shift as well—and returned to the observation room.

Sharon was watching TV with Chad once more.

The next six hours went by swiftly. Wallis took nearly three pages of notes, which he was reading over when there was a knock at the door.

Guru Rampal entered the room a moment later, dressed in the same tee-shirt and khaki shorts he'd had on earlier. The sunglasses were nowhere in sight. "Good evening, professor," he said, shrugging a backpack off his shoulder and setting it on the ground next to the table.

Wallis could smell McDonald's. "Bring some late-night snacks, Guru?" he asked.

"I did not know if I was going to get hungry or not." He looked through the viewing window into the sleep laboratory. "Did anything interesting happen?"

Wallis shook his head. "Their bodies are still in sync with their natural circadian rhythms. We shouldn't expect to see any deviations from their regular behavioral patterns until they've gone at least one night without sleep." He stood. "Take my seat. You're making me nervous standing over me like that."

"Thank you, professor." He sat in the chair. "Is there anything in particular I should know before you leave?"

"No, it's all pretty straightforward," Wallis told him. "Just keep watch on our two test subjects from Down Under and record their behavior. Have a read of my notes on the laptop if you want to get a feel for what you might want to jot down. Other than that…" He shrugged. "Just don't fall asleep."

"Do not worry about that, professor. I am a night owl. Uh, what if they want to talk to me?"

"Talk to them."

"That is okay?"

"Why wouldn't it be?"

"I do not know. I guess…I have never participated in a study with human subjects."

Wallis gestured to the touch panel controller. "There's a Talk button you press if you want them to hear you, and a Listen button if you want to hear them. That's about it."

Nodding, Guru tapped his fingers on the desk.

Wallis frowned. "Is there something on your mind, Guru?"

"Do you think I should shave my head?"

Wallis blinked, caught off guard by the question. His eyes flicked to Guru's Teddy Boys pompadour. "I like your hair," he said.

"It looks good from the front," he said, nodding. "I copied the hairstyle of a very famous pop star back home in India. But the problem is here." He bent forward and pointed to his balding crown. "Can you see?"

"A lot of men experience male-pattern hair loss."

He sat straight again. "But I am only twenty-two! If I had already found a wife, then no problem. But it will be much more difficult to find a wife when I am bald."

Wallis smiled. "You'll do just fine."

"Thank you, professor. But you have not answered my question yet. Should I shave my head? This is what all the advice online is telling me to do."

"As I said, I like your hair. It's you. But if you're self-conscious about the thinning on top—sure, shave it off, why not? It will always grow back."

Guru sighed. "The problem is, I am not sure if I have the face for a shaved head. I am not handsome like you. I do not have strong features."

"Maybe grow some facial hair to balance things out?"

"That is another problem! I cannot! I have tried. I get a few whiskers here and here." He touched his upper lip and chin. "But that is all. And with no hair or facial hair, I fear I will look like a brown alien."

"Ladies dig brown aliens."

Guru's shoulders sagged. "You are not helping, professor. You have a very stylish head of hair, and a stylish beard to match. You do not know what I am going through."

Now it was Wallis' turn to sigh. "I'm sorry, buddy, I shouldn't be making light of this. My best advice? Go to a good barber. Not a cheap one. A good one. I can recommend you mine if you would like? His name's Andre. He'll be able to tell you what products to use to give your hair some volume, and what cut might best suit your problem area."

Guru brightened. "Really?"

"His shop's in Union Square. You can't miss it."

"Thank you, professor! I will visit him first thing tomorrow morning!"

"You'll probably need an appointment…"

"Right. Well, I will phone him first thing tomorrow morning then."

"Now you're talking. Have a good night, Guru. And remember, any problems, any questions—check that: any *non-hair* related questions—don't hesitate to call me."

△△△

Seated in the black leather swivel chair, Guru Rampal looked around the small observation room, though there wasn't much to see. The table before him with the touch-screen panel and the laptop. A metal trolley loaded with a desktop computer and EEG equipment. And the five-hundred-or-so-liter tank that fed the stimulant gas into the sleep laboratory.

Curious, Guru got up and went to the tank. He placed a hand on the stainless steel surface. It was cool against his skin. He studied the different valves and pressure gauges but didn't dare touch any. Amphetamines and other psychostimulant drugs had to be ingested as pills or injected intravenously (or, when used recreationally, snorted as a powder or inhaled as smoke). He'd never heard of any that could be evaporated into vapors and breathed in as easily as if they were oxygen. Nevertheless, if this could be done with certain anesthetics such as nitrous oxide and xenon, he supposed it had only been a matter of time before someone figured out how to do it with stimulants as well.

And not just someone, he thought. *Dr. Roy Wallis.*
My professor.

Guru was beyond excited that Dr. Wallis had chosen him to assist in his groundbreaking research. He admired the man tremendously. Over the years he'd selected every one of the professor's courses that fit his schedule, and he would continue to do so when he undertook his master's degree next spring and, eventually, his Ph.D.

To call a spade a spade, Guru was an intellectual. This was due to both genetics and hard work. According to his mother, he had been walking and talking since his first birthday. By two and a half years of age, he could count to more than one hundred. When he was five, he solved a Rubik's Cube he'd found in the school's library on his first try. In grade six, he won the school's spelling bee contest, a feat he repeated every consecutive year until he graduated.

Nevertheless, even though learning came easily to him, he did not take his gift for granted. He always pushed himself to excel that little bit more, to become that little bit better than his classmates, because he'd known that doing so was the only way he would escape the slums into which he'd been born and provide a better life for himself and his mother and his brothers.

When he was accepted as a freshman to' UC Berkeley (thanks in part to a glowing letter of recommendation from the Chairman of Secondary Education in his home city of Dharamshala), his mother had urged him to pursue a degree in information technology. "Indians make very good computer programmers, Guru," she'd told him. "It is a very good job, and it pays very handsomely. I do not understand why you want to be a psychologist. Indians do not make good psychologists."

Guru, of course, disagreed that Indians did not make good psychologists, and as for why he wanted to work in the field of psychology, the answer was simple: it was what he was meant to do. His father had suffered from Alzheimer's, and his second-eldest brother was on the autistic spectrum, so Guru had spent much of his youth taking them to and from hospitals and serving as their primary caregiver. He became deeply invested in learning about their maladies, always pestering doctors and nurses with mental health questions, or cutting articles from whatever newspapers and magazines he could get his hands on. Over the years he became a veritable expert on both maladies, and when his father passed away from complications with Alzheimer's, he decided to devote the rest of his life to the psychology of the mind.

Guru was eager to begin this journey as soon as possible, but he still had a long road ahead of him. It would be another two years before he completed his master's degree, and four more years after that to become a chartered psychologist and gain his APA accreditation. On top of all this, he would need to spend another year or two in a fellowship program at the university to gain field experience. Only then—seven or eight years down the road—could he become a licensed clinical psychologist.

Originally Guru's dream had been to open a practice in California. However, he was now contemplating doing so in India, where he could also campaign for healthcare change at a grassroots level, for as he'd witnessed firsthand growing up, the country's healthcare was in an abysmal state of affairs. Hospitals and community organizations were understaffed and underfunded. Policies focused on curative measures rather than preventive ones. And in many of the villages and smaller towns, therapy and counseling were virtually unheard of. Yes, he would only be one voice in a population of 1.3 billion, but change always had to start somewhere—

"You there, doc?"

Jumping at the unexpected voice, Guru hurried to the touch-panel controller. "Uh, hi. This is Guru speaking."

"Elvis!" Chad said. He was standing directly before the two-way glass, grinning.

"Uh, yes, that is me." He wasn't yet comfortable using the intercom system.

"You wearing your sunnies? I can't see you in this mirror."

"My sunglasses?"

"Yeah, mate."

"No, I do not wear my sunglasses at night."

"I wear my sunglasses at night," Chad sang. *"So I can, so I can..."*

Guru recognized the song and realized the joke was on him. He didn't reply.

Chad stopped singing and said, "Hey, mate, where you from? India, right?"

"Yes, that is right. From a city named Dharamshala in the state of Himachal Pradesh. You might be interested to know the Dalai Lama's residence is located there."

"No shit? Didya ever meet him?"

"When I was a boy, yes. My class visited Tsuglakhang Temple while the Dalai Lama was present so we could listen to his preaching."

"Did he do any magic?"

"Magic?" Guru frowned. "No. The Dalai Lama is but a simple Buddhist monk. He has no magical powers."

"I thought he healed people and shit?"

"No, he could not even heal himself when he became sick and required the removal of his gall bladder."

"All right, mate. I hear ya. Hey, I have a question."

"About the Dalai Lama?"

"Nah. Food. Got any good recipes?"

"I—no." Guru shook his head, despite the fact the Australian couldn't see him. "I am not a very good cook."

"Come on, mate. You gotta know something? We got all this food in here and neither Shaz or I know shit about cooking."

"I make a great brekky!" Sharon said, looking up from the book she was reading on her bed.

"How hard is it to make bacon and eggs?" Chad remarked.

"I can do more than that," she protested.

"Anyway, Elvis," Chad said to Guru, "give me a recipe. Something elaborate that will help pass the fucking time in this box."

"The only dishes I prepare at home are curries. If you would like, I could give you one of those recipes. I learned them from my mother."

"Curry, awesome! Like a vindaloo or butter chicken or

37

something?"

"That would depend on whether you prefer it to be spicy or sweet?"

"Spicy, mate! The hotter the better."

"Do you have chili peppers?"

"We got an entire fucking supermarket in here, mate. But let me check." He went to the refrigerator. "Yup, got a whole package."

"Then check the pantry for these spices..."

△△△

Dr. Roy Wallis lived in the timeworn Clock Tower Building in San Francisco's South of Market neighborhood. Built in 1907, the brick-and-timber structure covered two city blocks at Second and Bryant Streets. It once housed the operations of the Schmidt Lithograph Company, the largest printer on the West Coast. In 1992 it underwent a facelift when visionary capitalists transformed the cavernous space into over one hundred trendy lofts, all of which featured soaring ceilings, concrete columns, and factory windows.

Wallis parked his bite-sized Audi TT in his reserved spot out back of the building and, forgoing the elevator to burn some calories, climbed the six flights of steps to the penthouse suite.

Home sweet home, he thought as he stepped through the front door into the 3,000-square-foot space. The brick walls and cathedral ceilings with their exposed steel beams were remnants of the building's industrial past, while Dr. Wallis' extensive renovations—including floor-to-ceiling windows, skylights, polished slate floors, and a black-and-gray color scheme—lifted the apartment's aesthetics into the twenty-first century.

Wallis would never have been able to afford the digs on his teaching salary. His parents, however, had been wealthy, and when they died in a yachting accident twenty years earlier, he had inherited their nearly twenty-million-dollar estate. At the time, he had been living in a modest studio apartment in SoMa, which had been a ghost town then, filled with empty warehouses festooned with smokestacks, few restaurants, and not a single grocery store. When he heard the penthouse suite in the nearby Clock Tower Building was hitting the market, he toured it out of curiosity and fell immediately in love. Not only was it airy and spacious, but it included exclusive access to the three-story Clock Tower. Wallis gave Sotheby's their asking price and moved in the next month. He had called it home ever since, and he couldn't imagine living anywhere else in the city.

Dr. Wallis hung his blazer on a wall hook, dumped his keys in a crystal dish on a table next to the door, then went to the bar, where he poured dark rum and ginger beer over ice, adding a slice of lime as garnish. He carried the highball outside to the twelve-hundred-square-foot wraparound deck, breathing the twilight air deeply. In the distance the downtown skyline glittered with lights, while the Bay Bridge appeared to magically hover above the fog-shrouded San Francisco Bay like a bejeweled necklace.

He was about to light a cigarette when his phone rang.

He withdrew it from his pocket, glanced at the screen, then answered it. "Are you downstairs stalking me?" he said. "You called as soon as I stepped in the door."

"You're standing on your deck with a Dark 'n' Stormy and admiring the night view," the female voice said.

"How did you know that?"

"I'm watching you."

Despite himself, Wallis scanned the windows of the buildings stretching away below him. "Am I that predictable?" he asked.

"As predictable as a grandfather clock."

"Is that a shot at my age?"

Brandy Clarkson laughed. "You look good for forty-one, Roy. Stop obsessing."

"I'm not obsessing."

"It's all you talked about on your birthday."

His birthday had been a month ago. Brandy had been in San Francisco, and she'd taken him to a dumpling restaurant in Chinatown, where, admittedly, he'd made a fuss about how old he was getting.

"You in town now?" he asked.

"Came for a conference tomorrow morning."

He glanced at his wristwatch: half past ten. "I can meet you at Yoshi's in twenty?"

"I'm not in the mood for jazz. I thought we could have a quiet night for a change?"

He was up for that. "You want to come over? Where are you staying?"

"The Fairmont. I'll grab an Uber and be there in fifteen."

Wallis hung up, finished his drink, then took a hot shower. He and Brandy had begun dating seven years ago when he was thirty-four and she was twenty-one—and a student in one of his senior classes. After about three years of exclusive dating, their relationship became serious. Too serious for him, and he broke it off, much to Brandy's dismay. She moved south to Menlo Park and got a job with Facebook as a behavioral data analyst. He didn't see her again for two years until they randomly bumped into one another during happy hour at the View, a lounge on the thirty-ninth floor of the Marriot, where they had often hung out when they were a couple. They had a few drinks together, reminisced, and ended up sleeping together. Since then they'd been hooking up whenever she was in the area, which was usually once a month or so. Twenty-eight now, Brandy was more of everything—independent, confident, sophisticated— and Wallis enjoyed her infrequent company.

Nevertheless, he *was* forty-one. He couldn't keep up his bachelor lifestyle forever, and he found himself thinking more and more about finding a proper girlfriend, someone he could spend each night with, build a future with.

He toweled off, shaved, dressed in black, and was pouring a second drink when Brandy knocked. He'd left the door unlocked and called out, "Come in!"

"Hello, my lovely!" Brandy sang, stepping inside, smiling radiantly. Holding a bottle of champagne in one hand, and a black handbag in the other, she closed the door with her tush.

"You look great," Wallis said.

"Thanks!" she said, crossing the living room, heels clicking on the slate, blonde ringlets bouncing against her shoulders, blue eyes sparkling. Flamenco-red lipstick matched the color of her dress, which clung to her breasts and hips and flaunted her long, tanned legs.

She planted a kiss on his lips.

"Mmmm," she said. "You smell good. I like that aftershave."

"You smell good too," he said. "Didn't I buy you that perfume?"

"You did indeed. Miss me?"

"I always miss you."

She pouted. "You do not. Otherwise you never would have dumped me. Here." She offered him the champagne.

"What's the occasion?" he asked, taking it and reading the label.

"Duh?" She slapped him playfully on the chest. "The first day of your big secret experiment you won't tell me anything about!"

"I mentioned it on my birthday…?"

"You did indeed, Mr. One-Too-Many-At-Dinner. And I do listen to you, Roy, believe it or not. I'm not just in this farce of a relationship for the sex."

Wallis led Brandy to the kitchen. He filled two flutes with champagne, then laid out a spread of red grapes, rye crackers, and goat cheese on the granite island.

"To the Sleep Experiment," he said, raising his glass.

Brandy tapped. "May it not be a snoozer."

"Touché," he said, sipping. The bubbly tasted light, fruity, and refreshing.

"So tell me about it," she said. "Are you hiding peas beneath a mattress in the hopes of finding your perfect princess-bride?"

"I'm studying the effects of sleep deprivation," he said simply.

She stared at him. "Is that it? That's all you're going to tell me?"

"There's not that much to it—"

"Oh, come now, Roy! You were just as cagey on your birthday! What's the big secret?"

"There is no big secret," he said. "I'm observing the behavior of two test subjects as they function without sleep." He shrugged. "And there's an experimental gas involved…"

"Here's the juicy stuff I wanted! What kind of gas?"

"A substituted amphetamine, which is to say, a class of compounds based upon the amphetamine structure."

"I didn't know you could inhale amphetamines?"

"The method is much preferable to taking pills because the subjects never miss a dose, and the gas is administered directly to the lungs, which limits systemic absorption, which limits side effects. I have so far observed zero negative central nervous system side effects in any of my clinical trials."

"*Zero* side effects? There are always side effects."

He shook his head. "Even administered in high doses, the gas has caused no neurotoxic damage to brain cells. I've only tested it on animals thus far, of course. But imagine, Brandy, if the human trials are successful—"

"You're going to have armies of meth-heads roaming the country!"

He shook his head again. "Unlike methamphetamines, the gas doesn't act upon serotonin or dopamine neurotransmitters. It provides no rush or euphoria. No addiction or withdrawal. No anxiety, depression, paranoia, or psychosis. You just…don't sleep."

"Like…for how long are we talking here?"

"Days." He shrugged. "Weeks."

Brandy appeared incredulous. "Bullshit, Roy."

"As long as you're inhaling the gas, you won't sleep. It's as simple as that."

"But we *need* sleep. You, me, everybody! You can't just *not* sleep."

Dr. Wallis smiled. "That hypothesis, Brandy, is what I intend to challenge over the next twenty-one days."

$$\triangle\triangle\triangle$$

Dr. Roy Wallis fielded several more questions from Brandy before steering her off the conversation and into the bedroom. Their sex was always loud, creative, and a little dangerous.

Straddling her on the bed now, Wallis peeled the red dress over her head and feathered her naval with kisses. She gripped tufts of his hair and thrust her pelvis into his. He slid his hands beneath her back and unclasped her bra—

There was a knock at the door.

Wallis straightened, wondering who it could be.

"Expecting company?" Brandy asked, smiling mischievously.

He shook his head. "Wait here."

Wallis crossed the penthouse, buttoning his shirt.

Who the hell would be coming by at this hour?

He paused at the front door. There was no peephole. He'd been planning on installing a security camera but hadn't gotten around to it.

"Hello?" he said.

"Roy? It's Brook."

Shit! he thought. Why was she here—?

They'd made plans the week before, only he'd completely forgotten about them.

Knowing he could not leave her standing on his doorstep, he opened the door and greeted her with his best smile. She smiled back.

"Hi!" she said.

"Hi," he said.

Physically, Brook Foxley was opposite Brandy Clarkson. Her black hair was cut in a short, straight bob. Her dark eyes possessed a skittish reticence. Her pale skin looked as though it had never been touched by the sun. She had none of Brandy's curves, but her svelte figure was somehow equally feminine, and she looked stunning right then in a silk blouse, skinny jeans, and nude heels a shade or two lighter than her beaded clutch.

Personality-wise, Brook and Brandy were also opposites. Brook was watchful, reserved, playful in a friendly manner. She was not one to immediately catch your eye, but somehow she became more beautiful each time you saw her.

Brandy, in contrast, was a flirt. She flaunted her sexuality, weaponized it to her advantage. When Dr. Wallis took her out, he practically shared the date with her phone. She insisted all the messages and emails were work-related, but he never really knew for certain. And when she wasn't on her phone, she was telling him about some celebrity or Silicon Valley so-and-so she had met at a gala dinner or yacht party or glitzy function. Her life was glamorous, narcissistic, exciting...and empty. She was an outsider relentlessly searching for a way into a world to which she didn't belong and would likely never be accepted, relentlessly positioning herself to be in the right place at the right time for that Big Break to transform her life, relentlessly searching for the quickest way up the social ladder, morals and happiness and empathy for others be damned.

She was, in fact, Wallis to a tee.

"I tried calling you," Brook said, smiling uncertainly, "but your phone was off."

"The battery was low all day. It must have finally run out," he said, remaining squarely in the doorway as his mind searched madly for a way out of the mousetrap he found himself in.

Sensing something was up, Brandy's eyes flicked past him. "I hope I'm not intruding...?"

"No, not at all..." he said. "Well, actually..."

The silence that followed spoke volumes.

"I see, I'm sorry," Brook said. "I shouldn't have just stopped by... But last week we made a date for tonight. You wanted to celebrate your new experiment..."

"I know, and I did—I do—want to celebrate...with you," he said, fumbling for the right words. "It's just that I've been so busy, and the date slipped my mind—"

"What's going on out here?"

Dr. Wallis' stomach dropped at the sound of Brandy's voice. He turned to find her crossing the room wearing nothing but her lacy white lingerie.

"Oh!" Brook said, her eyes meeting Wallis' before faltering to the floor. Yet in that brief moment he read in them heartbreak —the same sensation squeezing the inside of his chest. "Goodnight," she mumbled and retreated down the staircase.

"Brook!" he called after her.

She continued without stopping. He almost called her name again but didn't. What was the point? She wouldn't return, and even if she did, what would they talk about with Brandy standing in the living room in her thong and bra?

Brandy.

Goddammit.

Wallis stepped back inside, closed the door, then focused his frustration on his on-and-off-again fling, who now stood at the kitchen island, sipping her flute of champagne.

"What the hell did you do that for?" he snapped.

"She didn't have to leave," Brandy said. "I haven't had a threesome in, oh, far too long." She was acting nonchalant, her tone was conversational, but Wallis could tell she was pissed off, and he realized he wasn't the only one with a right to be upset.

He sighed. "Why didn't you just stay in the bedroom? I would have gotten rid of her."

"I wanted to see who you're fucking these days."

"Jesus," he said, shaking his head. He went to the bar, filled a tumbler with two fingers of rum, and swallowed the contents in one burning gulp.

Brandy asked, "Is she a student like I was?"

"No."

"She's young."

"She's thirty-three."

"Blessed with good genes. Dammit, Roy, you'll never change, will you?"

"Change?" He looked at her, surprised. "Change how? I can't

see other people? We're not exclusive. You know that."

"I know, but I thought…" Her blue eyes darkened. "I thought you were changing. I thought maybe…I don't know! But we've been spending a lot of time together…I thought… Oh, fuck it!"

She stormed off to the bedroom.

Wallis poured another couple of fingers of rum.

Brandy returned a minute later, fully dressed. She snatched her handbag from the island and went straight to the door.

"Where are you going?" he asked her.

"To the hotel."

"You don't have to…"

"Goodbye, Roy." She opened the door, looked back. "You know what's sad about this? I would have been good to you. I would have made you happy."

"Brandy…"

She left, slamming the door closed behind her.

DAY 2

TUESDAY, MAY 29, 2018

D r. Roy Wallis entered the observation room in the basement of Tolman Hall carrying his briefcase and two coffees in a pulp-fiber takeout tray. He set the tray on the table and said, "Cappuccino and vanilla latte. Your pick."

"Actually, I don't drink coffee, professor," Penny Park said. "Only tea."

"More caffeine for me then." He slumped into the second chair with a weary sigh. "I guess I could use it."

"Yeah, you look pretty tired, professor." She eyed him suspiciously. "Did you party late at a nightclub?"

"I'm too old for nightclubs, Penny. I just had a few drinks at home."

"By yourself?"

"Yes, by myself," he said, which was mostly true. After Brandy left, he'd stayed up well past midnight smoking pot and drinking his best rum and playing music way too loud. He rubbed his eyes and studied the two Australians in the sleep laboratory. Chad was lying supine on the weight bench, presumably resting between sets, while Sharon reclined in her bed, reading a book. "How've they been?"

"All good, mate," Penny said in a horrendous attempt at an Australian accent.

"My God," he said.

"Not good?"

47

"It's the effort that counts."

"Shaz taught me a lot of Australian expressions."

"Shaz?"

"It's her nickname."

"I know that—"

"She told me to call her that. It's what they do with names in Australia. Me, I wouldn't be Penz, because that sounds like something you write with—"

"Rather than a unit of currency."

"Ha, ha. Instead, Shaz said I'd be called Parksy. I don't know what you would be called. Probably not Royz. That sounds like the flower, which is too feminine for someone so manly as you."

"Manly as me?"

"You are a very manly man, professor. Hmmm…maybe you'd be called Wallsy? You should ask her."

"It's at the top of my list," he said. "What else did you talk about?"

"Do you know what a Map of Tassie is?"

"Yes, Penny, I do."

"Really? Prove it."

"It's an Australian colloquialism for a woman's pubic hair."

"Because the shape of Tasmania is—"

"Do you really want to spend the handover discussing this?"

"You asked what we talked about."

"I'll read your notes. Why don't you head off and relax? You've been up since the crack of dawn."

"I'm actually wide awake, professor. You know what's interesting? Chad used the bathroom at six thirty a.m."

"Why's that interesting?"

"Because that's nearly the time he would be waking up any other day. And when you wake up, you always have to pee. So it's interesting because he still had to pee at the same time, even though he didn't sleep. It means his liver is pre-programmed."

"It's simply his body's endogenous, entrainable oscillation acting on its twenty-four-hour rhythms."

"Say what, professor? English isn't my first language, you

know."

"His circadian clock, Penny. Endogenous means the daily rhythms are self-sustained. Entrained means they are adjusted to local environmental factors such as light and temperature."

"So his circadian clock will adjust to his new environment?"

"Certainly."

"He'll start peeing at all crazy hours?"

"He'll go when he needs to. Not when his circadian clock tells him it's the usual time to do so."

"Hey, professor? Can I ask you something?"

"You're not thinking about shaving your head, are you?"

"Huh?"

"Fire away."

"So this morning I was reading on my phone about sleep experiments. I had a lot of time to kill, right? Anyway, I came across a sleep experiment in the Soviet Union last century..."

Wallis smiled. "I was wondering when you or Guru were going to ask me about that."

She was referring to a paranormal legend that had been causing a stir on the internet the last few years. According to the most popular version of the tale, in the late 1940s, five political prisoners in the Soviet Union were offered their freedom if they participated in a government experiment in which they remained awake in a sealed environment for fifteen days—by breathing in an experimental gas-based stimulant.

"Because, you know," Penny said, "it sounds a lot like what we're doing..."

"I hope our gas isn't as toxic as theirs was," he said.

"Is that a joke?"

"The Russian Sleep Experiment is a legend, Penny. Complete fiction. What we're doing is careful, calculated scientific research."

"But do you think something...so awful...could happen in real life?"

"That remaining awake for an extended period could lead one to insanity, self-mutilation, murder, and cannibalism?

What do you think, Penny?"

"No," she answered sheepishly. "It's just that the story was so *creepy*. Maybe because I was here all by myself..."

"My advice to you, Penny? Bring in a good novel to pass the time rather than looking up nonsense on the internet."

"Yeah, right, good idea." She yawned. "Maybe I'm more tired than I thought." She collected her backpack and stood. "You work so much, professor. What do you do in your free time?"

"I have hobbies. I try to get to the gym now and then."

"Berkeley is so empty now, right? It's strange with no one around. All my friends went home to visit their families."

"I like the quiet. It's peaceful."

Penny nodded but made no move to leave. "What I'm wondering is, maybe *we* can go out for dinner this week?"

Dr. Wallis tried not to let his surprise show. Although he'd already concluded that Penny was attracted to him, he'd never imagined she would be so bold as to ask him out for dinner! Yes, he'd dated Brandy when she was his student, but he'd been a lot younger then. He was nearly twice Penny's age—a realization that depressed him enough to almost accept her invitation... almost.

"That would be nice, Penny," he said. "Except that I don't finish my shift until ten o'clock, by which time I'm rather exhausted. But, ah...thank you for asking."

"Yeah, no sweat," she said, her air a little too insouciant to be convincing. "I'll see you tomorrow, right?"

"Same time, same place."

She left then, easing the door closed behind her until the tongue clicked metallically in place.

Her exit was not half as dramatic as Brandy's door-slam the previous night, yet in the still basement room, the deliberately quiet action was somehow almost as emphatic.

ΔΔΔ

Chad Carter didn't know for certain how long he'd been cooped up in the sleep laboratory, but he reckoned it to be about one day or so now—and it already felt like a hell of a long time. Another nineteen or twenty days seemed like a bloody lifetime.

Initially, when he and Shaz were contemplating whether to participate in this wacko experiment, three weeks hadn't sounded too bad. But of course he hadn't known then just how fucked up it would be remaining awake for hours and hours on end.

He had pulled all-nighters before, of course, on more occasions than he could count. But it was different staying up around the clock when you were shitfaced and partying, compared to when you were sober as a judge with nothing to do but watch TV or work out or stare at the fucking wall.

Man, it was hard to believe last year at this time he had been partying his ass off in Europe...and now he was a rat in a box. He'd departed Melbourne in March with his good mate from uni, Shane Eales. They landed in London, where Shane's sister, Laura, worked for a marketing company. Laura had a lot of hot friends and connections, and on their first night on the town she took them to some posh club, all red leather and velvet, which featured glass fold-down trays in the bathroom cubicles not meant for holding drinks. Every time Chad went to the Men's to take a slash, he heard snorts coming from the occupied stalls. He wouldn't have minded doing a few lines himself, but he was on a budget that didn't include blow.

Later that evening, Kelly Osbourne, daughter of the Prince of Darkness, arrived at the pub and had countless blokes lining up to talk to her. Chad didn't get it. She wasn't hot. She was a spoiled rich brat. But all these guys wanted to talk to her just because she was famous becasue of her pop?

Always the larrikin, Shane decided to chat her up during a rare moment she was alone at her table. He sat down next to her, cracked an ice breaker—and she turned her back to him. The shutdown became an ongoing joke between them for the rest of the night.

Three days later they flew Ryanair to Spain, where they spent a few nights in Barcelona before heading to Pamplona. The small city was jam-packed with foreigners due to the annual festival Hemingway made famous in that book of his. There wasn't a single bed in any hotel or hostel to be found, so the only option was to buy tents and camp out in a huge field alongside thousands of other revelers.

It wasn't hard to find Australians when you traveled. You simply followed the beer and the noise. Chad and Shane quickly hooked up with a group of about twenty fellow Aussies that had set up base around a shitty RV with a big Australian flag taped to one side, and the next few days were a haze of drinking, tossing around a rugby ball, sleeping off hangovers, barbequing, and fucking in tiny tents.

Two days before the bulls were set to run, Shaz arrived at the field by herself. She had come to Europe with a friend, but the friend had returned to Perth. Shaz was easily the hottest in the ever-expanding group of Aussies, and Chad had tried his best that night to get some action, but she wasn't game, telling him she had a boyfriend back home.

The next morning, with everyone dressed in their whites with red sashes tied around their waists, they took a chartered bus into the city. The scene was fucking nuts. Streets and balconies packed with people. Everyone running around throwing sangria at everyone else.

The first order of business was to find beer, and by noon all two dozen or so Australians were smashed. Some Irish guy who'd ended up hanging out with them for much of the morning got so shit-faced he climbed a pole and leaped to his death. It wasn't intentional. Other people were leaping from the top of the pole into the locked arms of those below, sort of how rock stars belly-flop off the stage into a mosh pit of fans. The poor Irish bloke, however, jumped before anyone was paying attention to him. He landed on his head and was whisked away by paramedics. They heard later through the grapevine that he had passed away in the hospital.

Which, needless to say, was a major bummer and not exactly how you wanted to kick off a festival. But despite this, the rest of the day had come good, filled with drinking games, tapas, fights, and even conga lines. Most of those in their group passed out or returned to the field after dinner, but Chad and Shane kept partying throughout the night so they could secure spots along the fence that bordered the road which the bulls followed. Chad had planned to run, but that was before the Irish guy died, which had made the dangers of running with one-ton angry bulls a little more real and frightening.

In any event, the whole run went by ridiculously quickly, from the opening horn to the last bull charging past him lasting no more than a few minutes.

The following day the caravan of Aussies headed to Portugal, and Chad and Shaz went with them. They spent nearly three months traveling from small town to small town that lined the ocean, surfing and drinking and partying, until they broke up. The three blokes renting the RV were heading to Germany for Oktoberfest, while many of the others had already gone home or their separate ways. Sharon told Chad she wanted to see France, and for whatever reason (in the back of his mind he'd been thinking he could still get with her, boyfriend or not), he said he'd join her.

He parted ways with Shane, who was happy to check out Oktoberfest, and he and Shaz took a bus to Bordeaux, where they spent the night in an ancient, rundown hotel (same room, different beds). In the morning they rented a car and drove through the French countryside to Paris, which, up until that point, might have been the highlight of the trip. The Eiffel Tower, the Arc de Triomphe, the Louvre—all that shit you saw on TV was now right around every cobble-stoned corner.

Chad and Shaz remained in Paris for a month...and maybe the romance of the city rubbed off on her because she finally loosened up enough to make out with him one night, though she kept telling him "no" every time he tried to unbutton her jeans.

But whatever. Making out was kind of fun in itself, and the juvenile foreplay went on for another month before Sharon told him she was going to book a plane ticket to California. She didn't have much of a choice in the matter. She had to keep flying west on her around-the-world ticket. Chad's return flight to Melbourne was in three weeks, but he decided to fuck going home and booked a new ticket to California.

Shaz didn't exactly seem thrilled by this turn of events, and Chad figured it had something to do with her attraction for him warring with the guilt that came with cheating on her boyfriend.

Regardless, he tagged along to Cali, and they found accommodation in a house in Los Angeles, which they shared with three other Aussies and one Canadian.

LA quickly burned up whatever money they had left, so they both started looking for jobs. Sharon found work as a hostess at an Italian eatery, but Chad had a tougher time of it, eventually deciding to become a test subject for new drug trials. He participated in three clinical trials—two with the FDA and one with a pharmaceutical giant—before he came across the advert for the Sleep Experiment, which seemed like the motherlode of test trials.

Stay awake for three weeks, get a shit load of money. What wasn't there to love?

Given the professor running the show was looking for two test subjects who knew one another but were not romantically involved, Chad convinced Shaz to apply alongside him while coaching her not to mention their on-and-off-again make-out sessions.

And now here they were.

One or two days into the experiment.

Nineteen or twenty more to go.

No mornings, noons, or nights. Nothing to provide guidance or structure to the day. Just one unending slog of *Game of Thrones*, *Breaking Bad*, and all the other shit playing on Netflix.

Chad lay back down on the workout bench and gripped the

barbell suspended above his chest. *At least I'll be in shape when this is all over*, he thought, unracking the bar and performing the first of ten presses.

△△△

Dr. Roy Wallis was watching the Australians through the viewing window. Sharon was sitting on her bed, reading a hardback Rex Stout novel. Chad was lifting weights. He tapped the Talk button on the touch panel controller and asked, "How's everybody doing?"

Sharon glanced up sharply from the novel, apparently startled by the unexpected intrusion. "Hi, doc. You're back?"

"Enjoying the book?"

"I like the main character, Nero Wolfe. He's a brilliant detective who solves every crime right from his living room. He never goes outside. He just stays locked up at home reading books." She smiled sweetly. "Just like me right now, I guess."

"Perhaps I should bring you some orchids to tend for?" he said, referencing one of Nero Wolfe's favorite hobbies.

"Would you? That would be terrific."

Chad finished his series of reps, then sat up on the bench. "So we survived the first day, did we?"

"Does that mean it's about breakfast time?" Sharon asked.

There was no clock in the sleep laboratory to discourage the Australians from keeping track of how long they'd been sequestered. Having them count down more than three hundred hours until the experiment's end wouldn't be a great morale booster.

Dr. Wallis tapped the Talk button again. "You've been teaching Penny some interesting slang."

"She's a quick learner!" Sharon said.

"I was hoping we could try a couple of exercises today. If you'd like to eat first, go right ahead."

"What kind of exercises?"

"The first one involves tongue-twisters."

"I love tongue-twisters! Let's do it now. I'm not that hungry anyway."

"All right then. Nothing to it but to repeat after me…"

In total, Wallis recited six tongue twisters, and Sharon repeated them all back with relative ease. Chad made a few more mistakes than she did, but Wallis attributed those to the complexity of the phrases, not any faltering mental capacity due to sleep deprivation.

"Excellent," he told them. "The second exercise is a little more involved. I have a blindfold with me, along with a bag of random objects—"

"Kinky, doc," Sharon said, giggling.

"I'm going to bring them to the door now. Chad, I'd like you to meet me there. You can look in the bag, but Sharon, you cannot. Understood?"

"Too easy," Chad said, already heading toward the door.

From his messenger bag, Wallis gathered a silk shoe bag with a drawstring closure that had come with a pair of loafers he'd purchased recently. He also removed a red cotton bandana with a paisley design. At the door to the sleep laboratory, he handed both items to Chad and returned to his spot at the desk.

Although the stimulant gas was odorless and tasteless, he nevertheless thought he could detect a metallic scent.

My imagination, he told himself dismissively.

He pressed the Talk button. "Chad, I'd like you to tie the bandana around Sharon's eyes."

Chad did as instructed.

"Can you see anything, Sharon?"

"Nothing."

"Good. I'd like you to stick your hand in the bag Chad is holding and withdraw a single item."

"Better be no sheep brains or anything yucky in there, doc."

"Nothing of the sort," he assured her. "They're everyday items from around my house."

"What's all this about, mate?" Chad asked.

"I'd like to know whether Sharon is experiencing any initial signs of astereognosis due to sleep deprivation—that is, whether she has any difficulty identifying objects by touch alone without any other sensory input."

"You're the life of the party, mate. But whatever floats your boat. Shaz, you ready?"

"What if I fail?" she asked.

"The good doc pushes a button and you get incinerated," Chad said.

"You can't fail," Dr. Wallis told her. "Whenever you're ready…"

Sharon stuck a hand in the shoe bag and withdrew a Rubik's Cube. She identified it right away.

"Very good," Wallis said. Globes, pyramids, and cubes usually posed no problems. "Try again."

She set the Rubik's Cube aside and this time produced from the bag a porcelain teapot lid. She turned it over in her hand. "It's a lid of some kind."

"Can you be more specific?" Wallis asked.

"I don't know. Maybe for a teapot?"

"Excellent," he said.

"Two for two, Shaz," Chad said. "You're setting records."

"Try again," Wallis said.

This time she withdrew a novelty octopus flash drive.

She frowned. "God, what's this!"

"Try to identify it using your other hand."

She switched the flash drive to her left hand. "No idea…"

"Try using both hands."

"It's a bit squishy with some…things…at one end and something sharp at the other end…but…sorry, no idea, doc."

They continued the exercise until no items remained in the shoe bag. In total, Sharon correctly identified seven out of twelve objects. She removed the blindfold.

"So does she have that astro-disease?" Chad asked.

"It's not a disease," Dr. Wallis said. "And no, her tactile recognition exhibited no observable behavioral deficit. We'll see how well you do tomorrow."

"Can hardly wait, mate," Chad said and went back to lifting weights.

$$\triangle\triangle\triangle$$

Dr. Roy Wallis resumed his role as a silent observer, and over the next several hours the only sound in the small anteroom was the clicking of the laptop keys as he filled several pages with detailed notes chronicling the Australians' behavior and emerging symptoms related to sleep loss.

Guru Rampal arrived at nine forty-five p.m., holding his phone to his ear.

Wallis blinked in surprise at the young Indian.

His head was shaved smooth.

Guru held up a finger, to indicate he wouldn't be long on the phone. Dr. Wallis lit a cigarette. Guru hadn't yet spoken a word, and Wallis would have thought he was on hold had he not been able to hear a barely audible voice on the other end of the line. When he finished his cigarette and butted it out in the ashtray he'd brought from home, and Guru had still not spoken a word, he went to the bathroom. He returned five minutes later to find Guru still listening to someone jabbering away. He was about to say something when Guru abruptly spoke a few words in Hindi, waited, spoke a few more, then hung up.

"What the hell was that all about, Guru?"

"I was speaking with my mother in India."

"She's quite the chatterbox."

"No, she hardly speaks at all."

"But you only got in a handful of words in a ten-minute conversation."

"It was a group Facebook call with my mother and four brothers. My siblings and I must speak in order, from eldest to youngest. Because I am the youngest, I always speak last. Anyway." He pointed to his bald dome. "What do you think, professor?"

"Looking good, Iceman."

Guru grinned. "Andre had a last-minute cancellation this morning, and so I visited his barber shop. He told me he could help me style my hair with mousse and other products, but it would take a lot of upkeep on my part, and my hair would only continue to thin in the future. His recommendation was to shave it all off. I was hesitant at first, but Andre is bald too, and he looks very good, which gave me greater confidence to take the plunge myself."

"I'm happy you're happy, Guru," Wallis said. "It'll certainly be easier to manage now. Maybe pick up some sunscreen the next time you're at the drugstore?"

"Good point, professor. I will get some when I go shopping for my new clothes. Yes, I am ready for a complete transformation." He sat down in the free chair and set his backpack on the floor. "May I say, professor, you are a very good dresser, you have very good taste. Would you be willing to dispense some fashion advice?"

Beguiled, Wallis studied Guru's outfit. He wore an orange tee-shirt emblazoned with an anime character from Dragon Ball Z, a pair of plaid shorts, and the same brilliant white sneakers he'd worn the day before. He looked like a poster boy for Old Navy. "My best advice?" Dr. Wallis said, wanting to tread as tactfully as possible. "The shaved head makes you appear older. Nothing wrong with that. But the graphic tees you wear are a rather youthful style. To compliment your more mature shaved head, I would recommend you dress up a bit more. Think less casual, more...urbane."

"Excellent observation, professor!" Guru said, nodding enthusiastically. "More urbane. So no more tee-shirts? Not even nice ones? I do not want to look *too* mature."

"I'm not saying wear a jacket and tie, Guru, but simply spruce things up. I'd stick with button-down shirts from now on, well-fitted, neutral colors."

"And my shorts?"

"I'd probably avoid shorts altogether, to be honest."

"Only pants. Yes, I can do that. Jeans?"

"Jeans are okay. They work for almost any age. But they shouldn't have any holes, and they should be a darker rather than lighter color."

"And my shoes?"

"Eh…you probably need to let go of all of your sneakers too."

Guru seemed distressed. "*All* of my sneakers…?"

"If you *need* to wear sneakers, I'd go for a minimalist canvas variety. Personally, however, I'd stick with leather."

"Leather only?" Guru shook his head. "Jeez, professor. Maybe I am not ready for this new life quite yet. I feel like Tom Hanks in *Big*."

Wallis smiled. "It's heavy stuff, buddy. I feel for you. But remember, this is my advice only. You're perfectly free to continue wearing whatever you choose."

"No, professor, your advice has been very helpful."

Dr. Wallis sniffed. He glanced at Guru's backpack on the floor. "Did you bring McDonald's again?"

"I did indeed."

"Two days in a row. You might want to consider adding a healthier diet to this new lifestyle of yours too."

"I know McDonald's is not good for me. But it is the only food I can eat."

Wallis frowned. "What are you talking about?"

"My mother's cooking was the only food I ate growing up. I miss it tremendously. Since coming to America, McDonald's is the only food I have tried that I like."

"You've been here for two years!"

"Yes, I know. My diet is not enviable." He patted what Wallis had previously thought to be a beer belly but was clearly a McDonald's belly.

"You can't cook for yourself?"

"Yes, I cook at home. But when I am out, I eat McDonald's."

"There are so many great restaurants around, Guru. There's even an authentic Indian place not far from here that I'm sure—"

"On Solano Avenue? Yes, I have gone there. But the food tastes nothing like my mother's cooking—"

"Good grief!" Dr. Wallis blurted, shaking his head with incredulity. "Someday, Guru, you're going to be a very wealthy and successful man—but, brother, you're one strange duck!"

△△△

Instead of returning home, Dr. Roy Wallis drove the eight miles to the neighboring city of Oakland, and then to a commercial street in Dogtown—coined so by police officers due to the unusual number of stray dogs in the area. He tooled slowly past Café Emporium where Brook worked, peering through the large street windows. He couldn't see her among the over-twenty-one crowd. He parked down the block, then returned to the dive bar. The place had a good atmosphere, reminiscent of a wealthy eccentric's basement den, or perhaps an old hipster's antique shop. It was busy as usual, the bar staff pumping out Greyhounds, their marquee drink, to the thirsty throng. Wallis had tried a Greyhound once. The pour was heavy and the drink was strong, but all he could taste was the fresh grapefruit. Brook told him the bar used different grapefruit suppliers for each order depending on who could provide the sweetest fruit at the time. He believed her.

Dr. Wallis squeezed in at the bar and ordered a pint of a bitter IPA. He still didn't see Brook, though there were two other bars on the premises she could be tending. He took his beer outside and chain-smoked two cigarettes.

"What are you doing here?"

Wallis had been gazing across the dark, foggy bay to San Francisco's eloquent skyline on the far bank. He turned to find Brook standing behind him. Her knitted brow and crossed arms did not portend an easy reconciliation.

"Is this how you greet all your customers?" he said lightly.

"I'm serious, Roy. I don't know what you're doing here."

"I wanted to see you."

"Is a blonde bombshell going to pop out from behind a bush or tree?"

"That was rather awkward, I admit."

"Somewhat of an understatement, Roy." She glanced over her shoulder into the bar. "I have to get back to work."

"What time do you get off?"

"I'm just a simple girl, Roy. I liked you. I thought you liked me —"

"I do, Brook."

"Call me old-fashioned, but when a man and a woman like each other, and when they become intimate, they shouldn't be sleeping around with other people. Who was she anyway?" Brook shook her head. "No, I don't care. I don't want to know. I don't want to know how many women you're currently sleeping with—"

"Only her, Brook," Dr. Wallis interrupted sincerely. "We used to date, but we broke up two years ago. We just see each other casually now and then. That's it."

"That's it?" Brook repeated sardonically. "The fact you're having casual sex with your ex is actually a pretty big deal to me."

"I know, I understand," he said. "Bad choice of words. What I meant was, she's not important to me anymore. You are. I wouldn't be here if you weren't."

Something shifted in Brook's eyes. Hopeful calculation? "Are you going to see her anymore?"

"No," he said.

Brook's stiff body language relaxed. Her arms remained crossed, but she no longer seemed as though she wanted to throw the nearest drink on him. She chewed her bottom lip. "I don't know, Roy…"

"What time do you get off?"

"Not until the last call tonight."

"Could you get someone to cover for you?"

"I don't know…probably…"

"Great! I'll just wait out here until you do."

"Jesus, Roy." She shook her head.

"What?" he said, grinning.

"Just—*Jesus.*"

She returned inside.

ΔΔΔ

For the last year or so, Dr. Wallis had been coming to Café Emporium most Saturday or Sunday mornings to read the newspaper and sip a vanilla latte and occasionally nibble on a gluttonous pastry. Roughly two months ago, Brook had adopted the habit of serving his latte with a token chocolate cookie that he didn't order. He didn't give this much thought. He didn't give her much thought either. Until five weeks ago, when he glanced up from the sports section of the *Chronicle* and his eyes settled on her. She was dressed in her simple uniform of black tights and a black shirt, and she hadn't been doing anything more interesting than clearing a nearby table of dirty dishes. However, something triggered inside him. He stole several more glances in her direction before paying his bill. The next Saturday he engaged her in conversation whenever she approached his table, and before he left, he asked her to dinner. She seemed flummoxed and turned down his invitation. He persisted with a mix of stubbornness and friendly humor, and she relented. They met at a lively downtown restaurant, then watched a live show across the street at the Fox Theater. The evening couldn't have gone any better, and after a few nightcaps, Brook ended up spending the night at his place. Since then, they'd been seeing each other at least once or twice a week.

Dr. Wallis finished his beer and was thinking about going inside to order a second when Brook appeared.

"That was quick," he said.

"We're not that busy tonight," she said, though he found this hard to believe given the crowd inside. "Did you have anywhere in mind you'd like to go?"

"There's a good Spanish place over on Grace Avenue. I've been in the mood for tapas all day."

"Fine by me. But do you mind stopping by my place first so I can freshen up?"

"Sure," he said, surprised. He had never been to her place before.

It turned out Brook didn't live very far away—nor did she live in a landlocked house. She lived in a houseboat moored on the still waters of San Francisco Bay.

"Whoa!" Wallis said, taking in the squat, quaint structure on floats. "I didn't know you lived like Popeye!"

"Don't knock it, Roy. It's two-thirds the price of a single-bedroom apartment."

"I'm not knocking it. I love it."

The interior resembled that of a rustic mountain cabin: wood floors, wood walls, wood ceiling, wood cabinetry. A variety of wall hangings and throw rugs added splashes of color, while miscellaneous items—stacks of vinyl records, flowering plants, a battered guitar case leaning against a shiny black piano—lent the shoebox space a cozy, creative air.

"It's not much," Brook said, a bit self-consciously. "But it's comfortable."

"It's fantastic," Wallis said. "I feel like I'm suddenly on vacation."

"There's beer in the fridge. Help yourself. I'll have a quick shower."

"Why not just jump in the bay?"

"Funny, mister. Won't be long."

"Aye, aye, captain."

Rolling her eyes, Brook disappeared into the houseboat's only other room, closing the door behind her.

Dr. Wallis retrieved a Belgium beer from the compact fridge, twisted off the cap, and took a long sip. He was craving a cigarette but decided it wouldn't be prudent to smoke inside a house constructed entirely of hickory and oak.

Instead he studied the wall over the kitchen table. It was

studded with photographs, most in simple frames, a few pinned to the wood with thumbtacks. Some were portrait shots of a man and woman Wallis suspected were Brook's parents. Others were of Brook herself: as a big-eyed, pony-tailed child; as a pretty, awkward teen; wearing a mortarboard at her college graduation; partying with girlfriends indoors, outdoors, on a lake somewhere. And in five photos she was with the same man. He was Brook's age, handsome, and fit.

Dr. Wallis frowned. He didn't often experience jealousy, but right then a greasy fire warmed his belly.

The water clunked off and stopped running through the old pipes. A minute later Brook emerged from the adjacent room wrapped in a white towel. "Not much closet space in the bedroom," she said. "The dress I want is in here." She opened a door he hadn't noticed and removed a blue dress from a rack jam-packed with hanging garments.

"Who's this?" Wallis asked, pointing at the man in the pictures.

Brook joined him in the kitchen. "Oh him," she said cavalierly. "Just an ex I sleep with now and then."

Wallis stared at her.

She laughed. "You should see your face!"

"Who is he?" he demanded.

"My brother, Roy! *Sheesh.*"

Wallis' cheeks burned with embarrassment. "I didn't notice the resemblance." He finished his beer and set the bottle on the counter. "Now that you've mentioned your ex...I don't think you've ever told me anything about him?"

"You never asked." Brook shrugged her bare, slender shoulders. "He was a wild animal keeper at the San Francisco Zoo. He was headhunted for a senior position at the San Diego Zoo." She shrugged again. "He accepted the job, I didn't want to uproot and move, so we broke up. But is he really who you want to talk about right now?"

"No," Wallis said, sliding his arms around Brook's svelte waist and kissing her on her soft lips. He became immediately aroused. He slid his hands down over her buttocks, down her firm thighs, then up them again, beneath the towel. Her breasts pressed against his chest.

"I should get dressed," she mumbled.

"No," he said.

"The neighbors can see us through the windows."

He spotted a light switch within an arm's reach and flipped the nub, plunging them into shadows. He tugged Brook's towel loose and let it drop to the floor. Naked, she unbuckled his belt and undid the button and zipper of his slacks.

Kissing tenderly yet passionately, they shuffled through the moon-dappled boathouse to the cluttered bedroom, their bodies entwined in a slow, exotic dance.

They didn't make it to dinner.

△△△

Brook lay awake in bed that night, propped up on one elbow, watching Roy Wallis sleep. The windows and curtains were open, allowing a fresh breeze into the bedroom, as well as slices of silvered moonlight that cast Roy's strong features in a ghostly chiaroscuro effect. His bare chest rose and fell with each slow breath.

Such a handsome man, she thought, her eyes studying his straight eyebrows and thick-lashed eyes, his defined nose and chiseled cheekbones, his long and full beard. In her mind she pictured him on the cover of one of those trendy men's magazines wearing a checkered plaid shirt and suspenders with an axe resting on a shoulder.

The rugged, woodsy intellectual.

So different than her last boyfriend. Not that George Goldmark wasn't smart; he was. He was simply bland, both in appearance and personality. Standing at five-foot-ten, he was neither tall nor short. His chestnut hair, graying at the temples, was always parted on the left and brushed to the right and held in place with maximum-hold hairspray. Gray eyeglasses framing often unreadable black eyes, cleanly shaven jaw, dimpled chin. Friendly yet reserved, content to be a wallflower at a party rather than a mingler. Soft-spoken, polite, complimentary—boring.

Despite this mediocracy, Brook cared deeply for George. He was affectionate and accommodating to her needs. He didn't take drugs or smoke cigarettes. He only drank on occasion and didn't become drunk. He was never physically or verbally abusive. He was, she supposed you could say, safe.

They had met in a Costco food court of all places. She had finished her grocery shopping and had decided to spoil herself with a berry sundae. It was a Sunday afternoon, the place was busy, and George, carrying a tray loaded with a turkey provolone sandwich, French fries, and a large soft drink, asked if he could share her table. The last thing she wanted to do was eat with a stranger, but she nodded politely. She planned to finish her sundae promptly and get up and go, but George didn't start chatting her up as she'd expected. Instead, he produced a crossword booklet from his pocket, opened it to a half-completed puzzle, and began working away. She relaxed a bit and took out her phone, so she was doing something too.

"A small tropical fish that is a common pet and can live in brackish water?"

"Excuse me?" she said, looking up

He repeated the crossword clue.

"A goldfish?" she suggested.

"Only five letters, third letter an L."

She was about to tell him she didn't know when she said, "Molly?"

"Ah! Thank you." He scribbled down the answer. "As a vet, you'd think I would have gotten that one."

"To be fair, most people simply flush their sick fish down the toilet rather than take them to a vet."

"They do, don't they? But I don't run a practice. I work at the zoo."

"The Oakland Zoo?" she asked.

"The San Francisco Zoo."

"I haven't been there since I was a child."

"It's a great place to spend a day with the kids. They might even learn a thing or two about the environment and conservation."

"I don't have children," she said.

"No?" he said, his eyes going to her denuded ring finger. "I'm sorry. I didn't notice…"

"Why be sorry?" She took a final spoonful of her sundae and stood. "Good luck with that," she said, indicating the crossword puzzle.

"Uh…I'm George." He stood also and stuck out his hand. She shook but didn't offer her name. "Say," he added, "I've never done anything like this before…but if you'd ever like a tour of the zoo, I'd be happy to show you around. It is a great place to spend a day. Here, take this." He slid a business card from his wallet and passed it to her. She accepted it and cast the small print an obligatory glance.

"Thank you," she said.

She had never intended to take George Goldmark up on his offer. But the next week on one of her days off she came across his business card in a kitchen drawer where she threw all that sort of stuff, and after replaying her conversation with him in her head, she decided it couldn't hurt to call him.

He sounded delighted to hear from her and they made plans to meet at the main gates of the San Francisco Zoo at ten o'clock that morning.

The date was a pleasant change from the typical drink at a bar—there were lions and elephants and giraffes around every corner, after all—and Brook had enjoyed herself enough to accept George's invitation to dinner later in the week.

Fast forward three years and she had all but moved into his apartment building on Grand Avenue. She'd gotten to know most of his friends. She'd met his parents on several occasions. They'd adopted a cat from the animal shelter they'd named Leo. And they'd even begun talking about marriage and having children.

The relationship wasn't glamorous in any sense of the word. It was comfortable and predictable and, yes, *safe*, and there was nothing wrong with that.

Until Brook discovered George Goldmark was a two-faced slime-ball.

A coworker at Café Emporium, Jenny Stillwater, was a divorcee constantly singing the praises of the matchmaking app Tinder. One morning when she and Brook were on the same shift she said, "I've got to show you something, hon. Maybe I'm wrong. I *hope* I'm wrong."

She wasn't wrong.

The man in the Tinder profile Jenny showed her was calling himself George Cohen, but the photograph was definitely that of George Goldmark. According to his bio, he was single, financially secure, and looking for a serious relationship blah blah blah.

Needless to say, Brook had been devastated, but she didn't spend long feeling sorry for herself. She took off the rest of her shift, went home, and tossed all of George's stuff from the boathouse into the marina's dumpster. She refused to answer his calls, and by the time he stopped by, she'd already gotten the locks changed. He banged on the door, confused and indignant. She ignored him until he went away. He sent her a few messages over the next week, insinuating he knew why she was mad at him without admitting the reason, and insisting they could work it out. She deleted each message without replying, and eventually he stopped sending them.

That had been last autumn. Brook had gone on a date with a fitness instructor in December and another date with a construction worker in January, but neither man had been right for her.

Then Roy Wallis came along.

To be precise, he didn't come from anywhere; he had been right under her nose in the café every weekend morning. Always smartly dressed and groomed, he was impossible not to notice. Brook often greeted him with a smile, but she never attempted to make conversation. There was something aloof about him that intimidated her, that made her tiptoe around his table when he was reading his newspaper in order not to disturb him, something that reminded her she was his waitress, his servant, and nothing more.

Which was why she had been so utterly stunned when he asked her to dinner.

Brook had mixed feelings about what happened the other day at his apartment. They'd had dinner plans, granted, but she'd never confirmed them, and by showing up at his door unannounced, she'd been intruding on his privacy. On the other hand, had she not done this, she would never have learned about the blonde woman. Roy would still be seeing her behind Brook's back, and although they'd never agreed to date each other exclusively, this was unacceptable to her.

Brook didn't play games, and she wasn't going to let herself get hurt again.

So what are you doing in bed next to him?

He'd apologized. He'd said he'd ended it with the blonde.

And you believed him?

Yes.

Roy's eyes opened, startling her.

"Not morning, is it?" he asked sleepily.

She glanced past him to the digital alarm clock on the bedside table. "Only two."

"Good," he said, slipping his arm around her back, pulling her close to him. She rested her cheek on his chest and soon his breathing assumed the deep and regular rhythm of sleep.

She closed her eyes and tried to sleep too.

DAYS 3-5

LOGBOOK COMMUNICATIONS BY DR. ROY WALLIS, GURU CHANDRA RAMPAL, AND PENNY PARK (EXHIBIT A IN PEOPLE OF THE STATE OF CALIFORNIA V. DR. ROY WALLIS)

Subject 1 engaged me in conversation for nearly three hours. She's teaching me Australian slang and seems to enjoy reminiscing about her country. Subject 2 did not participate in the discussions. He divides his time watching TV, lifting weights, and cooking meals. For lunch he used cookbook recipes to prepare charred leeks with anchovy dressing, turnip tartiflette, confit of salmon with drizzled dill sauce, and sticky toffee parsnip pudding for dessert (made me hungry!). While eating, the test subjects discussed their plans when the experiment concluded. Subject 2 expressed interest in moving to Hollywood, where he hoped to land some gigs as a movie extra or even small roles with speaking lines. Subject 1 encouraged him in this endeavor, though she said nothing of accompanying him.

-Penny, Wednesday, May 30

Blood pressure, heart rate, forearm vascular resistance,

and muscle sympathetic nerve activity were measured this afternoon at rest and during four stressors (sustained handgrip, maximal forearm ischemia, mental stress, and cold pressor test). Results revealed an increase in the test subjects' blood pressure and a decrease in their muscle sympathetic nerve activity. Heart rate, forearm vascular resistance, and plasma catecholamines were not significantly altered. These data suggest that while sleep deprivation increases blood pressure, it does not increase heart rate or muscle sympathetic nerve activity and thus, contrary to much literature on the subject, sleep debt likely does not potentiate an increase in cardiovascular failure.

-R.W., Wednesday, May 30

For the first two days of the experiment, the test subjects were eating or snacking at three to four-hour intervals. Today, for the first time, they went six hours between meals, suggesting a decrease in appetite. Also for the first time, the test subjects demonstrated signs of ataxia (subtle abnormalities in their gait, speech, and eye movement). During a series of exercises assessing their mental acumen, they displayed frustration and irritation at their results, particularly Subject 2, who ended his participation prematurely. Subject 1 remained cooperative. Declines in her abstract thinking, reasoning, and working memory were observed.

-Guru Chandra Rampal, May 30

Subjects 1 and 2 butted heads in their first argument today. Subject 1 was reading on her bed while Subject 2 was lifting weights. Subject 1 glanced at Subject 2 in apparent annoyance several times at the noise the gym equipment made when metal struck metal. Eventually she asked him to take a break. He switched to using free weights. This, however, was a short-term solution, as Subject 1 soon became equally annoyed by Subject 2's heavy breathing and grunts. This time they raised their voices at each other and traded insults. In the aftermath Subject 2 continued lifting weights. Subject 1 slammed her book shut, got off her bed, and paced the perimeter of the room. By my count, she completed sixty-one circuits before settling down to read her book again! At this point, Subject 2 had commenced watching a movie wearing headphones.

-Penny, Thursday, May 31

Subject 1 displays normal orientation, but decreased self-care and reaction time. Her mood appears depressive and her posture is dysmorphic. Subject 2 also displays decreased self-care and reaction time. His answers to questions have become circumstantial and tangential. He exhibits a lack of interest and insight, and he has begun speaking apathetically. Subjects have become confrontational with one another without reconciliation, guilt, or shame. Episodes of grandiosity, fragmented thinking, and memory impairment have been noted, the latter suggesting that sleep deprivation leads to a loss of connectivity between neurons in the hippocampus.

-R.W., Thursday, May 31

The test subjects went seven hours between meals today. Decreases in attention and concentration, as well as severe memory impairment, were observed. Subject 1, for instance, could not remember anything of our conversations from the day before, complaining of feeling as though she had "early Alzheimer's disease." Subject 2's lapses in memory are more severe. Notably, he could no longer perform simple math. During one exercise, in which he was tasked with counting down from one hundred by subtracting seven, he only reached seventy-two, four subtractions, before stopping and becoming upset. When I asked him why he stopped, he said he forgot what he was doing. Both subjects appear to be struggling with muscle coordination and keeping their eyes focused.

-Guru Chandra Rampal, May 31

Wow, were they moody today! They barely wanted to talk to me, and when they did, they were slack-faced, irritable, and forgetful, barely able to finish their sentences. Subject 1 continues to read regularly, though now only in small bursts, sometimes for no longer than ten minutes at a time. When not reading, she becomes agitated. On one occasion she paced the room for fourteen minutes without ever looking up from the floor. Later, she sat on the edge of her bed for fifty minutes, unmoving except for her right foot, which she tapped rapidly. Subject 2 spent the majority of the afternoon watching movies. Aside from briefly talking to me, the only other activity he performed was a solo (and lethargic) game of basketball. This is the second consecutive day he has not lifted weights. Both test subjects complained to me of feeling nauseous and having very little appetite. All they seem to be eating is citrus fruit such as tangerines and oranges.

-Penny, Friday, June 1

Electroencephalography tests were conducted on the subjects' pre-frontal cortices, as this region of the brain has a greater restorative need than others and is thus more responsive to sleep deprivation. Both subjects are right-handed and have not consumed nicotine, alcohol, or xanthine-containing beverages (coffee, tea, soft drinks) during the past week. The electrodes were positioned according to the International 10/20 System, and all electrode impedances were kept below five kilowatts. EEG data were collected from twenty monopolar derivations for five minutes with the subjects' eyes closed to observe the cortex's electrical activity without any external stimuli. Visual inspection was employed for the detection and elimination of possible visual artifacts, and two minutes of artifact-free data were successfully extracted from the EEG's total record. Results indicate that prolonged total sleep deprivation causes a significant power decrease in the frontal, temporal, and occipital areas of the alpha and beta frequency bands. However, temporal delta and temporal-occipital theta T6, O2, and OZ exhibited power *increases*. Traditionally, increased theta activity correlates with an increased cognitive workload and tiredness. Why it has become more pronounced during the subjects' period of continuous wakefulness, when task demands have been relatively minor, is unresolved.

-R.W., Friday, June 1

DAY 6

SATURDAY, JUNE 2, 2018

Sharon Nash was really starting to feel like a guinea pig.

The first few days of the experiment had been a real slog with a lot of time on her hands and little to do to fill it. She spent countless hours lying down on her bed with her eyes closed, daydreaming. Sometimes she tried falling asleep, but this proved impossible. Her mind simply wouldn't shut off, and when she opened her eyes, she was always instantly alert.

Once Sharon got her head around the fact she didn't need or want sleep and wasn't going to get it for the next however-many days, she devoted herself to reading. Growing up, she had been a bookish girl. She recalled passing a lot of summers at her family's holiday house on the Avon River outside Toodyay reading Roald Dahl, R.L. Stine, the complete *Nancy Drew* series, and even a few *Hardy Boys* books to boot if there was nothing else interesting on the bookshelf. She continued reading voraciously throughout high school—mostly Danielle Steele and J.D. Robb and other women's fiction—but this all changed during her first year at Curtin University. Her courses required so much assigned reading that little time remained to fit in recreational stuff. Add partying and dating to the mix, and she probably averaged about one paperback novel a year during her three-year sociology degree. And if she thought she might've gotten back on track while backpacking through Europe, she was dead wrong, as most of her spare time was spent meeting other backpackers, visiting famous landmarks, playing drinking games, and bar hopping. The only real downtime she had was during hungover mornings, but the last thing she felt like doing while hungover was reading.

Sharon had not wanted to participate in the Sleep Experiment. She had been perfectly content working at the Italian eatery. Although she was only being paid about a third of what she would have made an hour in Australia, the tips more than compensated for this shortfall.

Chad, however, needed cash, and he pressured her into going to the interview with him.

Admittedly, after hearing what Dr. Wallis had to say about the experiment, Sharon's reservations largely vanished. It had been approved by UC Berkeley's Committee for the Protection of Human Subjects, and according to the doc, there were no long-term repercussions to sleep deprivation. Moreover, the pay was admittedly freaking awesome, and if she budgeted wisely, the money would last her until she flew back to Australia in September.

This last thought both excited and saddened her. She'd been away from home for about a year now, and she missed her parents heaps. She was, she had to admit, a little homesick. She wouldn't even mind seeing her brat of a brother again, who was currently in his second year at Curtin.

At the same time, however, Sharon had a total blast on her trip so far. She'd made some great friends she'd keep in touch with on social media, she'd had some wild experiences she'd likely never forget, and she knew in her heart the day she boarded the flight to Perth would be a sad one indeed.

She'd told Chad she had a boyfriend waiting for her back home, which wasn't true. But he'd been so damn hot to get in her pants those first few days they'd met in the park in Pamplona, she'd needed to say something to get him to cool off. It wasn't that he wasn't cute or nice. He was both. He was just too much surfy testosterone dude and not enough mellow thoughtful dude, which appealed more to the book nerd inside her. Anyway, the lie worked...for a while at least. Because when she tired of Portugal and decided to check out France, and he insisted on joining her, he got all hot again...and she gave in, and they'd been making out ever since.

Well, at least until the Sleep Experiment had commenced. She understood why Dr. Wallis hadn't wanted his test subjects to be romantically involved, given how relationships can fuck with people's heads sometimes.

Sharon didn't have to worry about this, though, because she no longer had any feelings for Chad whatsoever. Whatever attraction she'd developed for him over the last year had evaporated during their time stuck together in the sleep laboratory. He was beginning to drive her nuts. Just about everything about him now pissed her off. Like how he grunted like an ape during his workouts. Or mumbled to himself like a homeless person while he paced the room incessantly. Or bragged about his cooking, when all he did was follow a recipe in a book. The last time he fished for a compliment ("How good are the enchiladas, Shaz? Made 'em from scratch, hey!"), she wanted to throw her enchilada in his face. And she wasn't even going to get into all the TV he watched. Seriously, what a fucking couch potato! Hadn't he ever picked up a book in his life? She'd yet to see him do so.

Nevertheless, Sharon knew that as much as she was becoming fed up with Chad, her real gripe was with the Sleep Experiment itself. Because with each day that passed (or *perceived* day that passed, given there were no damn clocks or calendars anywhere), she was finding it harder and harder to cope with the mind-numbing boredom; the around-the-clock observation and the lack of privacy this entailed; and the relentless questions and tests, both physical and mental, that Dr. Wallis and his cronies put her through. Like, what was with that fucking EEG machine? Seriously, with all the electrodes stuck to her head she'd felt like a patient in an insane asylum.

Yes, she really was beginning to feel like a guinea pig.

Doesn't matter, Shaz, she told herself. *Can't be much longer until you're done with this shit. Another week maybe. Then you're home-free. You can ditch Chad and go visit Canada. Whistler-Blackcomb, mountain air, raw nature. Then home. Blue skies, the beach, Mom's lasagna and Dad's steaks on the barbie. Just a little bit longer—*

Someone was talking to her. Not Dr. Wallis or the Indian. The Asian. What was her name again? Jesus, how could she not remember her name?

The Asian—*Penny, that was it!*—kept talking in her stupid accent, pretending to be her friend to pick her brain...

Shut up and leave me alone! Sharon thought, refusing to look up from the book clenched tightly in her hands. *Shut up! Shut up! Shut up!*

△△△

"Morning, Penny," Dr. Roy Wallis said, setting the pulp-paper tray holding the vanilla latte and green tea on the table.

Penny, today dressed completely in white, took the green tea and said, "Thank you again, professor. You are very kind to bring me a drink each day. You're the most chivalrous professor I know."

"No problem, Penny," he said. "And I should compliment you on the fantastic job you've been doing this last week. I know it can't be fun waking up at whatever time you do to get here so early."

"Five o'clock, because I *always* shower in the morning."

Although this was an innocuous remark, the curl of Penny's lips and her inexplicable emphasis on "always" made it sound prurient, as though she'd wanted him to conjure a naked image of her in his mind.

Which, for a brief moment, he did.

Focusing his attention on twisting his coffee cup free from the tray, Dr. Wallis said. "I've been reading your notes, of course. They're well done."

"Thank you, professor," she said. "I've been doing my best—"

Something crashed into the viewing window.

Penny yelped. Wallis flinched, raising a forearm before his face in an instinctual gesture of defense. The reinforced glass remained undamaged. Beyond, in the middle of the sleep laboratory, Sharon was shaking a finger at Chad, her face flushed with emotion.

Dr. Wallis reached an arm across Penny—brushing the front of her chest—and jabbed the touch panel controller's Listen button.

"—disgusting!" Sharon was saying. "We have to share it for the next however long, so show a little consideration!"

"Take a chill pill, Shaz," Chad said. "It's just a little piss."

"Can't you lift the goddamn seat?"

"I never lifted the seat in the house."

"And I put up with sitting down on your piss in the middle of the night! Just because I didn't say anything then doesn't mean it was okay."

"Just wipe the seat down if it bothers you so much."

"How hard is it to aim your dick? Or is it too small to aim?"

Chad stepped toward her threateningly. "I swear, Shaz…"

While this exchange had been playing out, Dr. Wallis and Penny had swapped seats. Now Wallis pressed the Talk button and said, "Why don't you two give each other a little space?"

The Australians looked at the two-way mirror. Both were stormy-eyed and grimacing. Throwing up his hands, Chad skulked off to the lounge. He turned on the TV and clapped a set of headphones over his ears.

Sharon approached the mirror. "He's gross, doc! I mean, come on! Can you talk to him or something?"

Wallis pressed the Talk button again. "I think you made your position on the matter quite clear, Sharon," he said. "Let's first see how he responds going forward?"

"I swear," she said, fists clenching and unclenching at her sides, "if he doesn't start lifting the seat, or at least improving his aim, *I'm* going to start peeing all over the seat too!" She spun on her heels and went to her bed and picked up her book. She settled into her usual spot leaning against the headboard, facing the viewing window. After a moment she stood and pushed the bed in a counterclockwise direction. She maneuvered the headboard to about seven o'clock, then pulled the footboard until she'd turned the bed one hundred eighty degrees. She settled back into her spot leaning against the headboard—only now facing the rear of the sleep laboratory so Dr. Wallis and Penny could no longer see her face.

"Yikes..." Penny said. "She doesn't seem too happy, does she? What did she throw at us?"

"I'm not sure," Wallis said. "But it wasn't at us. It was at Chad. She missed him. Did they argue about anything else during your shift?"

"No, they didn't say anything. No, wait. Shaz spoke to me. She asked me how long they had been in the room. Don't worry, professor, I didn't tell her."

"Was she upset?"

"More like—indifferent. It was a very brief exchange."

"Still, I wonder whether this withholding of information contributed to her outburst. She has been severely limited in what she can do each day. Limiting what she can know too is no doubt a very frustrating situation."

"Should we tell her she has only been in there for a week?"

"Absolutely not. I am simply musing out loud, Penny."

Penny nodded, then said, "She's slurring her words. Did you hear when she was talking? It wasn't super noticeable, but...is that to be expected, professor?"

"It's one of the symptoms of cerebellar ataxia, which is also responsible for the deterioration in her coordination and balance that we've been witnessing, as well as the abnormalities in her eye movement."

Penny seemed contemplative. "That teenager you mentioned in the final class of the semester," she said, "the one who stayed awake for eleven days—"

"Randy Gardner," Wallis said.

"Yeah, him—you said he showed no side effects from lack of sleep. But Shaz and Chad, they're falling all over the place, not eating, their eyes are going crazy, now they're slurring their speech—"

"I know what you're getting at, Penny," Wallis said, "and you have a right to be concerned, so let me clarify. I never said Randy Gardner showed no side effects from sleep deprivation. I merely praised his motor skills and clarity of thinking after his experiment. Verbal sleight of hand, I admit. But Randy Gardner most certainly experienced side effects associated with tiredness. Yet it is important to remember that all his symptoms disappeared after a good night's rest, and he suffered no long-term physical or psychological repercussions."

"Was he also a grumpy bum like these two? Fighting and yelling with everybody?"

"Admittedly, no," Wallis said. "But unlike Chad and Sharon, Randy Gardner was not confined to a single room. He was permitted to venture wherever he chose. He went bowling and dined in restaurants. He interacted with other people. This would have considerably improved his state of mind." He glanced at his wristwatch. "Anyway, Penny, it's already ten past two. If you think you're getting paid overtime for hanging around past the end of your shift, think again."

"Okay, professor," she said, standing, "I know when I'm not wanted. I'll see you tomorrow!"

After Penny Park left, Dr. Wallis found himself thinking about her. Earlier, when his arm had accidentally brushed her chest, she didn't make any effort to move back. He was quite sure she had leaned *into* his arm before he suggested they exchange seats. So what was her endgame? he wondered. Was she simply flirting with him for the sake of flirting, or did she have the more audacious goal of sleeping with him?

Smiling thinly to himself—he couldn't deny it was a good feeling to know he was still attractive to twenty-something-year-olds—Wallis lit a cigarette and turned to his task of observing the Australians. Over the next two hours little occurred. Chad binge-watched an episodic series on Netflix, while Sharon read her book, paced the room, and showered. At one point Wallis put his feet up on the desk to get comfortable. Soon his eyelids grew heavy and he had to fight to keep them open—

He snapped awake, surprised he had allowed himself to nod off. He checked his watch and discovered it was already seven o'clock in the evening. Sharon, he observed, was now watching a movie, while Chad—Chad was nowhere in the sleep laboratory.

Alarmed, Wallis sat straight.

Did he slip out while I was asleep?

Goddammit!

He smacked the Talk button. "Chad? Where are you? Sharon, where did Chad go?"

"What, mate?" an irritated voice replied. A moment later Chad's head rose above the far side of the island in the kitchen.

Dr. Wallis relaxed. "What are you doing?" he asked.

"Lying down," Chad grunted.

"On the floor?"

"What's it to you?"

His head disappeared below the island.

Wallis made a note of the incident on the laptop, monitored Chad's heart rate for the next fifteen minutes to make sure he was not somehow sleeping, then he stood and stretched, cracking his back in the process. He went to the bathroom, but afterward, instead of returning to the observation room, he decided to visit his former office for old times' sake.

When he reached the fourth floor of the old cement building, he went left, passing empty office spaces that had served the faculty and graduate students, to his corner office at the end of the corridor. Stepping inside the twilit space, nostalgia bloomed in his gut. There was nothing to look at now, but he was seeing the office in his mind's eye as it had once been. Remembering some of the students he had counseled here, the faculty with whom he had debated and socialized. The nights he had worked late, composing lectures, grading essays and exams, writing papers. This little room had been his life—and now it was a soulless husk waiting to be demolished.

Dr. Wallis went to the north-facing window and drew a finger along the ledge, leaving a line in the dust. He looked out onto rain-soaked Hearst Avenue. The traffic lights glistened wetly. Puddles reflected the sinking sun on their pockmarked surfaces.

"Why do we get old?" he mused out loud. "Why does everything have to change? Why can't we just *be*?"

Somebody was down on the sidewalk.

Wallis leaned forward until his head touched the windowpane, but the person had angled toward Tolman Hall and out of his line of sight.

He backtracked down the corridor and descended the stairs to the main floor. He looked through the glass doors that opened to the breezeway. The person wasn't out there.

And what would it matter if he or she was? he thought.

Although the campus might feel like a ghost town, it wasn't off limits by any means. Anyone was free to come and go as they pleased.

Dr. Wallis returned to the building's basement and his ongoing experiment.

△△△

Penny and her friend Jimmy Su sat in the inky shadows at the base of a large pine tree, the inverted cone of boughs shielding them from the light rain.

"Another one!" Penny said, using a twig to poke a beetle doing its best to move through the wet grass. "This tree must be infested with them."

"It's a pine tree," Jimmy said, "and the beetles are pine bark beetles, so your deduction is spot on, Sherlock."

Jimmy was of Taiwanese descent, but he had lived in California since he was a kid, and he was about as Californian as you could get, with the gym body, the blond streak through his otherwise black hair, and the nose and tongue and helix piercings.

He and Penny had been friends since orientation week, and given he'd never once hit on her, she suspected he was gay, though he never admitted to this and she never asked. Because whether he was or not didn't matter to her. She simply liked having a guy friend she could hang out with now and then.

Ever since he'd started his part-time summer job as an assistant to an arborist, however, he'd been acting a little weird. He would stop before random trees, for instance, place his hands against their trunks and close his eyes like he was speaking telepathically to them. He would also bombard her with all sorts of stupid tree facts. Not five minutes ago he told her the pine sheltering them from the rain was one of more than a hundred different species in the genus *Pinus*, which were divvied up based upon their types of leaves, cones, and seeds, and—hold onto your hats, people!—they had once been the favorite snack of duckbilled dinosaurs.

Needless to say, she was looking forward to getting the old Jimmy back at the end of the summer.

Poking the beetle with the twig again, Penny said, "How do you know this thing's a pine bark beetle? It looks like any other beetle to me."

"It's a pine bark beetle," Jimmy assured her.

She squashed it beneath her heel.

"Hey! What the hell did you do that for?"

"I hate beetles. Besides, they're killing this tree."

"We don't know that for certain. Most pine beetles live in dead or dying hosts, which means there's a good chance the tree is already rotting."

Penny looked up at the towering pine. "Looks pretty healthy to me."

"You can't tell if it's sick just by looking at it. Bet if we peeled off a bit of its bark, the cambium layer would be brown and dry —"

"Holy God," she said, slapping her forehead. "Is this what my life has become?"

Jimmy frowned. "What's wrong with being knowledgeable about trees? You do realize that without them animal life would cease to exist?"

"Yeah, yeah," she said. "And I also realize it's time I get some more friends."

"Great! I wish you had more friends too. Then maybe it would be someone else other than me sitting out here cold and wet. What *are* we doing anyway?"

"I told you. Waiting for Dr. Wallis."

"Yeah, you want to jump his bones. But do you think stalking him like this is the best way to go about it?"

"I'm not stalking him!" she said indignantly.

"You're sitting under a tree at night, drunk, waiting for him to stroll past unaware. That sounds like stalking to me. Why can't you just go into Tolman Hall and meet him? You two work together, after all."

"Because Guru's going to be arriving any minute to do the handover."

"So?"

"So, I don't want him around when I make another—"

She cut herself off. She had been about to say *make another move*, but she hadn't told Jimmy that Dr. Wallis had already rejected her this morning. She was too embarrassed. The rebuff had stung, and it had continued stinging all day.

Even so, the more she'd thought about what had occurred, the more she became certain the only reason Dr. Wallis turned her down was because he was her professor. He was trying to keep to some moral high ground. But of course he secretly wanted her. He was forty-one. She was hot and young. No way he would say no again if she ditched the talking and simply presented herself to him, ready and willing.

Which was why she'd invited Jimmy up to her apartment earlier (he lived on the second floor in the same building) for a few drinks. The plan was to make it look as though she had been out partying all evening with a bunch of friends and had decided spur-of-the-moment to stop by Tolman Hall on her way home to say hi.

Penny took another swill of the vodka and orange juice from Jimmy's little silver flask, and she almost barfed it back up.

"Whoa!" Jimmy said. "You okay?"

Her eyes watering, she nodded.

"Take a deep breath..."

She swallowed the acid biting her throat and took a deep breath. "Whew..." she said, taking another breath.

"Maybe this isn't such a good idea right now," he said. "We've had a lot to drink. Maybe come back tomorrow—"

"*Shhhh!*" Penny said, spotting Guru crossing the breezeway toward the old building's front entrance. "There's baldy! Won't be much longer now."

△△△

Dr. Wallis checked his wristwatch when Guru entered the observation room: 9:45 p.m. Guru's head was as bald as ever, and he was dressed smartly in one of his new outfits, which consisted of a pink button-down shirt, navy jeans, and a pair of burgundy leather loafers sans socks.

"I'm digging your style, my man!" Wallis told him. "You look just like me on my day off."

"You flatter me, professor," Guru replied sincerely. "I owe all of my good fortunes to you."

"Good fortune? Have you found a suitable wife already?"

"No, not yet, though I am sure it will not be long now." He held up his backpack. "Can you smell it?"

Dr. Wallis sniffed. "I smell something, but it's not McDonald's."

"Not today! Look at this!" He set his backpack on the table and produced a paper bag with the Chipotle logo on it. "I present to you—Chipotle!" He pronounced the restaurant chain's name *Chee-pol-til.*

"It's called *Chee-poht-lay*, Guru."

"You've heard of it?"

Wallis raised his eyebrows. "*Are you mad?* It's one of the most popular fast-food joints in the country. You haven't heard of Chipotle before today?"

"No, never. I have never paid close attention to restaurants. But when I went for a walk this morning, and I saw Chee-poht-lay, I thought to myself, *Professor Wallis is right. I need to improve my diet.* So I went inside and ordered a burrito bowl, and much to my astonishment and delight, I was allowed to select the ingredients!"

"That's how they work, Guru. Sort of like a Mexican Subway."

"Subway? What is Subway? Ah! I got you there, professor! Of course I know Subway. But a big American sandwich never sounded appealing to me."

"But a big American burger did?"

"No, I only ordered the chicken nuggets from McDonald's."

"*Every* day?"

"Yes, every day. But now I have discovered Chee-poht-lay, and I will never return to McDonald's again."

"All right, I gotta get out of here, Guru, you're blowing my mind." Wallis stood and collected his messenger bag. "Chad and Sharon have been quiet for most of the day. They argued earlier. You can read about it in my notes. Looks like they've put their differences behind them. But if anything happens, you have my number."

"Do not worry about me, professor. I can hold down the fort."

ΔΔΔ

It had stopped raining, and the night was cool and wet, smelling of earth and rain. Dr. Wallis started east along Bayard Rustin Way when he heard heels clapping the pavement behind him.

"Professor!"

He turned to find Penny Park hurrying after him, sporting red pumps and a three-quarter-length jacket.

"Penny?" he said, surprised. "What are you doing here? You don't start until the morning."

"Of course I know that, professor," she said, coming to stand next to him. "I came here to see you!"

Dr. Wallis couldn't smell alcohol on her breath, but he could see it in her eyes, and hear it in the slippery way she was speaking.

"You look dressed to go out," he commented.

"I *have* been out. With my friend, Jimmy, and some others. But I got bored."

"So you came to see me?"

"Yes." She batted her fake eyelashes and took his arm. "Was that bad?"

Wallis looked past her but saw nobody else nearby. He looked back at Penny. She was smiling expectantly at him. "Penny, I can't go anywhere with you."

She sulked. "Why not?"

"I'm your professor."

"So? Professors are allowed to go out with their students. I'm twenty-one."

"It's not appropriate."

"Who's going to care!" she said. "Nobody's even going to see us! Nobody's around Berkeley right now."

Dr. Wallis actually found himself considering her words. Then: *No—no way!*

Penny, perhaps sensing his hesitation, pressed: "Come on, professor. We'll go somewhere small and quiet."

"Sorry, Penny," he said. "Not tonight."

"It will be *fuuuunnnnn*," she said softly, rocking forward on her toes to lean against him.

"No, Penny," he said decisively. "I'm going to call you an Uber."

"Awwww…" She hiccupped.

"How much have you had to drink?" he asked.

"Not much," she said. "And you can't call me an Uber."

He frowned. "Why not?"

"I don't trust them. You know how many girls go missing in them."

"They're just as safe as taxis."

"I don't trust taxis either."

"Then how did you get here?" He didn't think the bus, dressed how she was.

"Jimmy dropped me off."

Wallis' frown deepened. "How did you expect to get home then?"

She hiccupped again. "C'mon, professor. Let's go have fun!"

"I'll drive you home."

"But I want to go out!"

"Penny, you either let me drive you home, or you hang out here with Guru all night. Your choice."

"Oh, God! Fine! Where's your car?"

Wallis led her to where he had parked on nearby Crescent Lawn.

"An Audi!" Penny said. "What are you, rich or something, professor?"

"I don't have kids to spend all my money on." He immediately regretted the remark.

Penny seized on the opening and said, "So you're not married, right?"

"No," he said simply.

"Girlfriend?"

"In the car, Penny."

He pressed Unlock on the remote key, then slid in behind the wheel and closed the door. Penny climbed in shotgun, her door thudding closed a moment after his.

"Sporty!" she said.

"What's your address?"

"You don't have to put it into the GPS. I'll just tell you. Turn left on Oxford Street."

Dr. Wallis followed the instructions, his car the only one tooling through the night.

"So," he said, thinking of a safe topic to discuss.

"So?" she repeated mischievously.

The girl's incorrigible! he thought.

"I don't think I've ever asked you," he said. "What are your plans after you graduate next year? Workwise," he added quickly, so she didn't think he was propositioning her for marriage or something else equally ludicrous.

"I want to be a K-Pop star." She sighed. "But I'm not a great singer, so I don't think that's happening. Realistically? Something that lets me travel. I want to see Paris and London and Taiwan and Laos. I want to travel the world."

"You're in the wrong major then," he remarked.

"Psychology, you mean?" She smiled. "Oh my, professor. That's not my major. International affairs is."

Wallis glanced at her. "But you were in every one of my classes last semester. That must have eaten up most of your electives?"

"*All* of them. Want to know a secret?"

He wasn't sure he did, but he waited expectantly.

"I was in your first-year psych class too," she said. "You probably don't remember because that class was huge, like five hundred people."

He didn't remember.

"I liked it," she went on. "I mean, I only took it because it was one of those first-year classes every freshman takes. But, well, I developed a bit of a crush on you."

Wallis gripped the steering wheel more tightly. "Where am I turning?" They were approaching Bancroft Way.

"Next street turn right."

"Durrant?"

"Yeah, go straight on it for two blocks. Anyway, that was my secret."

"Right. Well, thanks for telling me, Penny. I'm, uh, flattered."

"Now it's your turn," she said. "Tell *me* a secret."

"I don't think so."

"Why not?"

"I don't have any."

She laughed. "Right! Everybody has a secret. Okay, stop! We're here."

Wallis tapped the brakes. "Here?"

She pointed out his window to a red, brown, and silver six-story student building. Above the double-door entrance, freestanding letters spelled: VARSITY.

"That's where you live? It's less than a mile from Tolman Hall!"

"You don't have to tell me, professor."

"What I mean is, you could have walked."

"In heels? No, thanks! Besides," she said, turning to face him, "I like being in your car."

"You should get some rest, Penny," he said.

"Do you want to come in?"

"No."

"Just for a little bit." She touched his arm.

"No."

"Why not?" She leaned closer, the throat of her jacket opening to reveal her cleavage in her low-cut dress.

"You're too forward for your own good," he said.

"I like getting what I want." She leaned ever closer.

"Penny, you need to go," he told her.

Her lips pressed against his. She kissed him forcefully, and he found himself kissing her back. She rested a hand against his chest, then attempted to relocate her body over the center console to straddle him. This proved too difficult in the cramped space, and she settled for sliding her hand down to his groin—

"Penny," he said, his voice husky. He gripped her wrist. Her eyes were inches from his, glistening, wild, alive. "You should get some rest."

He was sure she would protest, and he was steeling himself for an argument, but she simply slumped back into her seat. With a subtle smile, she said, "See you tomorrow, professor," and got out of the car and closed the door.

Dr. Wallis watched her until she entered the building, and

only then did he wonder if it had been Penny he'd spotted earlier from the window of his old office.

"Jesus Christ," he said in conflicted bemusement. He put the Audi in gear and headed home.

△△△

He didn't go home.

He wouldn't have been able to sleep. Instead, he stopped by The Hideaway, a pirate-themed pub in San Francisco's Fillmore District. The place might be decked out in Caribbean kitsch, but it was open late, always loud, and it boasted the largest selection of rum in the country.

Dr. Wallis managed to score a recently vacated stool at the bar, and he was promptly greeted by Julio, the always-smiling proprietor and head bartender, who was probably the only person in the state more passionate about rum than he was.

"Yo ho ho, Roy," Julio greeted him, speaking loudly to be heard above the chatter. "What's it going to be tonight? Your regular, or do you feel like continuing your voyage?"

The voyage he was referring to involved Wallis drinking his way through all one hundred or so drinks on the menu. He was about halfway there, having already tried everything from colonial tavern tipples to Prohibition-era Havana creations to complex ten-ingredient tiki cocktails.

"What's next on the voyage?" he asked.

"I don't believe you've had a Rum Flip yet? Whole egg, Demerara, freshly grated nutmeg, and of course a hand-picked premium rum."

"Dinner and drink in one. Sounds good, brother."

Julio went off to build the drink, and Wallis took out his phone. He opened the messenger app. The last text was from Brook thanking him for dinner the night before. He'd replied with a thumbs-up emoticon. It had seemed appropriate at the time, but now it seemed uninspired, underwhelming, and even a bit dickish, considering he'd also spent the night on her houseboat.

This interpretation was no doubt fueled by guilt due to the bizarre encounter with Penny, but he nevertheless typed:

Had a great time too. You looked spectacular. When are we going to do it again?

He set his phone down. The woman on the stool to his left said something to him.

"Excuse me?" he said. She was roughly thirty, dirty blonde, and had one hell of a rack.

"Rascal, scoundrel, villain, or knave. Which one are you?"

"All rolled into one," he replied.

She raised her elaborate cocktail in appreciation.

Julio returned then with a yellow concoction that looked like something you would drink on Christmas morning.

Dr. Wallis took a sip. "Excellent as expected, my man," he said.

Julio bowed with a flourish, identified the rum he'd used, and returned to serving other customers.

"Come here often?" the blonde asked.

"Where have I heard that before?"

"A girlfriend of mine recommended this place to me for the atmosphere." A smile lifted her lips. "She should have recommended it for the men."

Wallis studied the woman more closely. Her tight, knee-length green dress and gold stilettos straddled a fine line between slutty and elegant. However, her jewelry seemed real, and her makeup wasn't over the top…and he couldn't yet decide whether she was into him, or a lady of the night looking to offer her services.

"Is your girlfriend here with you?" he asked.

"I'm alone."

Dr. Wallis was chewing on this when his phone chimed and vibrated.

"Excuse me," he said, opening the messenger app.

The text was from Brook:

Hi Roy. I didn't work tonight. I made spaghetti and a salad earlier. If you want to come by, there are plenty of leftovers. But I understand if you've just got off work and are tired... Please let me know.

Wallis smiled to himself. Typical Brook: genuine, timorous, polite.

He felt worse than ever for what happened with Penny...and for the thought in the back of his mind that perhaps he should buy the woman next to him a drink.

He stood. "Unfortunately, business calls."

"Business...or pleasure?" the woman asked.

Wallis hesitated. "It was nice meeting you."

She extended a bony hand. "I'm Liz."

"Roy," he said, shaking.

"Maybe I'll see you around here, Roy?"

"It's one of my favorite hangouts."

"Lucky girl," she said, her eyes flicking momentarily to his phone in his hand.

"No, lucky me," he said, taking his leave then, and thinking, *Luckier than I deserve.*

DAY 7

SUNDAY, JUNE 3, 2018

D r. Wallis was having the dream that had stalked him throughout his childhood, adolescence, and adult life. He was seven or eight years old, walking down a street bustling with tourists and lined with dozens of kiosks all selling similar-looking jewelry, shot glasses, coffee mugs, and cheap magnets. A huge cruise ship, docked at port, loomed in the background like a modern-day castle.

Roy couldn't see what was following him, but he knew it was there. It was always there, and it always caught up to him. This was the reason for the cold terror in his gut: the inevitability and inescapability of his fate. The thing had caught him a thousand times before, and it would catch him another thousand times in the future.

Still, he continued to weave his way through the cheerful crowd, continued to look back over his shoulder for his unseen pursuer, continued to fight the tears brimming in his eyes. He had an almost overwhelming urge to approach one of the police officers in their meticulous uniforms directing traffic. He didn't because he had approached one before, in a previous dream, and the police officer had been unable to help him and had, in fact, only slowed him down, expediting his pursuer's arrival.

Roy started to run. He bumped into strangers and knocked over tacky souvenirs from tables and called for his mom and dad, but they couldn't help him either. They were dead. They had died here in the Bahamas. The capsized yacht had been discovered floating twenty nautical miles off Paradise Island by local fishermen. Their bodies were never found. This tragic event might not have occurred until Roy was a sophomore at UCLA, and he had never before visited any of the islands or cays in the archipelago, but chronology and logic mattered little to one's slumbering mind.

The throngs of tourists and locals thinned around him, and before he knew it he was alone on the street. On one corner rose the huge Roman Catholic church he used to go to on Sundays with his parents. He hurried through the gaping entrance into the structure's cavernous belly. The interior was not as he remembered it. No pews spanned the hardwood floors. Great swaths of uninhibited ivy climbed the stone walls and smothered the stained-glass windows. Chunks of missing ceiling and roof created great big skylights opening to the blue expanse above.

For some reason people had abandoned this church, leaving it to weather and fall apart, and God had abandoned it in turn.

Which meant there would be no safety for him here. He had to go. He had to find someplace better to hide—

He was too late.

The doors to the church no longer led outside. They led only to blackness.

"No," he whimpered, and a part of him knew he had spoken that same word out loud in the bed where his adult self slept.

The blackness beckoned him, and he moved toward it, unable to disobey. When he reached the doors, Roy could sense the size of the demon in the abyss beyond. He had only ever experienced it in spatial terms. Never a face or a body. No malevolent eyes or pointy teeth. It was only big. Monolithic. Making him in comparison feel no larger than a pebble at the base of a mountain—

Dr. Wallis jerked upright in bed, swallowing back the bile that had risen in his throat.

Bright sunlight seared his eyes. He squinted until they

adjusted and he made out Brook's bedroom. That feeling he always experienced when waking in a woman's bed—that he was in a place that wasn't his own, and maybe one where he shouldn't be—encapsulated him now. Yet this was lessened by another feeling: one of carefreeness. Nightmare be damned, it was simply nice to be waking in Brook's bedroom. The warmth of the sun's morning rays slanting through the porthole windows. The strawberry scent of her sheets. The gentle rock of the houseboat on the calm bay waters. All the natural wood and eclectic knickknacks that created the illusion of waking up in a beloved childhood tree fort.

Wiping beads of sweat from his forehead and dismissing any lingering dreamworld fear, Dr. Wallis called, "Brook?"

She didn't answer.

The houseboat wasn't big, and he couldn't hear water running, which meant she had likely gone somewhere.

He pushed aside the covers and hunted down his clothes, which he'd expected to find strewn all over the floor, but which he found folded neatly on the seat of a corner rocking chair.

Brook had left a note written on a small piece of pink paper atop them:

Another Saturday, another morning shift. Before I knew you, I always used to look forward to seeing you when you came in for your vanilla latte. Now what do I have to look forward to?

Help yourself to anything you'd like. Call me later.

xoxo

Wallis checked that his phone and keys were in his blazer pockets, then he left, making sure the door locked behind him. The morning was sunny and cool, the air crisp and moist with sea fog, and he felt absolutely dynamic. He spotted a bakery café across the street and realized he was famished, having eaten none of Brook's spaghetti the night before. He checked his wristwatch and found that it was almost nine o'clock. Rarely did he sleep in so late.

Wallis sat down at the bakery and ordered sourdough waffles with fresh whipped cream, seasonal fruit, powdered sugar, and maple syrup. Afterward he ordered a second coffee to go and detoured through a park redolent with the smells of eucalyptus trees and wild fennel. When he reached his car, he saw a slip of paper pinched beneath one of the wipers. For the briefest of moments, he thought Brook had left him another sweet note. He plucked free the parking ticket, which cited him eighty-three dollars for parking in a red zone.

Crunching it into a ball in his fist, he tossed it in the Audi's center console (*which Penny had tried to climb to straddle you, big boy*, he recalled with real contrition), then got behind the wheel. He had nearly five hours to kill before his shift at Tolman Hall commenced. Instead of driving home, he detoured to a boutique jewelry atelier a few blocks from his apartment where he had purchased a number of his custom-made rings and belt buckles. Inside the small, industrial space, focused spotlights hammered light onto silver pendants, stackable jeweled rings, necklaces, and numerous other creations by local metalsmiths and artisans.

"Roy!" Beverley St. Clair, the artist-in-residence, greeted him from behind the glass counter. White hair cropped and spiky, leathery skin tanned from the sun, she wore a pair of tortoiseshell Ben Franklin bifocals and about twenty pounds of silver around her neck. She had designed the gold signet ring engraved with his family crest that currently adorned the third finger on his right hand. "Wonderful to see you again," she added, her Eastern European accent always making him think of Count Vlad.

"Morning, Bev," he said, stopping before the counter.

"What sort of ring inspires your visit today? You know, you have so many calaveras, I have always believed a king lion design would suit you magnificently. Large, one hundred fifteen grams of solid silver. Diamond or ruby eye socket inserts. Or perhaps aquamarine for something fresh?"

"Actually, Bev, I'm not looking for anything for myself today."

"Oh?" she said, arching an inquiring eyebrow.

"Something for a lady friend of mine." He held up his hands, intuiting what she was thinking. "Not a diamond. In fact, nothing too flashy or glitzy. Let's say—unassuming yet tasteful. Can you help me out with that?"

"Most definitely, Roy. Most definitely. Just a moment while I get my sketchpad."

ΔΔΔ

"You're finally here!" Penny said as soon as Dr. Wallis entered the observation room. "Things are crazy!"

He set the hot drinks he'd brought on the table and looked through the one-way mirror—and found himself face-to-face with Chad. The Australian seemed to be in some sort of distress. His eyes stared at his reflection with haunted concern, the way one might upon finding the face of a stranger staring back. He held both hands to his head, slowly running them over and through his wavy (and unwashed) blond hair. Sharon was pacing the perimeter of the room, her eyes glued to the floor.

"What's going on with him?" Wallis asked, concerned.

"He says mushrooms are growing from his head."

"Mushrooms?" Wallis nodded. "He's hallucinating. This is not to be unexpected."

"This is normal?"

"Sleep deprivation exceeding forty-eight hours is considered unethical today by the prudish wing of academia, so there's not exactly a treasure trove of information on the effects of extreme sleep loss. But the studies I've read concerning individuals suffering from extreme insomnia all reported visual distortions, illusions, somatosensory changes, and, yes, in some cases, frank hallucinations, even in cases of people with no history of psychiatric illness."

"What we're doing is *unethical*?" Penny asked, apparently surprised by his a priori statement.

"Come now, Penny!" Dr. Wallis chastised. "We're depriving two individuals of sleep for potentially twenty-one days. We're not going to win the Noble Peace Prize. But when you're pushing the boundaries of scientific study, ethical matters are not always black and white. There's a lot of grays." He pressed the touch panel controller Talk button. "Chad? How are you doing, buddy?"

"Mushrooms are growing from my head, mate!"

"Why do you think that?"

"Shaz told me."

Wallis' eyes went to Sharon. She was passing in front of the exercise equipment, her eyes still downcast.

"I don't see any mushrooms," he said.

"You sure, mate? I can *feel* them."

"No, I don't see any. I think Sharon is simply trying to stir you up."

A hopeful look. "You think?"

Sharon's circuit took her directly behind Chad. She mumbled, "Outta the way, mushroom-head!"

"See!" Chad cried, his hands once more furiously probing his hair.

"There are no mushrooms, Chad!" Wallis said firmly. "Do you trust me?"

His brow knit. "I—I don't know."

"Do you trust Sharon?"

"Hell no!"

"Then you trust me more than Sharon?"

"Yeah, I guess."

"Then believe me when I tell you there are absolutely no mushrooms growing out of your head. You are perfectly healthy."

Sharon, now passing the kitchen, cackled: "Your head's rotting, and you got mushrooms growing out of it!"

Chad whirled on her. "Shut the fuck up, mate!" he exploded, his hands balling into fists. "The doc says there are no mushrooms, you're full of bullshit, so shut the fuck up!" He started toward her.

"Chad!" Dr. Wallis said. "Do you want to end your participation in this experiment?"

He faced the mirror, eyes wide. "End it?"

"You can leave right now. We'll continue with Sharon only."

"Leave? You mean, no more gas?"

"No more gas. You can go home."

His face ghosted. "No! I—I want to stay. Shit, I'm sorry, doc."

"You'll keep your temper in check?"

"Yeah, no problem, mate, I promise."

"Good," Wallis said. "That's good, Chad. Now why don't you go watch a movie? Put on your headphones. Relax."

"Yeah, I think I'll do that..."

He went to the lounge, put on a DVD of *Beverly Hills Cops*, dropped onto the sofa, and clapped the headphones over his ears. Sharon continued to pace the room, though now she was ignoring him.

Dr. Wallis sank back in his chair, pensive.

Penny said, "This is getting weird, professor."

"Seven days without sleep is quite an achievement, Penny. Only a few more days to go to surpass the Guinness World Records champ, Randy Gardner."

"You mean that guy, Randy Gardner...no one's ever beaten his eleven days?"

"Several people have. Guinness, however, stopped certifying attempts at his record, believing that going too long without sleep could be dangerous to one's health."

Penny was quiet as that sunk in.

"Their reticence is nonsense, Penny," Wallis assured her. "Unfounded in science. After Randy Gardner's experiment concluded, he was taken to a naval hospital where he slept peacefully for fourteen hours straight. Although the scientists monitoring his brain signals discovered his percentage of REM sleep was abnormally high, this returned to normal in a matter of days."

Penny nodded but said, "Chad and Shaz are a lot worse than

they were yesterday."

Wallis shrugged. "Chad had a mild hallucination, Penny. It is nothing to be too concerned about."

"Shaz hasn't stopped pacing my entire shift. Eight hours. She just walks in circles."

Wallis frowned. "She didn't stop once?"

"No."

"Did they eat anything today?"

"Only oranges. We're going to need to get some more."

Wallis contemplated this.

Penny said, "I don't know if they're going to make it two more weeks, professor. I don't even know if they're going to make it *one* more week."

"They very well might not."

"But how will we know when to end the experiment?"

"We'll know when Chad or Sharon tell us they want to end the experiment," he said curtly. "And you heard Chad just now. He wants to keep going."

ΔΔΔ

Dr. Roy Wallis watched in fascination while Chad reenacted scene after scene from the 1984 film, *Beverly Hills Cops*. In each he recited the dialogue of Eddie Murphy's character, Axel Foley, word for word.

He'd been doing this for the last hour.

"Look, cuz, don't even try it okay...?" Chad was saying now as he played out the scene in which Axel Foley confronted a wealthy art gallery owner and his thug in an exclusive men's club. "Get the fuck away from me, man," he said to the imaginary thug before performing some comical martial arts shit, adding all his own sound effects.

"Shut up!" Sharon shrieked suddenly and dramatically. For most of Dr. Wallis' shift she'd been sitting on the edge of her bed, her back to Chad, holding her hands over her ears and tapping her foot. "You're talking too much! Shut up! Just shut up!"

Chad seemed nonplussed. "I'm rehearsing, mate. Big role coming up. Gotta nail it."

"You're not a movie star!" she wailed. "You're nobody!"

"After I land this role, Shaz, everybody's gonna know who I am!"

She stood and faced him. "What's your name?"

"My name?" He shrugged. "Eddie."

Sharon cackled. "Eddie, right! Like Eddie Murphy?"

"Yeah, so?"

"He's black!"

"So?"

"Are you black, you dipshit? Look at your arms!"

Chad held his arms before him.

"They look black to you?" she said.

"Yeah, mate. What's your deal?"

"Your name's Chad! You're a white Aussie wanker with no job —unless you call this experiment a job—and no future prospects in acting! Don't believe me?" She snagged his wallet from the table separating their two beds. "Driver's license, right. I don't see a black wanker looking back at me. I see you. And, surprise, surprise, his name's not Eddie Murphy. It's Chad Turner."

Chad marched over and snatched the wallet from her hand. He flipped open the plastic sleeve with the driver's license and studied the identification closely. Different emotions rippled across his face. Then he stuffed the wallet into the pocket of his track pants. "Eddie's my *acting* name, Shaz. A lot of actors have acting names. You think *Spacey* is Kevin Spacey's real name, you fucktard?"

"Actors might change their names, but they don't change their race—"

"Don't know what you're yabbering on about—"

"You're not black! You're white! You're white! You're white! You stupid goddamn mushroom-head—"

Chad swung at her. She ducked, and his fist bounced off the top of her forehead.

Dr. Wallis smacked the Talk button. "Chad! Leave her be!"

Ignoring the instruction, Chad scrambled for Sharon, who retreated to the kitchen, where she kept the island between herself and Chad. She was screaming and laughing at the same time. Chad was seething and feinting left and right.

"Chad!" Wallis bellowed, shooting to his feet, wondering whether he was going to need to enter the sleep laboratory and physically intervene. "Chad!" A lightbulb: "Eddie!" he said. "Eddie Murphy!"

Chad swung his head toward the two-way mirror, his expression a mix of rage and bewilderment. "Who's that?"

Wallis' mind raced. "Your manager, Eddie. Your talent manager. Now you leave that woman alone."

Chad shook his head. "She's a fucking spaz, a shit-talking spaz. She called me—"

"You want to work in Hollywood again, Eddie?"

"What'd you mean?"

"You touch a woman, every major studio and director worth their salt is going to blacklist you. They don't tolerate that type of behavior. Not one bit."

Chad looked at Sharon, who was grinning wickedly at him, almost daring him to attack her. He snorted, then spat on the ground. "You're not worth it, Shaz. You're not gonna derail my career." He looked back at the two-way mirror and scratched his chin. "What was I doing?"

"Rehearsing," Wallis told him. "For your role in *Beverly Hills Cops*. The Harwood Club scene."

"Ah, righty-o." Chad grinned, his dark disposition immediately abandoned. "How was I doing?"

"You're very talented, Eddie. The role's as good as yours."

"I better keep rehearsing then—"

"Why don't you give it a break for now? Put on a movie perhaps?"

"Nah, don't feel like that." He raised his arms above his head and sniffed his pits. "Think I might have a shower. I stink. Can't go into an audition like this."

"Excellent idea," Wallis said. Chad's last shower had been three days earlier.

Whistling a tune—and completely ignoring Sharon—he grabbed a fresh set of clothing from the wardrobe, went to the bathroom in the back of the sleep laboratory, and closed the door behind him.

"He's crazy!" Sharon said, looking directly at the two-way mirror, her gaze so focused and intense for a moment Dr. Wallis had the uncanny feeling she was somehow seeing him beyond her reflection. "You locked me up with a crazy, doc!"

"How are you feeling, Sharon?" he asked her.

"Can't remember crap. Feel like a goldfish in a tiny, stupid bowl."

"Can you recall what you ate for lunch today?"

She glanced at the kitchen. "What?"

"Nothing," Wallis said. "You haven't eaten anything all day."

"Not hungry."

"You need to eat, Sharon."

She looked back at the mirror with those x-ray eyes. "We going crazy, doc?"

"Of course not," he said. "You both are performing exceptionally."

"Doesn't feel like we are. Feels like we're going crazy."

"What exactly do you mean?"

"Feels like there's somebody else inside my head. Somebody who wants to do the talking and everything."

Dr. Wallis leaned forward. "Does this person have a name?"

Sharon approached the viewing window. She stopped directly before it, less than a foot away. This close he could see that her eyes were dancing left and right. Her blonde hair fell around her oily face in tangled clumps. She glanced over her shoulder at the bathroom, then back at the mirror. She whispered, "I need to talk to you, doc."

"Why are you whispering?" he asked her.

"I don't want *him* to hear," she said.

"Chad?"

She nodded.

Wallis turned down the volume of the loudspeakers in the sleep laboratory so his voice too was barely more audible than a whisper. "He won't be able to hear anything now."

Sharon, her eyes dancing faster than ever, said, "He's faking."

"Faking what?"

"I don't trust him. He's *spying* on me."

"Spying? How so?"

"Like, I catch him watching me. Like, I'll look up from my book, and I'll catch him."

"What does he do then?"

"He looks away."

"Have you mentioned this to him? Perhaps tell him it makes you uncomfortable and you would like him to stop—"

"He *wants* something."

Wallis frowned. There was a violent inference to that statement. "What do you think he wants, Sharon?"

She smiled. "What do *you* think he wants, doc?"

The water in the bathroom stopped running. Sharon pressed a finger to her lips. After a long moment of silence, she whispered, "He's listening to us right now."

For a surreal moment Wallis became caught up in Sharon's paranoia and believed that Chad was not in the bathroom drying off but crouched with his ear pressed to the door, listening to them talk about him.

Nonsense.

He pressed the Talk button to reassure her of this conclusion, but before he spoke, Sharon went to her bed, picked up her book, and began reading. Chad emerged from the bathroom a minute later. His hair was wet but not brushed, his clothes fresh, though he wore no socks. He tossed his dirty clothes in the hamper by the bathroom door, then went to the lounge. He glanced at Sharon as he passed her bed. She remained intently focused on her book. He spent some time perusing the stacks of DVDs before selecting John Carpenter's *The Thing*. He clapped his headphones over his ears and slumped down on the sofa.

Sharon continued reading her book.

△△△

That night Dr. Roy Wallis stopped by The Hideaway on his way home from Tolman Hall. He continued his mixological voyage with two new rum libations and found himself both desiring and dreading a run-in with the woman in the tight green dress and gold stilettos. When he didn't find her at the bar —or during a very roundabout trek to the bathroom and back— he decided she wasn't there and that this was for the best.

At home he built a Dark 'n' Stormy but only took one sip before climbing into bed with all his clothes on and falling into a deep, dreamless slumber.

DAYS 8-9

LOGBOOK COMMUNICATIONS BY DR. ROY WALLIS, GURU CHANDRA RAMPAL, AND PENNY PARK (EXHIBIT A IN PEOPLE OF THE STATE OF CALIFORNIA V. DR. ROY WALLIS)

Subject 1 initiated a conversation with me today while Subject 2 was watching a movie wearing headphones. She refused to speak, instead using a pencil and pad to communicate. She reaffirmed her concern that Subject 2 was spying on her and had some sort of nefarious intention in store for her. However, when I asked if she wanted to end her participation in the experiment, she emphatically opposed leaving the sleep laboratory, appearing determined to complete the twenty-one days. Later, she complained of insects in her hair, noises that I couldn't hear, and a smell like burning food. She described the sleep laboratory as a magical, ever-changing forest, filled with creatures that speak to her and a meandering path that unfolds before her in whichever way she wants to go. I wonder if it is this forest and path she is seeing when she paces the room for hours on end?

-Penny, Monday, June 4

Significant changes in both subjects were observed today, including increased psychomotor activity, emotional lability, accelerated speech, and inappropriate smiling. Subjects have begun to exhibit paranoia, cognitive disorganization, and psychotic symptoms including auditory, tactile, and olfactory hallucinations of varying degrees.
-R.W., Monday, June 4

Subject 2 has become fully immersed in the vivid and sustained hallucination that he is the actor Eddie Murphy. He repeatedly performs scenes from the actor's films and bits from his stand-up comedy routines, effectively adopting the actor's mannerisms and manner of oral expression. The test subjects have not spoken to one another during my shift. Subject 1 mumbles to herself and is prone to interchangeable bouts of laughter or crying, nervousness, and excessive excitability. She has also displayed perplexing and concerning behavior such as throwing objects around the room, spitting on herself, and pulling down her pants. She continues to experience instances of paranoia. Although she believes Subject 2 to be spying on her, I have observed no evidence of this. Contrary, it is Subject 1 who frequently and fervently glances at Subject 2. Neither has eaten any food for more than eighteen hours.
-Guru Chandra Rampal, Monday, June 4

Physical examinations today documented weight loss, pupillary dilation, lacrimation, rhinorrhea, fever, and sweating in both subjects. Other changes noted were variances in body temperatures, decreased thyroid hormones, increased metabolic rates, high pulse rates, high plasma norepinephrine levels, an elevated triiodothyronine-thyroxine ratio, and an increase of an enzyme that mediates thermogenesis by brown adipose tissue. The changes in body temperatures are attributable to excessive heat loss and an elevated thermoregulatory set point, both of which increase the thermoregulatory load, while the other changes can be interpreted as responses to this increased load.

These data indicate sleep serves a thermoregulatory function in humans and suggests that continued total sleep deprivation can result in flu-like symptoms.

-R.W., Tuesday, June 5

DAY 10
WEDNESDAY, JUNE 6, 2018

C had was becoming worried.

He'd been working so hard memorizing his lines, feeding the right amount of emotion into them, really embodying the character of Axel Foley, the street-smart Detroit cop trying to solve the murder of his friend…and now it could all be for naught if fucking mushrooms started sprouting from his head.

Martin Brest would never cast him with fruiting fungi all over his face, and the role of the lifetime, the role that would catapult him to stardom, would go to some other actor.

Chad ran his fingertips over his forehead for the hundredth time, feeling for the bump he'd noticed earlier.

There it was, over his left eye, right between his hairline and his eyebrow.

He applied pressure. The bump mushed a bit, or at least he thought it did.

Was there even a bump there?

Yeah, there was. The mushroom wasn't big yet, but it was there all right, and it could pop up fully grown at any time, just like the fuckers did after heavy rainfall.

Chad was tempted to check himself out in the two-way mirror, but he didn't want the professor or his two fruitloop assistants asking him what he was doing. They might call up Martin Brest and tell the director Chad wasn't fit to make it to the casting call.

He rubbed the bump again and noticed Shaz watching him.

"What the fuck you looking at?" he asked her.

She quickly returned her attention to her book.

Chad glowered at her for another few seconds, then turned his back to both her and the observation window.

He continued rubbing the bump on his forehead.

ΔΔΔ

Sharon tried to focus on the Dean Koontz novel open on her lap, but the words weren't making any sense. They hadn't been for a long time, but she kept staring at them and turning pages so everyone spying on her would think she was okay.

But she was definitely not okay.

Not only was she hot all the time lately like she had a fever, but she was also was getting a pretty bad sore throat that made it painful to swallow. Her stomach wasn't great either. It felt bloated and full even though she couldn't recall the last time she had eaten anything of substance.

When she had been sick as a kid, her mom would stay home from work to take care of her, making her chicken noodle soup and letting her have ice-cold cans of her dad's Canada Dry ginger ale. At nighttime, she would tuck Sharon in beneath her bedcovers and apply Vicks VapoRub to her chest and read to her until she fell asleep.

Sharon missed her mom and her dad and her brother so much, but she knew she would not be able to see any of them again until the Sleep Experiment finished. She simply had to deal with the fever and sore throat and bloated stomach until Dr. Wallis told her she was free to leave.

You're not a prisoner, Shaz. Just tell him you want to go. He'll let you.

Yeah, right. As soon as I step out of the sleep laboratory, I'll fall asleep. And who knows what he'll do to me then. I'll probably wake up strapped to a table with my stomach cut open.

Why would he want to cut your stomach open?

To see what's inside me.

What's inside you?

"Shut up!" Sharon shouted abruptly, launching the paperback novel across the room. She leaped off the bed and began pacing.

Someone was speaking to her. The Indian. Asking what was wrong.

"Leave me alone!" she shrieked, grabbing an avocado from the basket on the kitchen counter and smashing it against the ground. It kept its pear shape. She crushed it with her heel. The green skin split and the fleshy golden meat squished out from both sides of the fruit like lumpy mucus. The big seed rolled across the floor, stopping at the base of the oven.

The destruction made Sharon laugh, and when she laughed, she stopped thinking about missing her family and what was growing inside her and all that other stuff she didn't want to think about.

ΔΔΔ

A few minutes later, sitting stone-faced on the kitchen floor, the fever and other symptoms returned, the feeling of being spied on returned, the darkness of her thoughts returned.

All worse than before.

She wept.

ΔΔΔ

Guru checked the gold-plated Casio wristwatch his mother had gifted him upon his acceptance to the University of California. It was 5:45 a.m. Another fifteen minutes to the end of his shift. He yawned. It was getting harder and harder to remain awake throughout the night. Neither Chad nor Sharon spoke to him anymore. They didn't do much of anything lately. Chad sat on the weight bench or the sofa staring at a middle distance, while Sharon sat on her bed staring at whatever book was open on her lap, sometimes not turning the page for extended periods. Every now and then they'd do something noteworthy. Chad would jump up and begin rehearsing a scene from *Beverly Hills Cops*. Sharon would spontaneously crack up laughing or crying like she'd done earlier in the morning. But for the most part they just sat around doing nothing, which meant Guru was just sitting around watching them doing nothing.

For eight long hours.

Nevertheless, while Guru and Penny might have been reduced to little more than babysitters, Dr. Wallis was still conducting important cognitive tests on the Australians, bolstering his research into the effects of the stimulant gas on human subjects, and Guru remained proud to be a part of the experiment.

He heard footsteps approaching. A moment later the door to the observation room opened and Penny appeared dressed in one of her eccentric mix-and-match outfits that made Guru think of how a six-year-old might dress a Barbie doll. She was smiling and seemed to be in a spunky mood.

"Morning, Guru!" She rubbed his smooth head. "I wish for a new Lamborghini."

"*I* wish you would stop doing that to me every morning."

She skipped to the observation window. "How're our little rats doing?"

"Unfortunately, Sharon had another meltdown earlier."

"I really mean it," she went on as if she hadn't heard him. "They're just like rats, aren't they? Put a person in a room for a long time with nothing to do, and they lose what makes them human. They just sit around like dumb rats. Why do we think we're so special?"

"You sound as though you might be having an existential crisis."

She turned to look at him. "Why do you talk like that?"

He frowned. "Like what?"

"So formal all the time. And so fast. Your speech pattern— way too fast. Gobble, gobble, gobble. You need to slow down."

"*You* are giving *me* speech advice? You cannot even pronounce my name properly."

"Gulu?"

"It is Guru! Guor-*roo*!"

"That's what I said. And what kind of name is Guru anyway? Isn't 'guru' a common noun?"

"'Guru' is a Sanskrit term for a teacher of a certain field."

"So, like, you're some kind of teacher?"

"I am not a guru, Penny. Guru is simply my name, just as Violet or Rose can be a woman's name without any connotation to the flowers."

"I bet you're a *sex* guru."

Guru stood. "I think I will be leaving now."

"But we haven't done the handover yet!"

"Yes, well, if you will be serious for once—"

Penny dropped in the now vacated chair. "I don't care about the handover," she said, putting her sneakered feet up on the desk. "I need to ask you a question."

"Yes?" he asked, eyeing her feet disapprovingly.

"Do you know where the professor lives?"

Guru blinked. "Dr. Wallis?"

"What other professor would I be talking about?"

"Why do you want to know where he lives?"

"I'm just curious, that's all."

"I am sorry. I do not know."

"But you can find out online, right?"

"Why would you think that?"

"Because you're Indian, and Indians are really good at computers and stuff."

Guru rolled his eyes. "You sound like my mother. And Indians are no better at IT than any other race. There are just more of us —"

"I'm kidding!" she said, cutting him off. "But you *are* good with computers, right?"

"I am no computer guru."

"Oh God, please shoot me. You are *so* not funny so don't try to be."

Guru's smile vanished. He thought it had been a pretty good joke.

"So come on," Penny pressed. "Can you help me out or what?"

"I think we should respect Dr. Wallis' privacy."

"Aww, I knew you would be a huge nerd about it." She dropped her feet to the ground and swiveled the chair so her back was to him. "See you tomorrow, *nerd*."

Guru was surprised by the venom in her tone. He contemplated the predicament for a moment, then said, "Have you searched for Dr. Wallis on social media sites?"

Penny spun around. "Yeah, of course. He has a LinkedIn account, but I can't see any of his personal information because the account is private."

Guru shrugged. "Given we already have his phone number, we could try a reverse lookup," he said. "If Google has ever crawled his number on a publicly accessible webpage, we might be able to pull it up, as well as any information related to it, such as an address..."

Penny cracked a smile. "Then let's do it!"

△△△

Dr. Roy Wallis hadn't seen Brook since the night he'd slept over in her boathouse, and he was looking forward to their date this evening tremendously. After showering, he dressed in a simple monochrome outfit along with a pair of wool loungers with cream soles. He stepped through a spray of cologne, then added some pomade to his hair and worked a dab of cedarwood balm into his beard. In the living room, he played background music on the stereo, adjusted the lighting to a pleasing ambiance, built a Dark 'n' Stormy, then went to the wraparound deck for a cigarette. He was about to light up when the doorbell rang. He returned the smoke to the pack, carried his drink inside, and opened the front door.

Brook, channeling a 1920s debutante with a long pearl necklace and beaded dress in bold Art Deco colors, looked ravishing.

"Welcome, my dear," Wallis said, kissing her on the cheek.

"My, don't you smell nice," she said. "Woody."

"Remind you of home?"

"Does my houseboat smell *that* much like wood?"

"No, it smells *only* of wood. Drink? I have a great California Syrah I've been saving for just such an occasion."

"Sounds lovely."

Dr. Wallis poured her a glass of the single-vineyard wine in the kitchen, then said, "Come on, I want to show you something." He led her to the clock tower room, then looked at her heels. "Are you going to be able to climb three stories in those?"

"Three stories?" She frowned at the staircase. "Don't tell me this place has *three more* levels?"

"No, only this tower."

"Tower—?"

He took her hand and led her up the powder-coated steel staircase. She seemed pleasantly surprised by the first level with its pool table, pinball machines, and city views through the four large picture windows. She oohed and aahed over the second-level library/office/garden solarium. But it was the third level— where star- and moonlight filtered through the four giant clock faces, setting the room aglow in an eldritch light—that took her breath away.

"Oh, Roy, I love it!" she said, peeking through a clear pane of glass in the east-looking clock face. "I feel like a princess in her fairy-tale castle!"

"I'm glad you like it," he said, topping up his drink at his second bar. "It's what sold me on the place twenty years ago."

"If you don't mind my asking, Roy...how can you afford such an apartment? I mean, I know professors get paid well, but this must have cost millions…"

"I received a large inheritance when my parents passed away. I had to spend some of the money on something. Real estate seemed a good bet."

"Oh, Roy," she said, expressing regret. "I'm so sorry…I knew I shouldn't have asked—"

Dr. Wallis pulled her close and kissed her on the lips. They continued kissing for several long seconds until he stepped back to give his libido some space. He wanted to enjoy the evening with Brook, not rush right to the hanky-panky.

They returned to the main floor and set about preparing dinner. Wallis had stopped by the local supermarket that morning to pick up the ingredients to make a Caprese salad, bruschetta, and the simple yet classic pasta carbonara. His enjoyment of cooking didn't extend to baking desserts, however, and he'd opted to purchase a tiramisu cake rather than attempt to bake one from scratch.

They were finishing up their meal on the deck when his doorbell rang.

Wallis flashed immediately back to the evening with Brandy nearly two weeks before when Brook had come by unexpectedly.

Could it now be Brandy at the door in some karmic twist of fate?

"Excuse me," he said, dabbing his lips with a napkin and standing. Unable to offer Brook any explanation, he promptly returned inside and went to the front door, trepidation expanding in his chest with each step.

He gripped the doorknob, paused a beat, then pulled open the door, hoping for the best, which right then would have been anybody but Brandy.

It was Penny Park, all K-popped up in an oversized sweater, frilly scarf, and miniskirt.

Dr. Wallis blinked. "Penny?" he said, careful not to raise his voice too loudly. He looked past her, saw nobody else. "What are you doing here?"

"I wanted to hang out." She smiled. "You free, professor?"

"How did you get my address?" he demanded.

"Not too hard if you know your way around online."

Wallis restrained a surge of anger at the blatant invasion of his privacy. "This isn't a good time, Penny," he said simply.

"Come *on*, professor," she said playfully. "I mean, I'm not drunk tonight. I'll behave."

"This is *not* a good time, Penny," he repeated meaningfully.

Comprehension flickered in her eyes, and she peered into the apartment, drawing a connection between the bottle of wine on the kitchen island, the mood lighting, and the background music.

Her face darkened.

"Go home," he added gently. "We'll talk tomorrow."

For a terrible moment Wallis thought Penny might burst into tears, or worse, throw some sort of scorned lover's temper tantrum. Thankfully, she merely hurried down the stairs.

Badly shaken, he returned to the deck. Brook had not touched any more of her food and was standing by the railing that bordered the deck, gazing out at the night.

"It was my assistant from school," he explained. "She wanted to update me on the experiment."

Brook turned. "At close to midnight?"

Wallis scratched his head. "Look, it's bizarre. I don't know what to make of it."

"She knows where you live?"

"I'm baffled, Brook. I swear, she's never been by before, and nothing is going on between us." He couldn't believe he was speaking these words, feeding Brook such a clichéd defense, but he nevertheless added: "She's my *assistant*, for Christ's sake! She's twenty-one."

"I think I should go," Brook said tightly.

"Brook, no—hold on! Look, she has a crush on me, okay? That I know. She's made it pretty clear. But there's nothing between us! I swear to you, nothing!"

Brook studied him for a long moment, then, in a disconcertingly blasé tone, she said, "Okay, Roy. I believe you. I don't know what's going on, and I don't think you're telling me everything, but I believe you're not romantically involved with this assistant of yours. Still, I can't stay tonight. I'm sorry."

She marched past him and went inside. Wallis followed, at a loss for what to say or do to right the situation.

"Brook..." he said lamely when she opened the front door to leave.

She didn't reply. The door swung shut behind her.

After a long moment of thoughtful silence, Wallis returned to the deck to finish his dinner—and smashed his pasta-laden dish on the slate tiles, followed shortly by his Dark 'n' Stormy.

DAY 11
THURSDAY, JUNE 7, 2018

D r. Roy Wallis did not bring Penny Park a green tea the following morning. He set his vanilla latte on the desk and got straight to business. "How were they?" he asked, looking through the viewing window. Chad sat on the workout bench, slumped forward, his head held in his hands. Sharon was nowhere to be seen.

"Is Sharon in the bathroom?" he inquired.

"Yup," Penny said, not looking at him. She was wearing a denim jacket over some sort of multi-colored court jester's shirt. Jovial, however, she was not. More like royally pissed.

Dr. Wallis didn't appreciate the attitude. He'd done nothing wrong the night before. She was the one who'd tracked down where he lived and busted up his date.

"How long has she been in there?" he asked.

"A couple of hours."

"*A couple of hours?*"

"They're bad," Penny said. "Like, really bad. Way worse than yesterday." She finally glanced up at him, but instead of the anger he'd expected to find in her eyes, there was a concern. "We made them sick, professor," she continued. "And I think we need to end the experiment."

Dr. Wallis straightened in shock. "*End it?* Penny, we can't end —"

She cut him off. "These last few days, I haven't been

122

comfortable with the experiment. I've been worried about Chad and Shaz. Now I'm *really* worried about them. What we're doing, stealing their sleep, isn't right. You said this yourself—"

"The experiment was approved by the university's Institutional Review Board. Chad and Sharon both provided written informed consent. Most importantly, they've displayed no willingness to end—"

"Stop it!" Penny cried. "Stop talking and listen to me, okay? Chad and Shaz are not well. Look at them! Watch them! See for yourself."

△△△

Dr. Wallis and Penny Park observed the two Australians for the next twenty minutes. Chad remained on the weight bench holding his head in his hands. When Wallis coaxed him into a conversation, his replies were curt and slurred, and he complained of dizziness, nausea, and the "fucker of all fucking headaches." When Sharon returned from the bathroom, she appeared gaunt, clammy, and unsteady on her feet. She curled into a ball on her bed and wrapped her arms around her knees to stop her body from trembling. She refused to speak at all.

Dr. Wallis tried once more. "Sharon?" he said. "I would like to perform another EEG. Would that be acceptable?"

When she didn't reply, he got up and rolled the metal cart with the EEG equipment into the sleep laboratory.

Neither Australian paid him any attention.

He stopped next to Sharon's bed.

"Sharon?" he said in a clinical voice. "Open your eyes please."

She cracked them open. They were red and watery. "What?"

"Remember this machine?"

She looked at the EEG equipment. "No."

"We used it a few days ago."

"What does it do?"

"It will help me find out what's bothering you. Sit up please."

She didn't respond for a long moment. Then slowly, like an old woman suffering osteoarthritis, she sat up, shoulders rolled forward.

"I'm going to place this on your head now," he said, picking up the electrode headband. After smearing some gel on her forehead, he slid the headband in place so the smooth sides of the metal discs were in contact with her scalp, and the adhesive ground patch was behind her ear. "We're all set. You can lean back against the bed's headboard if you'd like?"

She only closed her eyes.

Dr. Wallis adjusted the photic stimulator so the lamp was directed at Sharon's face, flicked on the amplifier, and began recording her brainwaves.

△△△

While Penny Park watched Dr. Wallis perform the EEG on Sharon, the questions that had consumed her thoughts all morning returned:

Who was that woman he'd been with last night? Is she prettier than me? Is she some big-shot professor too? Are they dating? Can I compete?

Penny totally regretted going to the professor's house last night. She'd made such a fool of herself. She cringed each time she recalled the disapproving look in his eyes when he found her on his doorstep, and how he'd sent her home like she was nothing but a silly little schoolgirl.

She was furious with him for making her feel as lousy and worthless as she did. She wanted to hurt him the way he'd hurt her, which was why she'd taken so much satisfaction in telling him the Sleep Experiment had to end. The dismay on his face had been priceless! But she was not motivated to end the experiment by her embarrassment and jealousy alone.

Sharon and Chad really were sick, and they really did need medical attention.

When Penny had taken over for Guru at six a.m., the Australians were their normal sedentary selves. By midmorning, however, Sharon began sweating and shivering, while Chad swatted at invisible objects and mumbled gibberish. By noon Sharon had curled into a fetal position on her bed where she rocked and moaned and sobbed, and Chad could hardly stand for a few minutes without losing his balance and falling over, looking for all the world like a drunk after an all-night binge.

Penny had nearly called Dr. Wallis then, to tell him about the Australians' rapid decline in health, but her pride did not allow this. She didn't want to show weakness. She didn't want him to view her once again as a silly little schoolgirl; despite her anger with him, she still craved his respect.

So she stuck out the last two hours on her own, checking her wristwatch every ten minutes, silently urging the hands to move faster.

Dr. Wallis, Penny noticed now, was removing the electrodes from Sharon's head.

The EEG test was done.

Penny knew the professor was going to try to spin his findings in the best possible light and insist everything was okey-dokey. She would like to believe this, because deep down she didn't want the Sleep Experiment to end, as that would mean her relationship with Dr. Wallis, however rocky, would end also.

But what she wanted didn't matter anymore.

It's not about me, she told herself, realizing how selfishly she'd been behaving lately. *It's about Chad and Shaz. It's about doing what's right for them.*

△△△

"The electrical activity in Sharon's brain is exceedingly abnormal," Dr. Wallis admitted to Penny when he returned to the observation room. "It's similar to what you might expect to observe in someone with epilepsy, and very severe epilepsy at that, multiple seizures a day."

"See!" Penny said, appearing vindicated. "She's sick! Something's not right in her brain. She needs to see a doctor...a medical doctor."

"Bah!" Wallis said, brushing these concerns aside with a wave. "You're overreacting."

Penny seemed taken aback. "You're not going to do anything to help them?"

"What can we do right now, Penny?"

"For starters, professor, we shut off the gas and take them to the hospital."

Wallis blinked in surprise. "You were serious about wanting to end the experiment?" He shook his head vigorously. "Where is the scientist in you, Penny? We do not shy away from the unknown; we embrace it."

"Not at the expense of two people's health, professor."

"Penny, Penny, Penny," he said, alarmed at her flip of allegiance to him. "Does this newfound moral compass of yours...have something to do with last night?"

"No! God! They're *sick* in there!"

"They may be, but simply letting Chad and Sharon out of the sleep laboratory is no magic solution, I'm afraid. They won't instantly and miraculously recover. Their symptoms may worsen."

Penny frowned. "What do you mean? You don't *know* for certain? The stimulant gas, professor...you've tested it before, right?"

"Of course I have, Penny. Extensively. On mice."

"On *mice*? Only mice? And what happened to the mice?"

"They didn't sleep, naturally," he told her. "And then, unfortunately, they died."

"Died!" she cried, shooting to her feet.

"Penny, calm down."

"But what if Chad and Shaz *die*?"

"Humans aren't mice, Penny! They'll be fine. I'll reduce the amount of gas being vented into the room each day," he lied, giving her a chance to come back to his team. "We'll wean them off it during the last week of the experiment."

"No! No way, professor! This has to end." She took her phone from her pocket.

"Who are you calling?" he demanded.

"Guru."

"Guru? Why?"

"So he can talk some sense into you—"

Dr. Wallis grabbed her phone and stuck it in his blazer pocket, steeling his nerves for what he now was convinced had to be done. Penny had left him little choice. Her mind was set in opposition to him. She could no longer be trusted to do his bidding and keep her mouth shut. She had become an existential threat to the experiment. "You're not calling Guru, Penny," he said, "so stop being such a melodramatic twat."

Penny stiffened as if he'd slapped her. The cloudy confusion and hurt in her eyes quickly focused into sharp fear as she read his intention on his face.

"Professor...?" she said, back-stepping toward the door.

"Why couldn't you have been a good girl, Penny? Why couldn't you have simply nodded your head and gone along with me, Penny? I don't want to do this. I don't."

"Professor...?" Her back bumped into the door. She turned— fast. Got the door open, but that was all before Wallis grabbed her from behind and swung her about. She cried out in alarm. He shoved her to the floor and fell on top of her.

She screamed.

Dr. Wallis covered her mouth with one hand. The scream became a strangled muffle. She writhed back and forth beneath him and swatted his sides with her hands. He worked his weight forward until his knees pinned her biceps to the floor. Tears smarted her eyes and her body shuddered as she sobbed into his palm. With his free hand, he pinched her nostrils closed.

Her eyes bulged. She went wild, bucking her hips and thrashing her head from side to side and biting his skin.

Wallis didn't watch her die. He wasn't a sick man. He was an ambitious man, and he couldn't allow anybody to sabotage his life's work.

Not when I'm so close to uncovering the truth behind the human condition.

So he lowered his lips to her ear and told her in a soothing tone that her suffering would soon be over, that she would no longer feel any pain, that she would be at peace.

Wallis continued telling Penny Park this for a good minute after she had stopped moving.

△△△

At nine-thirty p.m. Dr. Roy Wallis left the observation room and waited out front of Tolman Hall for Guru to arrive for his ten o'clock shift. Swollen storm clouds robbed the night sky of the moon and stars. Rain fell in a steady drizzle, and a nippy wind rustled the wet leaves of the nearby trees. Dr. Wallis chained smoked and tried not to think too much about Penny, or the work ahead of him to dispose of her body. When he spotted Guru approaching through the dark, he crushed out the smoke beneath his heel and met the Indian in the middle of the breezeway.

"Professor?" Guru said, surprised to see him outside. "What are you doing out here?"

"Nice night, isn't it?" Wallis said. "I like it when it rains. Everything is clean and fresh."

"I like rain too, but not so much when I have to walk through it."

"At least you don't have to worry about it messing with your do anymore."

"That is true, professor. I continue to reap the rewards of my transformation."

"You don't have a car?"

"I do not even have a driver's license. Should we go inside? It is rather chilly."

"Here's the thing," Wallis said, stroking his beard. "I'm not sure the best way to break this to you, buddy, so I'll just spit it out. The Sleep Experiment is over."

Guru's eyebrows arched. "Over? Did something happen to—"

"The Australians are fine. But since your last shift their conditions deteriorated demonstrably, and I decided, in the interest of their health, to take them off the gas."

Guru's shoulders slumped as he digested this information. He looked like a lost puppy dog that had been kicked in the side. "I should have expected this. Their health had been declining for days. Have they begun to reacclimatize?"

"They're still in the basement. Once I turned off the gas, and the air in the sleep laboratory approximated the ambient air in the building, they quickly fell asleep in their beds. I suspect when they wake sometime tomorrow their symptoms will have decreased significantly, if not have resolved altogether."

Guru sighed. "Well, this is unfortunate. I was enjoying assisting with the experiment very much. I am sad it has come to a premature end."

"Look on the bright side, my man. The experiment lasted eleven days. We tied the Guinness Record. That should be something to celebrate." Dr. Wallis clapped him on the shoulder. "Your contribution has been greatly appreciated. Go enjoy the rest of your summer. Of course, you'll be compensated for the full twenty-one days, so don't worry about that. Just email me your bank details, and I'll wire the money tomorrow."

"You are too generous, professor." Guru stuck out his hand awkwardly. "I must thank you for this experience. I will not forget it."

Dr. Wallis shook. "I hope to see you in a few of my classes next semester."

Guru frowned when he noticed the compression bandage wrapped around Wallis' right hand, which hid the teeth marks on his palm.

"Spilled some hot coffee on it," Wallis said by way of

explanation. "Nothing to worry about. You take care now."

DAY 12

FRIDAY, JUNE 8

D r. Roy Wallis spent the next several hours observing the Australians and recording notes as usual. Cloistering himself in the small observation room 24/7 for the foreseeable future was not going to be ideal, but he would put up with the discomfort in the name of his research. He would purchase an inflatable mattress to sleep on, and he would eat most of his meals at the nearby cafés and restaurants in downtown Berkeley. He would have to return home to shower and shave, but that shouldn't cause any problems. The Australians had displayed no desire to leave the sleep laboratory. All would be fine.

At two o'clock in the morning, Wallis walked through the wet night to his car and parked it out front of Tolman Hall. He returned to the empty basement room where he had stored Penny's body and carried it under the cover of darkness to his car, where he laid it across the tiny backseat.

Slipping behind the wheel, he pressed the ignition button and spent some time plugging his destination into the GPS. A minute later he was about to put the transmission in gear when a knock on his window made him jump. He peered out to see the round face of campus police officer Roger Henn. He was smiling beneath his waxed Monopoly Man mustache, so Dr. Wallis didn't think he'd seen Penny's body. Moreover, the Audi TT was a two-door coupe, and the back side windows were little more than tiny triangles, which made it very difficult to see into the backseat. Still, Wallis played it safe and got out of the car.

"Rodge, my man," he said, digging his cigarettes from his pocket and leading the bigger man away from the car.

"How ya doing, doc?" Roger Henn said. His ball cap—stamped with *POLICE: University of California*—was pulled low over his forehead, the bill keeping his bright blue eyes in shadows. He had the ruddy cheeks and nose of a seasoned drinker, and he smelled strongly of spearmint gum.

"I'm good, my friend. Catch any students making out in the bushes tonight?"

"Pepper sprayed the shit out of them."

They laughed. Wallis lit a cigarette.

"So how's that experiment of yours going?" Roger Henn asked. "What you doing down there anyway?"

"Oh, you know, what all scientists do. Run rats through mazes and mess with effervescent test tubes."

"While cackling evilly and striking dramatic poses."

"Exactly." Doing his best imitation of Gene Wilder in *Young Frankenstein*, Wallis spread his hands and said, *"It's alive!"*

They laughed again.

"So how are you, Rodge?" Dr. Wallis asked. "Quiet night?"

"We got an interesting feller back at the station on remand," Henn said. "Says he's a pickpocket, and you gotta hear how he allegedly spends his weekends. Takes his local train to San Francisco International Airport Saturday morning, dipping all the way. At the airport, buys a pack of envelopes and stamps and posts what he calls his 'takings' back to his home address. Then he dips some more around the departures lounge before taking a cheap flight to Phoenix, Santa Fe, fucking Topeka—wherever he feels like sightseeing for a day or two, still dipping and posting the cash back, so none of his ill-gotten gains are on him if he ever gets busted. And he says he never does 'cause if anyone ever notices they've been pickpocketed, he drops the wallet instantly and points it out to the person, like a Good Samaritan. Says he's lost count of how many people fucking thank him."

Dr. Wallis tapped ash from his cigarette. "So how'd he get caught tonight?"

"DUI."

"Ah, yes. The bane of the midnight shift patrolman. Speaking of which, how does a cop get stuck on graveyard duty anyway?"

Henn shrugged his beefy shoulders. "We got a shift bid policy. Patrol officers bid by seniority."

"But you're what? Thirty-five? Thirty-six? You must have a fair bit of seniority under your belt?"

"Thirty-seven, and yeah I do. But I don't mind the dark side. Less nuisance report calls, and most of the other cops, being more junior, are less cynical about life than the guys on the other shifts. But shit." He yawned. "I do get tired sometimes."

"Because what you're doing isn't natural, Rodge. Humans are diurnal. We're not meant to stay up all night and sleep during the day. It works against our circadian clock."

"That's right, you're the Sleep Doctor. Got any recommendations on how to make me feel less tired?"

"Sure, get enough sleep."

"Easier said than done. You ever try sleeping in the daytime?"

"Your brain can be tricked into going to sleep under the right conditions. Get some blackout shades for your bedroom or an eye mask. Earplugs too for when your neighbor decides to weed whack or mow in the middle of your night."

"Yeah, I might try that, doc. Neighbor has a dog that never shuts up."

"You can try changing out your lights as well. Get some low-wattage ones. Maybe even red ones."

"Shit, no! I ain't gonna turn my house into a brothel."

"You asked for my advice."

"I'll stick with the eye mask and ear plugs."

Dr. Wallis shredded his cigarette beneath his toe. "All right, Rodge. It's been fun, but I have to get home myself. Have a good night."

Roger Henn continued his patrol east along Hearst Avenue, and Wallis returned to the Audi, pleased at how calm he'd remained while speaking to a police officer with Penny's body hidden a dozen feet away.

Making a U-turn, Wallis left Berkeley and drove west along I-580. Thirty minutes later, just past the prison where Johnny Cash recorded an album live, he continued west along Sir Francis Drake Boulevard to Samuel P. Taylor State Park.

He had been an outdoorsman in his younger days, and he'd discovered the park quite by accident a dozen years ago while driving to Point Reyes National Seashore. It quickly became a favorite place of his to spend a solitary weekend camping, hiking, and mountain biking. He couldn't remember the last time he'd come out this way, but it must have been more than five years ago now.

The park, as Wallis recalled the lore, was named for a man named Samuel Penfield Taylor, who hit it big during the California Gold Rush and used some of his gold to buy a parcel of land along Lagunitas Creek, where he built the first paper mill on the Pacific Coast. When a stretch of the North Pacific Coast Railroad was constructed nearby, the ever-entrepreneurial Taylor built a resort alongside the tracks catering to city-weary San Franciscans. After Taylor died, the State of California took possession of his property for non-payment of taxes, and he became immortalized as the modern-day park's namesake.

Dr. Wallis parked the Audi about a mile west of the Camp Taylor entrance, in a pullout on the side of the road. At this hour there were no other cars. He removed Penny's body from the backseat. Thankfully rigor mortis had yet to affect her muscles, and he flopped her body over his shoulder like a bag of potatoes.

Across the road, he knew, were trails leading up to Devil's Gulch. He had no intention of following trails. Instead, he started west off the beaten path into the old-growth forest.

The towering redwoods blocked any celestial light penetrating the clouds from reaching the ground, but the torch app on his phone served well to illuminate his way. Despite the fact he was in good shape and Penny's body was thin and light, the trek was not easy. Steep hills and winding creeks impeded his progress, while a light fog shrouded roots and rocks, causing him to stumble on more than one occasion. After ten minutes he was panting and sweating. After another ten minutes he stopped to catch his breath. However, this was not the occasion to be lazy or sloppy. The deeper into the forest he brought the corpse, the better.

In the end, he pressed on for what must have been another thirty minutes before deciding he had gone far enough. He dumped Penny's body onto the leaf litter with a sigh of relief. He wiped the sweat from his forehead and eyes and shook the numbness out of his shoulders and arms. Then he withdrew the hunting knife he had collected from his home on the way to the park. He'd only used it before to cut rope and clean fish. Tonight's activity would be very different, and for a moment he worried he didn't have the stomach to decapitate Penny. But he knew it was a necessary horror. He didn't own a shovel, and he hadn't been about to go purchasing one in the middle of the night. Even if he found somewhere that sold them well past the witching hour, he would have to use cash to avoid leaving a paper trail, and the transaction would be suspicious as hell. The clerk would remember him and could potentially provide his description to the police. He supposed he could have waited until morning and popped by Home Depot. But the store had CCTV cameras, and being caught red-handed on camera was worse than any eye-witness account.

Besides, he didn't need a shovel. The park was full of carnivorous wildlife. Black bears, cougars, gray foxes, and bobcats were all opportunistic predators that would jump at a free meal. And Penny in the belly of a bear was better than Penny buried beneath the ground, where, if ever discovered, her remains could be identified.

The problem was her head.

It was too big for any animal to consume, and even if the elements and decomposition reduced it to a whitewashed skull over time, forensic technology could reconstruct her face.

So he had to dispose of it properly.

Crouching, Dr. Wallis commenced the gut-churning job of detaching Penny's glossy-haired cranium from her body. The five-and-a-half-inch serrated steel blade made relatively easy work of this, even when it came to severing her cervical vertebra, though he did get blood all over his hands.

Standing, Wallis thought he might be sick. But a few deep breaths stayed his nausea.

He picked up Penny's head by the locks and made his way back to one of the creeks he had passed earlier. He set the head on the bank, then waded into the water to test its depth. It came nearly to his shoulders at the deepest point, which would be good enough. He scrubbed the blood from his hands, then returned to the bank. Bacteria in the gut and chest of a deceased person will eventually create enough gas to float a submerged body back to the surface of any body of water. You didn't have this problem with a head though. Still, to be safe, Wallis stuffed Penny's mouth with small river rocks. Then he lobbed the ghastly thing into the middle of the creek.

It sank promptly out of sight, and Dr. Wallis continued to his car, satisfied with a job well done.

ΔΔΔ

He returned to his penthouse apartment just as dawn was painting the rain-scrubbed sky amber, apricot, and vermillion. He showered and changed and was planning to head out to purchase the necessities he would require in the coming days, but the sight of his king bed was too tempting.

Just for an hour, he told himself in a moment of weakness, flopping down on top of the duvet.

During the latest REM stage of his comatose-like slumber, he dreamed it was daytime in Samuel P. Taylor State Park, the forest still and silent. He was hurrying through the shadows cast by the giant coastal redwoods, glancing back over his shoulder for his unseen pursuer, when a thick fog materialized from nowhere, and within it, a decrepit stone church sprouting from the rotted-out stump of a felled tree. The stone walls were cracked and crumbling in places, and a trail of white smoke, nearly indistinguishable from the fog, wafted from a chimney.

He crept into the hybrid structure through a gap in the jagged stump. The interior was much larger than should have been possible, and he hurried across the nave and took refuge beneath the cloth-draped altar. Yet even as he hid, the air was shifting and thickening, darkness was gathering, and when he worked up the courage to peek out from beneath the altar cloth, he found himself suspended in an abyss so vast it would reduce even the tallest redwoods to toothpicks. He was not alone, for the amorphous, monolithic demon now shared the darkness with him, and he knew his time was almost up—

Dr. Wallis snapped awake with a breathless gasp. The night filled the bedroom windows, disorienting him. It had been morning when he'd lain down. Surely he hadn't slept all day?

He sat up and checked his wristwatch. It was eight-thirty p.m.

"Fuck," he mumbled. Then, like a zap from a live wire, he recalled his middle-of-the-night excursion, and what he'd done to Penny's body, and he cursed again in remorse.

Wallis went to the bathroom, splashed cold water over his face, brushed his teeth, then returned to the bedroom. He collected his phone and was heading to the front door when he saw on the display that he had missed a call from Brook.

He paused in the living room, conflicted. He rang her back.

She picked up on the second ring. "Hey," she said, sounding neither upbeat nor upset to hear from him. Had it only been the day before yesterday when she had been over and Penny had paid the unannounced visit? That seemed like an eternity ago.

"Hi," he said, trying to sound more chipper than he felt. "Missed a call from you."

"I'm sorry, I shouldn't have disturbed you while you're working—"

"I'm not working right now," he said promptly. He had to

get back to Tolman Hall, he knew. The Sleep Experiment had been unsupervised for more than eighteen hours now. Yet...he was depressed and anxious, and the sound of Brook's voice was familiar and comforting. He wanted to see her. He wanted to experience the normalcy that her company would offer, even if it was false normalcy, for the murder of Penny was going to be a stain on his conscience for a long time to come. "What are you doing?" he asked.

"Sipping a glass of wine and looking out at the bay."

"Sounds nice."

A pause. Then: "Would be nicer if you were here with me."

He didn't reply.

"Roy?"

"I was just thinking... Have you eaten?"

"Yes, but I could eat again, something light."

"How about that izakaya restaurant on San Pablo Avenue. That's not too far from your place."

"We'll need reservations."

"I know the owner. He should be able to squeeze us in. Say, a half hour?"

△△△

With the Audi's top down, Dr. Wallis sped across the San Francisco-Oakland Bay Bridge, enjoying the roar of the wind in his ears and the great black expanse of night sky overhead. The moon shone bright and full amongst the scattering of stars.

He parked in downtown Oakland and walked a few blocks to the izakaya. He remained anxious and on edge, worried Brook was going to read in his eyes what he'd done. This was nonsense, of course, just his guilt distorting his judgment, and he told himself to get his shit together.

The hostess—an Asian woman channeling an Edo-period ninja with her headband, loose black clothing, and slippered feet —led him to a corner table. Brook hadn't arrived yet, and he took the opportunity to order a drink. The restaurant didn't stock rum, so he settled for a twelve-ounce carafe of sake. David, the owner, came out from the kitchen to say hello. They'd gotten to know each other on a small-talk basis by the sheer number of times Wallis had patronized the establishment over the years.

When the waitress brought the sake, David returned to the kitchen and Wallis ordered a second carafe before he had even touched the first. The waitress, God bless her, didn't bat an eye.

The izakaya restaurant was dark, minimalist, and not very large. All the tables were occupied with middle-aged well-to-dos enjoying a night out without the kids. The smells of deep-fried tempura and teriyaki sauce and grilled pork belly aromatized the air, and Wallis realized he hadn't eaten since yesterday afternoon.

Brook arrived ten minutes later in strappy sandals and a sleek cocktail dress. The waitress had cleared the carafe he had polished off, so only one remained on the table, albeit half-full.

"Sorry I'm late," she said after they kissed and sat. "I couldn't decide what to wear."

"You look great," he said.

"You always look great."

"It's easy when all you have to do is throw on a jacket."

Dr. Wallis poured Brook a cup of sake, then ordered another bottle, along with some house-made pickles, edamame, mushroom tempura, and beef skewers.

"Cheers," he said, tapping cups and drinking.

"So I just want to get this out of the way first," Brook said. "I'm not mad about the other night. I probably overreacted a little by going home. I can hardly blame your assistant for having a crush on you. I have a crush on you. It was just that..."

"You don't have to explain anything, Brook," he said. "And you might be happy to know, I've dismissed her from the experiment."

"You dismissed her? Oh my, Roy, you didn't have to do that!"

"Yes, I did. It was completely inappropriate for her to come by my house like she did. She looked up my address online somehow. That's borderline stalking."

"Well…as long as *you* think it was the right thing to do, and it had nothing to do with my reaction."

"It was the right thing to do," he assured her. "However, I'm going to have to pick up her eight hours, which means I won't be available much if at all until the experiment concludes."

"Which is, what, another week?"

Dr. Wallis had told Brook the duration of the Sleep Experiment was twenty-one days, as he had told Guru and Penny and the Australians, but the reality was it would last as long as was necessary to either prove or disprove his revolutionary premise.

Regardless of this, he said, "Yes, another week."

She pouted with put-upon exaggeration. "What am I going to do without you?"

"Hey, I got you something. Close your eyes."

"Really?" Smiling, she closed her eyes.

"Hold out your hand."

She stuck her hand out, palm upward. "Okay."

Wallis produced from his jacket pocket the ring Beverley St. Clair had made for him. He tried slipping it over Brook's middle finger. The fit was a little tight, so he slipped it over her ring finger instead.

"All right," he said.

Brook opened her eyes, which lit up in delight when she saw the ring. "Oh Roy!" she said, holding her hand before her face to admire the piece of jewelry. "It's lovely! It really is."

The ring was sterling silver with green quartz. On the bottom left corner of the gemstone, as if perched on the edge of a leaf, was an eighteen-karat rose gold ladybug.

"I wasn't sure of your size…"

"It's perfect." She took his hand in both of hers and squeezed it affectionately. "Thank you, Roy. I don't think I'll ever take it off."

The waitress arrived with the third carafe of sake and the food. Dr. Wallis ordered several more dishes, which he ate almost exclusively over the next hour or so. During the leisurely meal, he and Brook spoke about everything under the sun. Their conversation was easygoing and pleasant. They had a natural synergy. They liked the same things. They had a similar sense of humor. What Wallis enjoyed most about spending time with Brook, however, was the way she always put his mind at peace. Her life was simple, which made her simple by extension, but in a desirable way. This was why, he believed, she had cast such a spell over him. She had no pretenses. She didn't play games. She had no grand aspirations in life and didn't desire to have any. She had her job, which she liked; she had her friends, the ones he had met down to earth and genuine; she had her silly little houseboat, which she adored; she had her health.

She lived *in* the moment, not for some greater moment, and he found himself not only enchanted by this paradigm but envious of it too.

"So they're saying we're going to be getting a month's worth of rain in the next week," Brook was telling him now, taking the last edamame from the dish and delicately sucking the soybeans from the salty pod. "Three storms in seven days. Can you believe that?"

"We talking winter-level storms here?" he asked her.

"Not that heavy, but it will be raining nearly nonstop."

"Good thing I'll be cooped up inside Tolman Hall."

"I'd love to see it."

"Better be quick. It's going to be torn down later this summer."

"I mean your experiment."

Wallis blinked in surprise. "Really?"

"Sure. Can I?"

"There's nothing to see. It's just two people sequestered in a room."

"I know you don't like talking about it much, Roy, but I really would like to see it. I'm a mess if I don't get my eight hours of sleep each night. And your guinea pigs have gone two weeks?"

Wallis hedged. "I don't know, Brook...I'm not exactly running a freak show, a penny a peek."

"I won't interfere or anything, I promise. Didn't you say there was a two-way mirror? So they won't even see me."

"When did you want to come by?"

"We're not doing anything right now."

Wallis contemplated this as he chugged what remained of the sake.

"All right then," he decided, dabbing his bearded lips with a serviette. "Let's do it."

△△△

"Jesus H. Christ!" Dr. Wallis exclaimed as soon as they stepped inside the observation room.

"Oh my God... Is that?" Brook spun away and made a retching sound.

Wallis couldn't take his eyes away from the viewing window. One or both of the Australians had torn hundreds of pages from the books in the library and plastered them to the two-way glass with their feces. Their work was so thorough he couldn't see into the sleep laboratory at all.

He hit the Talk button on the touch panel controller. "Hey, guys...?" he said, a singsong intonation to the question.

They didn't answer.

Brook came to stand beside him. She didn't speak

"Chad?" he tried again. "Sharon? What's going on in there?"

He heard susurrate whispers and witchy laughter.

"Roy...?" Brook said, her voice careful.

"This is unprecedented," he told her.

"Is it a joke? Why would they...do this?"

"They've been experiencing mild hallucinations. This must be some sort of extension of their distorted perception."

"Like they saw something in their reflections they didn't like so they covered up the mirror?"

Wallis thought of Chad's hallucination that mushrooms were

growing from his head and nodded.

"I don't like it, Roy," she added. "Should we...I don't know... should we get them help?"

"*No*," he said harshly as he experienced a sickening sense of déjà vu. Nevertheless, he quickly dismissed any notion that he would have to serve Brook the same fate as Penny. Brook wasn't impulsive or disloyal or motivated by self-interest. She would never go behind his back to the Board of Trustees. "I mean, not right away," he added. "I'll keep watch on them for a bit, let them outside to get some fresh air, give them some time to clear their heads."

"You think that's all they need? What they've done is..."

"I'm ninety-five percent sure it's all they need, Brook. Maybe I'll even take them for ice cream?" He smiled. "Anyway, if for whatever reason they don't shape up, I'll drive them over to Alta Bates Summit myself. Their health, of course, is of the utmost importance."

"You don't want me to stick around with you until you know for sure that everything is okay...?"

"Everything *is* okay, Brook." He smiled again, only this time it was a little tighter. "Trust me. I've been spending eight hours a day with these guys for the last two weeks. I know them inside out. They just need to be let out of the room for a while. Now why don't I drive you home? It's late, and you have work tomorrow morning, don't you?"

"Well, okay then. I guess...well, I won't be seeing you for another week, will I?"

Dr. Wallis kissed her on the cheek and led her from the observation room. "Hopefully we can find time before that. Maybe you could even come back in a couple of days to see the Australians when they're back to their boring old selves reading books and watching TV?"

"Yes, I would like that." They started up the stairs to the main floor. "Thank you for the lovely evening, Roy." She glanced over her shoulder the way they had come, laughing. "I mean, it *was* really lovely...up until *that*."

"You're getting off easy," he said, laughing too. "I'm the one who's going to have to figure out how to clean it all up."

DAY 13

SATURDAY, JUNE 9

Sharon was happy they could no longer see her. All their spying had been driving her crazy. Her hands smelled like crap, the entire sleep observatory smelled like crap, but the privacy was worth it. She felt giddy with the success of what she and Chad had done…giddy and *free*.

They can't see me! They can't see me! They can't see me!

A series of giggles escaped her mouth.

Chad, across the room, looked at her. She thought he was going to start yelling like he always did, but instead he giggled too.

She scampered toward him on all fours.

"They can't see us!" she whispered.

"Fuck them!" he said.

They both broke into titters.

"Chad…?" she said quietly.

"Yeah…?" he said.

"Can you hear the voices…?"

"Yeah…"

"But they're not coming from the speakers…"

"No…"

"They're coming from inside me…"

"Me too…"

"They want me to…do stuff…"

"Me too…"

"They want...out..."

"I know..."

"Should we let them...?"

He began laughing then, his fouled hands clamped over his mouth, and after a moment of watching him, she joined in.

△△△

Chad and Sharon refused to communicate with Dr. Wallis, and all he could hear via the microphones in the ceiling of the sleep laboratory was shuffled movement and the occasional rustle of secretive laughter.

He didn't know if they still wore the smartwatches he'd given them, but the devices were either turned off or out of batteries because the touch panel controller was no longer displaying their heart rates or blood pressure.

He pressed Talk once again, but this time he said, "Guys? I'm coming in, okay? Just to make sure everything is okay."

Laughter.

Dr. Wallis went to the door to the sleep laboratory.

It didn't budge.

He tried the handle again, realized the door was blocked from the other side and threw his shoulder into it.

No good.

What the hell had they moved in front of it?

He returned to the desk and sat down. Although frustrated he could no longer visually observe what was going on in there, he was also brimming with excitement.

The Sleep Experiment had entered the next phase.

△△△

At 1:43 that morning, Sharon began to scream.

ΔΔΔ

By 3:00 a.m., her screaming and crying had stopped.

ΔΔΔ

Half an hour later, after repeated attempts at communication with the two Australians, Dr. Wallis made a call.

"Professor?" Guru Rampal said, sounding sleepy.

"I need you to come to Tolman Hall. Right now."

ΔΔΔ

As soon as Guru Rampal stepped into the observation room, he stopped flat-footed as if he'd run smack into a wall. "Yikes!" he said, staring at the violated viewing window. "*What have they done?*"

Dr. Wallis stood and offered Guru the chair. "Sit down, Guru. We need to talk."

He sat down, frowning. "Have I done something wrong, professor?"

"No, this concerns the Sleep Experiment. Details that you don't know, and that you need to know if you are to help me."

"What would you like me to do?"

"You are a bright young man, Guru. You must understand that no great progress is ever made without sacrifice."

"Yes, I do understand that, professor. I made a great sacrifice to leave India and my family to study in America."

Wallis nodded. "I too have sacrificed much—a social life, marriage, children—all in the name of my work. For the last ten years I've been consumed with a theory that, if proven correct, will change the world forever. Success is tantalizingly close. But it all hangs on the success of the Sleep Experiment."

"But you said you ended the experiment, professor?"

Wallis stroked his beard. "When I was a child, Guru, my parents took me to church every Sunday morning. I remember the services well. They always began with a procession down the aisle. The big old Hammond organ would blast out rusty notes while the altar boy, carrying a giant cross, would lead the slow-moving line. Following him came the candle bearers and the priest and finally the deacon with the Gospel Book. The congregation would join them in a hymn. Although it was played in the upbeat major key, and meant to be joyous, and everybody gave it their best falsetto, I was always confused by the verses. They implied that Satan wasn't trapped in a fiery lake in the middle of the earth as I'd believed up until that point in my young life. He was, in fact, loose upon the world, leading an invisible army of demons. When I asked my mother about this, she quoted the Scriptures, telling me, 'Satan has desired to have you.' This is what Jesus told his apostle Peter in the Garden of Gethsemane because Peter was prepared to fight bravely for Jesus against flesh and blood enemies, but he was unprepared to meet Satan on the battlefield of the heart and mind. And that's where Satan and his minions will get you, I learned that day, where he will always get you, wherever and whenever he wants, perhaps without you ever even knowing. In the heart and mind." Wallis lit up a cigarette. "Growing up, the inexorableness of this concept terrified me. In fact, to this day, I still have dreams that play to these fears. My point here? It was this simple statement —'Satan has desired to have you'—that set the course of my life. It's what got me interested in psychology." He pondered this for a long moment. "You see, Guru, my parents died when I was only a little younger than you," he continued. "They were sailing in the Bahamas when pirates attacked them if you can believe that. Fucking pirates. The swine boarded my parents' yacht, stole everything of value, then sent my parents overboard. That's what the local police believe happened, at any rate, and I don't have any reason to doubt them. I went to a dark place after that, I won't lie. A very dark place. I didn't care if I lived or died. I had suicidal thoughts. Once, when I was driving down the freeway, I had a nearly irresistible urge to swerve my car into oncoming traffic with no thought for the others I would kill in the process of killing myself—and it was that moment I realized Satan had already gotten me." Wallis took a long, hard drag, exhaling smoke through his nostrils. "I turned my life around then. I did my best to banish the darkness inside me. I changed my major to psychology to understand better why people did some of the awful things they did, to help them if I could. Nevertheless, it was the science of sleep that proved to be my true calling. I joined the wave of researchers endeavoring to uncover what went on in our brains when we slept. Before the 1950s, everyone thought sleep was a passive activity, but then electroencephalographs changed the game, revealing that our brains have a clear four-stage routine that repeats over and over until we wake at the end of a bout of REM, our minds full of melting clocks and impossible places and faces we can't remember."

"Here is an interesting fact, professor," Guru said. "One of the first researchers to study REM found that he could predict when an infant would wake by watching the movements of its eyes beneath its eyelids."

Dr. Wallis nodded, twisting his cigarette out in the ashtray. "A party trick to liven up any Tupperware party, no doubt. Now, here's an equally interesting fact: every single creature you can strap electrodes to and keep up past their bedtimes—birds, seals, cats, hamsters, dolphins, you name it—all experience this four-stage routine when they sleep."

"Hamsters dream when they sleep?"

"Dream and a lot more, brother. Golden hamsters wake from hibernation—just to nap. So something pretty damn significant —essential, I would say—goes on when the lights are out. The question is, what? What the hell is going on during sleep that is so vital to every creature's survival?"

"May I remind you, professor, that in your Sleep and Dream class, you argued that we sleep out of habit. We sleep, to paraphrase you, because we have always slept."

"That certainly makes an interesting talking point, doesn't it? Not to mention packs my lecture halls with inquisitive young minds. But do I believe this?" Wallis began to pace in the small observation room, his hands clasped behind his back. "Ten years ago—during the summer of 2008—I conducted my first sleep deprivation experiments on mice. At the time, most of this research was being conducted on fruit flies due to the fact they're much cheaper and easier to maintain. But the benefit of mice is that they can be hooked up to an EEG machine. In the experiments, I stimulated the mice just as they were about to enter a bout of REM, causing an escalation of sleep pressure. Later, when I let the mice sleep undisturbed, I isolated the ones that were displaying odd behavior and dug into their genomes. Eventually I discovered they all shared a mutation in a specific gene. Their EEGs revealed an unusual number of high-amplitude sleep waves, suggesting they were unable to rid themselves of their sleep pressure and were consequently living a life of snoozy exhaustion. Although I have never been able to understand the full relationship between the mutated gene and sleep pressure, my research ultimately allowed me to engineer a preliminary version of the stimulant gas—which changed everything."

△△△

Guru was leaning forward in his chair. "What do you mean it changed everything, professor?"

"Control mice exposed to traditional sleep deprivation lived for anywhere between eleven and thirty-two days. No anatomical cause of death was ever identified; they simply dropped dead, which I speculate was due to stress or organ failure. The mice exposed to the stimulant gas, however, all died within fourteen days, and they didn't merely drop dead. They died extremely horrible deaths."

"I must ask how a mouse can die horribly, professor?"

"During the initial five or six days of the experiment, they behaved similarly to the control mice. They experienced a loss of appetite while their energy expenditures doubled baseline values, which resulted in rapid weight loss and a debilitated appearance. All to be expected. But then, between ten and fourteen days, they began spontaneously attacking one another with tooth and nail. These were not minor skirmishes due to tiredness, Guru. They were fights to the death—fights beyond death. Because whenever one mouse died, the survivors would attack its corpse for no apparent reason. Chew out its eyes, gnaw off its feet and tail, eviscerate its gut and remove its innards. Behavior antithetical to mice, and indeed to all animals, save for perhaps the most depraved of our species. And then when only a final mouse remained, it would turn on itself, performing acts of self-mutilation until it was incapacitated by mortal injury." Dr. Wallis paused theatrically. "*That*, my friend, is how a mouse can die horribly."

ΔΔΔ

"But if the control mice behaved normally until they died of natural causes," Guru said, "why would the mice under the influence of the stimulant gas act so bizarrely?"

"I asked myself that same question daily for months on end," Wallis said. "Until one morning the answer stumbled onto my lap. I had been out for breakfast when a priest sat down at the table next to mine. Soon he was joined by another man, a friend perhaps, or another priest not wearing his collar. In any event, they engaged in a theological discussion I had no interest in overhearing but could not help but listen to given their proximity to me. I did not stick around for my usual second cup of coffee, and as I returned home, I began thinking about all the Sundays I had spent in church as a child. The song the congregation used to sing came to me. My mother quoting the

Scriptures, warning me that Satan has desired to have us and that the way he would get us was in our hearts—"

"And *minds*," Guru said meaningfully. "Do not tell me you believe the mice under the stimulant gas were *possessed*, professor?"

"Possessed?" Dr. Wallis shrugged. "I am no longer a religious person, Guru, but I suppose 'possessed' is an adequate description of what happened to those mice, because what is possession other than the expression of a chaotic mind? And this is my point, my young friend. Every living organism—from tiny multicellular bacteria and viruses to mammals and human beings—we're all chaos wrapped in order. In other words, we've all been born with madness inside us, though it's kept in check by innate, fixed-pattern behavior."

"You mean instinct?" he said.

"Exactly, Guru. Instinct—the instruction booklet on how to act sane, if you will. Because imagine if a lioness had no maternal instinct to raise her cubs? Or if a newly hatched sea turtle had no instinct to run to the ocean and relative safety? Or if a marsupial, upon being born, had no instinct to climb into its mother's pouch? Indeed, without instinct a spider would never know how to spin a web. A bird would not know how to build a nest or hunt for worms. A bear would not hibernate during winter and likely starve to death. A dog would not shake water from its coat and likely fall ill. Without instinct, you see, existence would be chaos."

"But what of us? Humans? We are not puppets of instinct—"

"Of course we are, Guru!" Wallis said. "Fear, anger, love. Instinct rules almost every moment of our lives. But you are right in one regard. With our complex brains and our capacity for reason and free will, we're in the rare position in the animal kingdom to sneak a peek behind Mother Nature's curtain to get a taste of the madness bubbling inside us. Because let me tell you, buddy, instinct has never told someone to jump off a bridge, drive a van into a group of shoppers, or kidnap and torture a child. That's the crazy inside us talking, the madness, unfettered by instinct."

Guru's expression was a mask of studious disbelief. "Even if this is true, professor, even if nature is balanced on a knife-edge between chaos and order, I still do not understand what this has to do with the mice and the stimulant gas?"

"Because instinct was not Mother Nature's only tool to provide us sanity. She had one more powerful trick up her sleeve."

Comprehension dawned in his eyes. "*Sleep...?*"

"Why does every biological lifeform experience sleep pressure? Why do we have a failsafe in the form of microsleep to guarantee we will nod off even when we try our hardest not to? What are our brains doing for a third of our lives that is so important and requires so much juice that, at the end of each day, they essentially render us unconscious and paralyzed? What evolutionary advantage is worth the risk of the brain taking itself mostly offline for a good chunk of each day? I'll tell you what, my good friend. Our brains are doing their damned best to keep the madness inside us at bay. It's true. I've witnessed firsthand what happens during the total and prolonged absence of sleep and microsleep. Yes, admittedly only in mice thus far, but now..." He looked at the feces-smeared viewing window.

Guru looked too, and he gasped. "Chad and Shaz are not sleeping as you said?"

"No, Guru, they are not."

"They have...peeked behind Mother Nature's curtain?"

Dr. Wallis nodded. "And they need our help."

ΔΔΔ

"Chad, Sharon, I'm coming in," Dr. Roy Wallis said.

He didn't expect an answer and didn't get one.

To Guru: "We're going to have to bust the door in."

"What about the viewing window?" he said. "Would it not be easier to break that?"

"Easier, yes, but then the stimulant gas would contaminate the antechamber. Now, on the count of three, you and I are going to shove this door open. Ready?"

They shoved. Something sounding like metal on concrete squealed from the other side of the door.

"Keep pushing!" Dr. Wallis said.

Inch by inch the door cracked open until Wallis could see that the large seven-hundred-liter refrigerator lay on its side in front of it.

"A little more," he grunted. And then: "Okay, that should do it." He studied the narrow space they'd created between the door and the frame. It would be a tight fit. "I'll go first."

With his back flush with the door, Wallis placed his right knee on what was now the top of the toppled fridge and allowed himself to fall sideways. His upper body cleared the narrow space, and then it was simply a matter of dragging his legs through after him. He stood, dusted off his hands, and surveyed the room.

"Oh, shit," he said.

△△△

Dr. Roy Wallis approached the middle of the sleep laboratory, which smelled ten times worse than the filthiest restroom he had ever had the misfortune of visiting. Chad was crouched in a far corner, near the lounge, watching him with eyes that almost seemed to shine with an inner glow. But it was Sharon who Dr. Wallis was focused on. She lay on her bed, on her side, naked from the waist down. Across the center of her forehead either she or Chad had carved a straight incision from temple to temple, which had bled tremendously, painting much of her face red.

Her eyes, like Chad's, seemed to shine catlike, though whereas his were guarded and watchful, hers were intense and manic, conjuring the image of a woman in the final few minutes of childbirth.

"What the *fuuuuck*?" Guru said from behind him.

"Sharon?" Dr. Wallis said. "Did you cut yourself? Or did Chad?"

Her lips curled into a smile.

"Where's the knife?" he pressed.

"There it is, professor," Guru said, pointing.

A steak knife, the stainless steel blade and black plastic handle covered in blood, lay on the floor ten feet away from the bed.

"Go get it," Wallis said. "Don't startle Chad."

Guru went to the knife slowly, his eyes never leaving Chad. When he reached the knife, he crouched—and hesitated. "Are you sure I should touch this, professor? It is evidence."

"If you leave it there, Guru, either Chad or Sharon might use it again—to do something worse."

Guru picked up the knife and stood. "What now?" he asked.

"Take it to the observation room and bring back the first-aid kit."

Guru did as he was told, and Dr. Wallis returned his attention to Sharon. The incision across her forehead was deep but not excessively so. It most definitely required stitches, but this was not a service he could offer. Her hands, he noted, were smeared with dried excrement and blood, the latter leading him to believe she had been the one who did the cutting.

"Why'd you cut yourself, Sharon?" he asked her.

Her smile returned, the corners of her mouth twitching upward in a sinister rictus. Wallis did not like that smile one bit. He looked back to the door. Guru was squeezing through the crack to reenter the sleep laboratory. He scrambled over the fridge and came to the bed.

"Here you go, professor," he said, handing Wallis the bright red first-aid kit. "What should I do now?"

"Get some warm soapy water from the sink and bring it over."

Dr. Wallis unzipped the kit and set it on the bed. By the time he had snapped on a pair of blue Nitrile gloves, Guru had returned with a glass of soapy water and a roll of paper towel.

"This might sting a little, Sharon," he said.

"Okay, doc," she replied, her voice as dry as the rustle of October leaves, her manic blue-green eyes never leaving his.

Wallis wetted some paper towels and gently dabbed the long incision. Sharon didn't flinch.

"Does it hurt?" he asked her.

"I like you touching me, doc."

Wallis paused for only a moment before he resumed cleaning the incision, which he then misted with antiseptic spray and smeared with a liberal amount of antibiotic cream. He placed four small Band-Aids perpendicularly over the cut in the hopes of holding it together in the absence of sutures. He wrapped her head with the same compression bandage he'd used on his hand. He then used more paper towels and water to wipe the dried blood from her forehead, face, and neck.

"That's about the best we can do for now," he said, studying his handiwork. "How does the bandage feel? It's not too tight, is it?"

"All good, doc," she said. "But what about my tummy?"

She wore one of the nearly two dozen identical navy sweatshirts he'd purchased for her. He'd been so focused on her forehead that he hadn't realized the sweatshirt was saturated with blood.

"Can I take a look?" he asked her.

Sharon sat up in the bed and raised the oversized garment —it was clearly one he'd purchased for Chad—to just below her breasts.

A second gaping incision divided her taut stomach an inch above her belly button. Blood, much of it still wet, smeared her lower abdomen, pubis, and inner thighs.

Guru inhaled. Wallis swore.

"Guru," he said tightly, "go get me some more water."

When the Indian returned, Wallis used nearly the entire roll of paper towel to clean the incision and surrounding skin. The wound was still bleeding, but there was nothing he could do about that.

"Do you like touching me there, doc?" Sharon asked abruptly.

Wallis was wiping down her left inner thigh. "I can think of a myriad of other activities I would prefer to be performing right now, believe it or not."

"*I* like it when you touch me there. You don't have to use the gloves."

"Guru, pass me the antiseptic spray, then go get her a fresh set of clothes."

Dr. Wallis sterilized the incision, taped it closed with the largest Band-Aides available, and looped the compression bandage several times around her torso.

"Do you need help changing," he asked her when Guru brought him the clothing, "or can you manage yourself?"

Sharon pulled the sweatshirt swiftly over her head so she sat on the bed stark naked.

"You're going to need to stand up," he told her, holding out his hand in assistance.

She took it and stood with little trouble despite her injuries. Guru passed him a pair of white underwear. He crouched before her. "Lift your left foot," he said. She lifted it. "Right foot." She lifted it. He pulled the underwear up and over her thighs. The band snapped snugly around her waist. He repeated the same procedure with the sweatpants. "Do you want to wear a bra?"

"No," she said simply.

"Arms up."

She raised them in the air, and he pulled the sleeves of the sweatshirt over each, then lowered the neck hole over her head, careful to avoid touching her forehead.

"You can sit back down," he told her.

"Can we dance?" she asked him.

"We're not dancing."

"Please, mate? I *wanna* dance."

Dr. Wallis packed up the first-aid kit, then requested Guru's help to return the refrigerator to its upright position. On small wheels, it was easy enough to push back into its place in the kitchen. "Collect the rest of the knives from the cutlery drawer," he told Guru, "and wait for me in the antechamber. I'll be there in a minute."

Wallis went to the viewing window, crinkling his nose in distaste at the smell and sight of it. He peeled free three stained pages from the two-way mirror and rubbed the surface clean with what remained of the paper towel.

He turned to find both Australians watching him with their strangely gleaming eyes. Chad had joined Sharon in smiling at him.

"I believe this small portal to be a fair compromise," Wallis announced loudly. "You both have more privacy than before, yet we are still able to look in here now and then to check up on you."

Neither of them spoke.

"You are both extremely malnourished and need to eat. If you would like anything specific not provided for already, please let me know."

They began to giggle—awful, high-pitched batty sounds as unnerving as fingernails scraped down a blackboard.

"At least drink water to stay hydrated," he added. "It's essential for your health."

Now the giggles became full-throated, hyena-like, hysterical.

Dr. Wallis returned to the observation room.

∆∆∆

"What time is it, professor?" Guru asked. "Am I asleep? Because I feel as though I am trapped in a nightmare."

And it's only going to get worse, my friend, Dr. Wallis thought, but didn't say.

They were in the observation room, Guru slumped in the chair as if exhausted, Wallis sitting partially on the table, his arms folded across his chest.

"Why would Sharon do that to herself? No, you do not have to explain, professor. I know why. It is the madness." His shoulders sank. "How can this be?"

"The proof is right in front of you, Guru. They've gone insane. Or they're very, very close to the tipping point."

"Should we not try to help them? Should we—"

"It's too late for that. They're beyond the point of help."

"But we cannot just sit here and let them go insane—or go *more* insane."

"That's exactly what we have to do."

"But professor! They are not lab animals. They are humans!"

"I'm well aware of that fact, Guru. But you have to think of the greater good here. Over the next couple of days the evidence we document will be invaluable. Think about it. We will have demonstrated that you, me, the entire human race, *all animal life*, is essentially mad."

"Is this something we *want* to make known to the world?"

"Of course! It may seem like a pessimistic revelation at first glance, but it is quite the contrary. We once thought the universe was ordered because it appeared to run on a set of rules that we termed the laws of physics. But quantum theory has shown us that these laws, at their core, are actually random and unpredictable. Chaotic. However, far from diminishing our view of the universe, this knowledge has enlightened it tremendously. We now know matter can essentially be in an infinite number of places at any given time. We know there may be many universes, or a multiverse. We know that when subatomic particles disappear they reappear somewhere else, which sounds preposterous but is a proven fact and one day might lead to the tantalizing prospect of time travel. And speaking of the future, in the coming century mastering quantum theory will enable us to master matter itself. We'll create metamaterials with new properties not found in nature, and quantum computers that operate at millions of times the speeds of computers today. Invisibility, my man. Teleportation. Space elevators. Limitless energy. Advances in biotechnology and medicine we can't even begin to comprehend."

"What are you saying, professor?"

"I'm saying, Guru, that no scientific discovery has ever set us backward. Imagine the new fields of psychology our research will open up, the new fields of quantum theory applied to the *mind*. Jesus, our research may set in motion the steps to one day crack the code of consciousness—and with that, *reality itself*. Can you dig that, my man? *Can you dig it?*"

"Oh my, professor. This is almost too much for me to process."

"What matters, Guru, what matters right in this moment, is that while it's unfortunate what's happening to Chad and Sharon, certainly, it's for the greater good. Remember—no great progress is made without sacrifice. You told me you understood that?"

"I do, professor, I do." His face dropped. "Oh my..."

"Penny could not grasp the big picture. She was too close-minded. This is why I had to dismiss her from the experiment. But you're not like her, buddy. I know that. I've always known that. You're a scientist at heart. The search for knowledge and truth is in your genes. So you're not going to make the same mistake she did, are you? You're not going to walk away from what will arguably become one of the greatest intellectual triumphs in the history of human civilization, are you?"

Nearly a full minute of silent contemplation followed this grandiose statement, but then the tormented indecision in Guru's expression hardened into fierce resolve.

"No, professor," he said finally. "I am not."

DAY 14

SUNDAY, JUNE 10

D r. Roy Wallis left Tolman Hall at 7:00 a.m. to purchase a pair of air mattresses, pillows, sleeping bags, and any other necessities he and Guru might need in the coming days. He was pleased with his decision to bring the young Indian into the know. Not only did Guru take the around-the-clock pressure off Wallis, but it was simply a great relief to finally confess to someone the true purpose of the Sleep Experiment, and with this, the theory he had been working on for much of the last decade.

On the walk to the Audi, Dr. Wallis bristled with life. Everything about the day seemed fresh and wonderful: the magenta and coral dawn sky; the warm rays of the waking sun; the scent of grass and, beneath this, nutmeg and cloves, which was probably the organic herbicide that the campus employed to control the weeds in the block-pavement walkways.

You're so, so close, buddy, he was thinking excitedly. *Another day, perhaps two, to discover if your theory will be proven correct.*

And if so... Well, the implications simply could not be understated. Overnight *Roy Wallis* would become a household name, spoken in the same sentences as Newton, Einstein, Tesla, Galileo, Aristotle.

It was all a little unreal right then. But he'd get his head around it.

He would thrive in the spotlight. He was born for it.

△△△

Dr. Wallis' voice echoed inside Guru's mind:

We're all chaos wrapped in order.

Guru shivered.

Did he believe this extraordinary claim? Truly believe it?

If anyone other than Dr. Wallis had told him this, the answer would have been an emphatic no. But the professor was one of the world's foremost experts on the science of sleep. He knew what he was talking about.

Moreover, Guru had witnessed the changes in Chad and Sharon himself. They were going mad before his eyes.

We're all chaos wrapped in order.

Guru was not a spiritual man. When he pondered the vastness of the universe and the wonders of the natural world and the mysteries of consciousness, he did not search for a divine power to give meaning and purpose to it all. He accepted a material world that could be understood through the logical reasoning of science.

Consequently, even if he did believe Dr. Wallis' extraordinary claim—and he thought perhaps he did—he did not necessarily share the professor's description of the chaos as some sort of 'demon.' However, whatever it was, the chaos in question was clearly not benign.

It was dark, twisted, wicked.

Just look at what it had done to the Australians.

Guilt and shame filled Guru at the thought of the raving lunatics that Chad and Sharon had become. When the experiment concluded, they would be carted off to a mental institution where they would spend the rest of their days in straight jackets. This image was all the more terrible when Guru contrasted it with the smiling, healthy, easy-going people they had been less than two weeks before. Sharon especially. She had been so friendly to him, so inquisitive, always smiling and asking him questions.

And look at her now...all cut up and mad as a hatter.

Nevertheless, nothing could be done about this. The damage to her mind had already been inflicted. There was no rewind button.

If Dr. Wallis and Guru walked away now, Chad and Sharon's sacrifices would be for naught.

So the professor was right. There was only one course of action available to them.

They had to see what they'd started through to the end.

△△△

After tossing everything he'd purchased from a Target in West Oakland into the small trunk of the Audi, Dr. Wallis slid behind the wheel, stuck the key in the ignition...but didn't put the car in Drive. His libido was revved up with blinkers on. It had been more than a week now since he'd slept with Brook, and after that whole episode with Sharon stripping in front of him, he was having a tough time getting sex off his mind, and he knew it would soon begin affecting his ability to work and concentrate.

Dr. Wallis didn't like the term "sex addict." It sounded dirty and unbecoming of someone of his position in society. Not that the clinical designation of "hypersexual disorder" was a much better alternative. Nevertheless, Wallis couldn't deny that he was addicted to sex. He didn't have the cravings as bad as some people did, but he thought about sex—and engaged in it—a lot more than most.

The addiction began when he was a young man of twenty-two, shortly after his parents were murdered in the Bahamas. Sex, he discovered, helped to numb the pain of their loss. At first he was paying for one or two prostitutes a week, but it wasn't long before he was blowing two grand every other night in strip clubs. The next step in his disillusioned pursuit of happiness was the local sex club scene. Even when Brandy came into the picture a few years later, he spent many nights with other women. The thrill of everything that came before the sex —the flirting, the conversation, the drinking, the dancing, the thoughts of *will we or won't we?*—filled him with adrenaline and became almost as important as the sex itself. Orgies, BDSM parties, swinging, exhibitionism, dogging, he'd done it all—and was always searching for more extreme and exciting iterations of sex. Brandy never knew of his nighttime doppelgänger, of course. He supposed it hadn't been fair to have strung her along in a dead-end relationship for as long as he had, because no matter how much he liked her as a person, he had become detached from the emotional value of sex and relationships in general. She had offered him a sense of belonging and nurturing, which he'd so desperately desired, she had made him feel wanted, which he'd so desperately needed, yet despite all of this...it inevitably amounted to a false intimacy. He had a hole in his stomach, and he had a compulsive need to fill that hole, and one woman was never going to be enough.

The unfortunate situation was repeating itself with Brook now. He enjoyed spending time with her, and he enjoyed the attention she gave him and the serenity she exuded, but in the back of his mind he was already preparing for when he would have to cast her aside and move on.

Brushing these thoughts aside, Dr. Wallis drove to an upmarket twenty-four-hour bordello in Oakland's Financial District. It was not one of the seedy brothels posing as a massage parlor you could find all over any city. On the contrary, it was an invitation-only establishment that served a very select list of clientele.

Wedged between a bank and a nail salon, the bordello resembled an old European hotel, and for tax purposes it doubled as a boutique short-stay hotel. Wallis entered through the front door into a small, dimly lit lobby filled with plants where a receptionist he didn't recognize welcomed him with a smile.

"Good morning," she said. "Are you looking for a room for the night?"

"No, I am not," he said.

"Have you been here before?"

"I have."

"May I have your name?"

He told her, she entered it into the computer, then said, "It's very nice to see you again, Mr. Wallis. Would you follow me?"

She led him to a private waiting lounge that resembled an elegant Victorian men's bar. There were more plants here, while portraits of abstract female nudes in muted colors decorated the walls. A few minutes later the madam of the house, who Wallis did recognize, appeared with three primped women in skimpy yet elegant clothing.

"Hello, Roy," the madam said, shaking his hand. Unlike the prostitutes, she was dressed in regular clothing and cute sneakers. "How are you, darling?"

"Just fine, Janet."

"Which one of these lovely girls would you care to join you this morning? If you'd like to spend some time in private with each to get to know—"

"Not today," he said.

"Of course. Girls?"

Obediently, they took their leave.

"So who will it be, Roy?" Janet asked.

Dr. Wallis had been with the African before, and the Asian was too overly augmented for his liking, so he decided on the Scandinavian.

"Excellent," Janet said. "She's only been with us for a month or so now, but everybody loves her. She's part of the family. Cash or credit?"

Dr. Wallis paid with a credit card for a thirty-minute booking. The madame placed the girl's cut into a folder of the sort restaurants use for the bill, handed it to Wallis, then picked up a telephone. "Vivian, darling? Thirty minutes with Roy." She hung up and said, "You have a very special time now, and please come back soon."

She left the waiting room and the Scandinavian returned shortly thereafter.

"Hi!" she said brightly. "I believe you have something for me?"

Wallis handed her the folder, and she led him deeper into the house, which quickly morphed from Victorian to Greek décor. Her room featured four corner columns, a hot tub, and a statue of Venus.

"Shower's right in there," she said, indicating a door that led to a marble bathroom. "I'll be right back."

Wallis had a hot shower and returned to the bedroom with a white towel around his waist.

Vivian held a box in her arms and was neatly arranging an assortment of condoms, toys, and lubricants on a small table.

"Have you been here before?" she asked, smiling at him.

"Yes," he said, obliging the small talk. "Janet mentioned you're new?"

She nodded. "This is my first month...in the business."

Dr. Wallis put her in her early thirties, which meant she was late to prostitution.

"I was in sports medicine," she said.

"What led to the change in profession?"

"The money."

He nodded.

"What do you do, Roy?"

"I dabble in psychology."

"Is that so? Have you met Lisa before?"

"I don't believe I have."

"She's been here for about a year now. She used to work as a licensed psychologist. She once told me she felt as though she helped more people here than she had at her previous practice."

"I can imagine," he said, making a show to glance at his wristwatch. "In any event, and in the interest of expediency, the faster we drop the charade and fuck, the better for me, as I have somewhere rather important I need to get back to."

ΔΔΔ

Dr. Wallis returned to the observation room in the basement of Tolman Hall at 9:15 a.m.

"They've behaved?" he asked, going immediately to the small portal and surveying the sleep laboratory. Chad sat in the same corner he'd been in earlier, only now he was facing it, his back to the viewing window. Sharon was lying on her side on her bed, in a slightly fetal position.

Guru nodded. "They have hardly moved since you left."

"Good," Wallis said, grateful he had not missed anything. "Now come step outside with me for a moment." In the hallway where he'd left the two large Target bags, he added, "Take one of those, my friend, and choose a room where you would like to set up."

Guru retrieved a bag and said, "Which room do *you* want, professor?"

"Doesn't matter to me." He poked his head into the room adjacent to the sleep laboratory. "This will do fine."

"I will go this way a little then." Guru started down the corridor, sticking his head into one room after another before stopping at the fourth one down. "I like this one."

A chill feathered the nape of Wallis' neck. Guru had selected the same room where he'd stored Penny's body.

"Make yourself at home," he said with a forced smile. "Mattresses have an in-built pump, but give me a call if you need a hand."

Dr. Wallis unpacked and inflated his mattress, unrolled his sleeping bag on top of it—and stared at the bed longingly. He hadn't slept all night, and the Australians weren't doing much of anything right now. Perhaps he could squeeze in a couple of hours...?

ΔΔΔ

Brook never did too much of anything on her days off from work. She began the mornings with a homemade breakfast after which, Karl the Fog permitting, she would embark on a forty-five-minute walk along the bay. At the end of the walk she would often stop by the library to browse the head librarian's recommendations. Back home it would be something simple for lunch, then the outstanding chores (cleaning, laundry, emptying the septic tank if it was full), then...well, it would be time to start preparing dinner, and where did the day go?

Today Brook had spent the morning puttering around the marina and feeding and watering her plants, and now she was in the kitchen, making a half dozen devilled eggs...and thinking about Roy.

She hadn't been able to stop thinking about him and his Sleep Experiment ever since returning from the university campus the night before. That the two young people Roy was employing would smear their excrement over that window was not only mindboggling but worrisome. They were clearly not in a very healthy state of mind.

Roy had appeared shocked at what they'd done, but he'd quickly brushed it aside as no big deal.

Why?

Had he been downplaying their behavior for her benefit, or had he come to expect such conduct from them? Was psychosis a side-effect of remaining awake for a substantial period? And if so, had Roy's Sleep Experiment been sanctioned by the proper authorities? Because it was hard to imagine how any ethics review board would sign off on an experiment that drove the test subjects crazy.

Then again, this certainly wouldn't be the first experiment involving human test subjects to cross ethical red lines. Brook, as an avid reader, could cite all sorts of examples off the top of her head. The physician who'd developed the smallpox vaccine deliberately exposing children to the deadly disease to advance his research. Project MKUltra, a CIA-sponsored research initiative plying unwitting Canadian and American citizens with LSD and other mind-altering drugs to develop chemicals that could be used in clandestine operations. Nurses at the University of California employing cruel and unusual techniques to study blood pressure and blood flow in newborns as young as one day old. The Imperial Japanese Army's covert biological and chemical warfare research experiment, Unit 731, in which scientists removed the organs and amputated the limbs of Chinese and Russian prisoners to study blood loss. A South African army colonel and psychologist who was convinced he could cure homosexuality via electric shock therapy. The chief surgeon at San Quentin State Prison performing testicle transplants on living inmates using the genitals of executed prisoners, and in some cases, goats and boars. The United States Army releasing millions of infected mosquitos in Georgia and Florida to observe whether the insects could spread yellow fever and dengue fever. And, of course, everything that was revealed during the Nuremberg trials concerning Nazi experiments on Jews, POWs, Romani, and other persecuted groups.

Brook shook her head at these thoughts as she sliced another egg in half lengthwise. It was ridiculous to compare Roy to the Imperial Japanese Army or the Nazis. He wasn't committing crimes against humanity; he was merely keeping two test subjects awake for an extended period with that mysterious gas of his.

Besides, who was she, a waitress, to question UC Berkeley's Chair of Psychology? Roy knew the laws and codes that governed his work better than anybody. He would not skirt them. She simply had to trust in him.

Brook focused on the culinary task before her. She dumped the yolk from each hard-boiled egg into a small bowl and added mayonnaise, Dijon mustard, apple cider vinegar, and salt and pepper. She stirred the mixture into a creamy paste and scooped a spoonful of it onto each egg white. She placed the finished deviled eggs in the refrigerator, made herself a tea, and then went to sit on the sheltered deck out front of the boathouse. She gazed out at the menacing storm clouds and the slanting rain pockmarking the bay, but her mind was a million miles away.

She was thinking about Roy again.

He'd told her he'd dismissed one of his assistants. Was this truly the case? Perhaps she had not been let go but had instead quit. Perhaps she'd disagreed with the direction the experiment had been heading.

Who cares, Brook? What's gotten into you?

She didn't know. She simply felt as though something was… wrong.

In any event, Roy was working double shifts. Which meant he was now spending sixteen hours a day in that dingy little basement room.

It would be extremely boring.

And lonely.

Brook sipped the tea without tasting it. A raft of fluffy white clouds eased in front of the sun, stealing the brightness from the sky.

I should make him something for dinner, she thought. *Bring it over for him later in the afternoon.*

He would appreciate the food and the company.

And she would get a second look at this experiment of his.

△△△

Dr. Roy Wallis shot upward out of sleep. All was dark and quiet. His heart was beating quickly in fear of a dream that he couldn't remember. He was about to get up and go to the observation room to check on Guru and the Australians when he felt an itch at the back of his skull. Frowning, he reached a hand behind his head to scratch it—and discovered a small protrusion in the little valley where the occipital bone met the cervical spine. He probed it with his fingers. It was hard and unyielding. Concerned, he picked at it until he felt blood smear his fingertips. He knew this wasn't doing him any good, but he couldn't stop himself.

When all the skin was removed, he realized the protrusion was made of metal.

A zipper, he thought a moment later.

He gripped the slider between his index finger and thumb and pulled it up. It moved slowly along the parallel rows of teeth, creating a Y-shaped channel in his skin in its wake.

The zipper terminated at the very top of his skull. Still unable to stop himself, he slid his bloodied fingers beneath the dangling flaps of skin and peeled them forward. The skin came free easily, almost like the shell of a hard-boiled egg.

Fascinated, repulsed, and alarmed, he stared at the folded clumps of hair and skin cupped in his hands, which also included his shapeless face—

"Professor?"

Dr. Wallis opened his eyes. For an awful moment he thought he was in a prison cell. Then he made out Guru crouched above him, aglow from the hallway light.

He sat up quickly. "Has something happened?" he demanded.

"No...not exactly. But that may be the problem."

"What the hell are you talking about, man?"

Before Guru could answer, Wallis was on his feet and hurrying to the observation room. He peered through the portal in the viewing window.

Chad remained seated in the same corner as before, his back to Wallis. Sharon was not on her bed.

"Where's Sharon?" he asked, even as his eyes went to the closed door at the back of the room.

"She went to the bathroom nearly two hours ago," Guru said. "She has not come out."

"*Two* hours ago?" He glanced at his wristwatch. It was 10:13 p.m. "I've been asleep all day!"

"I did not want to wake you..."

Dr. Wallis sniffed. Then he saw the brown paper bag with Chipotle branding sitting on the desk. "You left them unsupervised to get food?"

"I would never do that, professor. I ordered Uber Eats. There is a steak burrito in there for you."

Famished, Wallis dug out the burrito, tore away the aluminum foil wrap, and sank his teeth into it.

Guru smiled. "Is it not delicious?"

"Pretty damn good," he said around a full mouth. "Now you say Sharon's been in the bathroom for two hours?"

"Yes, roughly."

"Have you tried communicating with her?"

"She doesn't answer."

Dr. Wallis swallowed, licked some adobo sauce from his fingers, and pressed the Talk button on the touch panel controller. "Sharon? How you doing?"

No answer.

"Sharon?"

Nothing.

Wallis turned to Guru, his concern growing. "Why didn't you wake me earlier?"

"I did not think there was anything to be concerned about, professor. If she was cutting herself again, I would have…heard her."

Wallis nodded but didn't mention the possibility she could be in there hanging from the shower head.

Suddenly no longer hungry, he set the burrito down on the table, wiped his mouth and beard with a paper napkin, and said, "I'm going to check on her."

$$\triangle \triangle \triangle$$

The sleep laboratory still reeked powerfully of excrement and body odor, and beneath this, the sweet scent of blood.

As Dr. Wallis crossed the room, he noticed Chad turning to keep his back to him.

He stopped. "Chad?"

The Australian made a phlegmy, broken sound.

Giggling?

Wallis said, "How about turning around for me, brother?"

He went very still.

"Chad, buddy?"

When the Australian refused to respond, Wallis decided to deal with him later. He continued to the bathroom and rapped his knuckles on the door.

"Sharon?" he said. "It's Dr. Wallis."

Giggles—although unlike Chad's, these were deceptively childlike.

"What are you doing in there?"

More childlike giggles.

"I'm going to come in."

"No!" Sharon screeched suddenly.

Dr. Wallis pushed the door inward. It moved two inches before slamming back shut. She had her back or feet to it.

"Why don't you want me to come in?" he asked her.

"I don't want to leave!" Her voice was raspy, frightened yet excited, like a gasper's voice during erotic asphyxiation.

"You don't want to leave the bathroom or the sleep laboratory?"

"The sleep lab!"

"Don't worry about that, Sharon. I have no intention of making you leave the sleep laboratory. Why would I do that?"

"I've been bad."

"What have you done?"

Giggling.

"Sharon?"

Mumbling, as though she were talking to someone.

"I don't care what you've done, Sharon," he said. "But I'm coming in whether you like it or not. I suggest moving away from the door."

He didn't hear her move.

He threw his shoulder into the door.

It barely budged.

"Sharon?"

Laughter now, high-pitched and impetuous.

"All right then," Dr. Wallis said. "You've left me no choice. I'm going to have to turn off the gas."

"No!" she screeched.

"Then let me in."

Sobbing—or was it more laughter?

This was accompanied by lethargic, laborious movement.

He waited until he heard nothing more, then tried the door again.

It swung inward easily.

Dr. Wallis had been expecting a macabre scene, but what he found defied anything he had imagined.

Blood covered the floor, perhaps an inch-deep where it had pooled in the recess around the drain, which was plugged with... chunks of flesh. Sharon sat slumped against the toilet, her elbows hooked over the seat, keeping her upright. She resembled a cross between a woman who'd had five too many tequila shots and one who'd survived—barely—a rabid wild animal attack.

"My Lord, Sharon," Wallis breathed, fighting to keep the burrito down.

The tension bandages that had been around Sharon's head and stomach now lay on the floor in the spilled blood, which had turned them bright crimson. The incision across her abdomen was much larger than before, revealing glistening white hints of her bottom ribs. Her gastrointestinal tract had spilled (or been pulled) onto her lap, a messy pile of wormy spaghetti. Her small intestine, Wallis noted in horror, was digesting food before his eyes, muscles contracting and fluids flowing behind the thin pink membrane. Even in the enormity of the moment, he wondered how this could be possible when she had not eaten in days—until he realized what she was digesting must be her own flesh.

"Hi, doc," Sharon said, her brazenly glowing eyes meeting his, and her mouth creeping into a smile.

"What have you done to yourself?"

"I'm letting it out."

"Letting *what* out?"

Sharon commenced that godawful giggling—only it was more harrowing than before because the sweetness had left it, leaving behind only a bitter cackle. Her eyes remained locked on his, impossibly bright and alert. Then she coughed, a fine red mist spraying the air before her. A sustained round of coughing followed, sending thick rivulets of blood trickling over her lower lip and down her chin and neck.

Yet her health was no longer of concern to Dr. Wallis. His inner scientist, detached and clinical and craving answers, had taken over. "What is it, Sharon?" he demanded. "What's inside you?"

The smile returned. "I think you know, doc."

He thought he did too, and he cursed himself for not bringing the EEG machine with him. He needed to see inside her head. He needed evidence of *what* was inside her head.

"Guru!" he shouted over his shoulder. "Bring the EEG in here! Now!"

"Want me to show you, doc?" Sharon asked.

"What?" Wallis snapped, returning his attention to her.

"Want me to show you what's inside me?"

"No, don't! Just wait... Just wait, goddammit!"

Dr. Wallis heard the door to the sleep laboratory open and then the clatter of the cart carrying the EEG equipment.

"Look, doc. *Look.*"

"Guru! Hurry!"

Sharon reached a hand into the cavity in her gut that had once held her gastrointestinal tract. Screaming—in what sounded as much ecstasy as pain—she shoved it upward and beneath her ribcage.

"Sharon, no!" Wallis yelled, lurching forward to stop her. His foot slipped in the pool of blood and he fell to the floor. His head cracked against the tiles. Darkness washed over him in pounding waves, though he fought to remain conscious.

Nevertheless, he could do little more than watch in slow-motion despair as Sharon's wrist and forearm followed her hand deeper into her innards with the sloppy slurping of two virgins kissing.

All at once her body stiffened. Spasmed. She yanked her arm out of her stomach triumphantly.

Dr. Wallis had managed to prop himself up on an elbow, though he knew he could no longer stave off the darkness.

The last thing he saw before passing out was Sharon holding her still-beating heart before her in a clawed fist.

ΔΔΔ

Dr. Wallis' phone, which the professor had left on the table in the observation room, was ringing. Guru ignored it. He was frozen in terror as he listened to what was happening at the far end of the sleep laboratory. He could only see the broad backside of Dr. Wallis as he stood inside the bathroom door, but he could hear everything clearly.

What have you done to yourself?

I'm letting it out.

Letting what out?

Guru's blood went cold at Sharon's words because he knew what she wanted to let out, even if he couldn't fully accept the reality of the possibility.

This cannot be happening, he thought. *Demons do not exist—*

"Guru!" Dr. Wallis' voice blasted through the intercom. "Bring the EEG in here! Now!"

Guru raced to the corner, grabbed the metal cart with one hand while opening the door to the sleep laboratory with the other. He backpedaled through it, dragging the cart behind him.

"Guru!" Dr. Wallis shouted. "Hurry!"

Guru swung the cart around in a circle, so it was now in front of him. He pushed it toward the bathroom as fast as he could.

Just as he reached the door, Dr. Wallis slipped in blood coating the floor and went down hard.

"Professor!" Guru said, leaving the cart and rushing to his aid.

Yet when he saw Sharon slumped next to the toilet, sliced open and holding her heart in her hand, he hit an invisible wall. He watched as she convulsed a final time, her heart sliding from her blood-greased hand and dropping to the floor with a wet, fat sound.

Wheezing on air that was suddenly sauna-dry, Guru tore his eyes away from the ghastly corpse and knelt next to Dr. Wallis. With trembling fingers, he checked the professor's pulse and was immensely relieved to find it beating fast and strong.

His first thought: *Call an ambulance.*

His second thought: *Call the police.*

He dashed back to the observation room, grabbed his phone from his bag, was about to dial 9-1-1—but hesitated.

There was no emergency.

Sharon was dead. No paramedic could bring her back to life. Dr. Wallis had suffered a bump to the head but was breathing. He'd come around soon—and be furious with Guru if he panicked now and called for help.

He needed to calm down and *think.*

Stuffing his phone in his pocket, Guru went to the adjacent room and brought Dr. Wallis' air mattress to the antechamber. Then he reentered the sleep laboratory. Chad was sitting on the floor by the TV, his back to the room. How he could remain indifferent to all that was happening, Guru couldn't fathom, but it didn't matter right then.

He went to the bathroom. Keeping his eyes averted from Sharon's body, and careful not to step in the puddle of crimson-black blood, he gripped the professor's wrists and dragged him back to the antechamber, a streak of red marking their progress.

Breathing heavily—Dr. Wallis had been much heavier than Guru would have imagined—he hooked his hands beneath the professor's body and rolled him up and onto the air mattress.

Guru wobbled over to the chair and dropped down into it, the events of the last few minutes finally sinking in.

Sharon was dead by her hand, and he had defiled the suicide

scene.

Was this a crime?

He hadn't called 9-1-1.

Was this a crime too—?

Guru heard approaching footsteps in the hallway. The police! He leaped to his feet, ready to flee, but there was nowhere to go. Trapped! He spun toward the door, bracing for a SWAT team to bust through it, assault rifles locked and loaded—

"Hello?" someone said at the same time a knock sounded.

A moment later the door opened and a pale-skinned woman with short black hair and dark eyes peeked into the room.

Guru swallowed. "Who—who are you?" he managed.

"I'm Brook. Roy's friend. You must be—" Her eyes nearly doubled in size when she saw Dr. Wallis, covered in blood, sprawled atop the air mattress. "Roy!"

△△△

When Dr. Roy Wallis returned to the world of the living, he found himself lying on his back on his air mattress in the observation room. He sat up, groaning as an icy needle poked his brain.

"Professor!" Guru exclaimed, appearing next to him. "He's awake! Ma'am, he's awake!"

Ma'am?

Dr. Wallis sensed movement from the other half of the antechamber, and a moment later Brook was crouching next to the air mattress, her face tight with concern, her eyes red and wet, as if she'd been crying.

"Roy," she said, taking his hand gently in hers. "Don't move too much. You have an awful gash on your head."

He pulled his hand free and touched the left side of his head, discovering a large Band-Aid taped to his temple. He winced as the icy needle poked a little deeper.

"What...?" He was about to ask what happened, but the

gruesome images of Sharon's self-mutilation came flooding back in vivid glory. "What are you doing here, Brook?" he asked instead.

"I tried calling you a little while ago," she said, "and again on my way over here, but you didn't answer your phone. I, well, I thought you would be hungry, and I just wanted to bring you some food!" A sob escaped her then, and she turned away while she collected herself.

"It's okay," he told her. "Take a deep breath—"

"It's not okay!" she said. "Your assistant told me she's dead! The girl working for you! That's her blood on you! She's in that room back there, and she's dead!"

Dr. Wallis glared at Guru, wondering why he couldn't have kept his fucking mouth shut. Nevertheless, he realized the Indian would have been hard-pressed to explain why Wallis looked as though he had just spent the evening partying with Jeffrey Dahmer.

Buying himself time to wheel out a plausible explanation for Sharon's death (telling Brook the girl had torn her beating heart from her chest was simply not an option), he said, "His name's Guru, and—"

"*Why's she dead, Roy?* How did she die? What in God's name is going on here?"

"She committed suicide," he told her.

"But all that *blood*."

"She slit her wrists." It was the best he could come up with. "I slipped in the blood when I was trying to help her."

"Why did she—"

Wallis cut her off. "I'd like to change," he said. "I'll explain everything after that."

Brook rubbed her eyes. "I'll go get some clean clothes from your place—"

"No," he said, not wanting her to leave his sight in the event she did something foolish like call the police. "One of Chad's tracksuits should fit me."

Despite protests from both Guru and Brook, Wallis lumbered

to his feet. A spell of dizziness almost made him fall backward onto his ass, but it passed after a few disorienting seconds. He entered the sleep laboratory, feeling more surefooted with each step. Chad, he noticed immediately, sat facing the same corner as before. He had pulled the sweatshirt's hood up over his head, and with his slumped shoulders, he resembled a beggar on a street corner unable to face the world.

He was no threat. Not right then.

At the wardrobe, Wallis withdrew a pair of boxers, sweatpants, and a sweatshirt. He stripped off his bloodied clothes and glanced momentarily at the bathroom. He would have liked a shower, but he wasn't going to start messing around moving Sharon's body with Brook in the next room. He pulled on the fresh clothes and returned to the antechamber, feeling slightly better.

Guru was pacing anxiously. Brook stood by the door, her arms folded across her chest, staring at the floor.

"You shouldn't have come here," he told her.

She looked up. "What happened to that girl, Roy? Why did she kill herself?"

"She was having hallucinations. She—"

"It was that gas, wasn't it? Your assistant told me—"

"His name's Guru."

"Guru told me the gas made them go crazy. So why, Roy? Why didn't you stop this experiment if you knew what was happening to them, if you knew—"

"I *didn't* know," he snapped. He closed his eyes for a moment against the flare-up of pain in his head. "I didn't know she was going to kill herself," he added more reasonably, despite the statement being a bald-faced lie. "She was hallucinating, yes, but that's to be expected in severe cases of sleep debt. It's been well documented."

"And *that*?" Brook said, waving her hand at the feces-splattered viewing window. "Was that to be expected? That's just…sick. And the young man in there, is he hallucinating too? Is he going to kill himself too? Because he's just sitting in the corner staring at the wall. That's not normal, Roy!"

"Of course it's atypical behavior. He's gone fourteen days without sleep, Brook. *Fourteen days*. We're in uncharted territory here. Regardless, from this moment onward, I'm going to keep an eye on his every waking minute to make sure he doesn't…do anything rash."

"You're continuing the experiment?" she said, aghast.

"It's nearly over. Just another day or so and—"

She was shaking her head. "I can't believe I'm hearing this!"

"Hearing what, Brook?" Dr. Wallis asked calmly, though her melodramatics were beginning to piss him off.

"That girl is dead, Roy! Your experiment killed her! We've got to call the police."

Wallis clenched his jaw. "We *will* call the police, Brook," he said. "*After* the experiment has concluded. One more day—"

"What's so important about this experiment, Roy?" she demanded. "What's so important about it that it's obscured your values and decency?"

Dr. Wallis considered explaining everything in detail to her as he had to Guru. But he found he couldn't be bothered. Besides, Brook wasn't an intellectual like Guru. She wouldn't appreciate the magnitude of his revelation. She wouldn't be able to get her pedestrian mind around the fact that no great progress was made without sacrifice. That the lives of one, two, a dozen individuals meant nothing in the grand scheme of things. Across the globe thousands of people were dying every hour due to old age, disease, accidents, and plain old stupidity. So who gave a shit if one or two more joined them? One or two more dying not in vain but in the name of knowledge—knowledge that would change the world forever? They should be honored to serve humanity so, and anybody who could not understand this was, as far as Wallis was concerned, a simpleton who had no purpose existing themselves.

He tried a smile. "One more day, Brook," he said. "That's all I'm asking. One more—"

She threw her hands in the air. "You're crazy, Roy! This

experiment has made you crazy too! Those aren't lab rats in there! They're people."

"You have two options, Brook," he said in a perfectly reasonable tone to contrast her hysterics. "You can stay here and calm down while I check on Chad and make sure he's all right, or you can leave and call the police and royally fuck everything up."

Brook glared at him for a very long moment, her dark eyes smoldering even as her face struggled for aplomb. Then she opened the door to leave.

"Aw, fuck, Brook," Wallis mumbled under his breath, sincerely wishing she hadn't called his bluff. As she stepped into the hallway, he snagged her by the shoulder and pulled her back into the antechamber.

She whirled in surprise. "Let go of—"

Dr. Wallis drove his fist into her jaw.

△△△

"Professor!" Guru cried.

Dr. Wallis looked at him. "I couldn't let her go to the police, buddy," he said. "You know that."

Guru clapped his hands against the sides of his bald head in an absurd imitation of the figure in Munch's *The Scream*. "This is too much for me. Too much."

Dr. Wallis stepped over Brook's body and gripped Guru by his forearms and shook him hard. "You know how important this is, Guru! You know what's on the line here! Don't wimp out, man!"

"I know, but..." He tore his arms free and backed away. "We will go to prison."

"No, we won't," Wallis said, encouraged that his assistant was thinking in terms of the practical rather than the ethical, because the practical, at least, could be appealed to with reason. "Look," he added. "I just need to hook Chad up to the EEG machine. After I get the evidence I need..." He shrugged. "That's it. We won't need him anymore. Not that he's going to last much longer. He's going to take his life just as Sharon did. So how are we culpable? We didn't force their hands. They did what they did to themselves."

"But we *allowed* it, professor."

"Bah! No one will know that. Just yesterday, did you believe they were suicidal?"

Guru frowned. "They were experiencing hallucinations and —"

"Yes, yes, but did you think they were suicidal?"

"No," he said simply.

"No," Wallis repeated. "Their final decline, their descent into madness, happened quickly. Literally overnight. So we simply... fudge some of the facts."

"Fudge some of the facts?"

"I get what I need from Chad's head, then you and I go out for dinner to celebrate the conclusion of the experiment. We turn off the gas and leave Chad and Sharon to catch up on some much-needed rest. And when we return in the morning...they've done what they've done. They've done it in our absence. Some side effects of coming off the gas. I don't know. I'll spin it in scientific terms. The bottom line is, the experiment was all above board on our watch. We couldn't have foreseen what was to happen to them, and we weren't around to prevent it."

"You want us to lie," he stated.

"Shiva, Krishna, and fucking Christ, Guru! Don't be like the rest of them, my man. Lie? If you want to call it that. I call it a pretty near representation of what happened, fudged a little to cross the Ts and dot the Is. And what's wrong with that? You want to wallow in ethics? How about philosophical consequentialism then? Judging whether something is right by what its consequences are. And I'd say, given what the consequences of the Sleep Experiment will be, we are pretty damn square in the right."

"What about her?" Guru looked at Brook.

Dr. Wallis looked too. Brook was sprawled on the floor where she had fallen. Truth be told, he wasn't quite sure what he was going to do with her yet. He couldn't dispose of her as he had Penny. He was her boyfriend. He had met some of her friends. Most of the staff at Café Emporium knew they were dating. He would be the first and perhaps only suspect if she went missing. And two people close to him disappearing within a matter of days? No, offing Brook was out of the question. "I'll talk to her," he told Guru. "When she hears everything I have to say, she'll come around. She might not be happy about Chad and Sharon's deaths, but she loves me. She'll—she'll keep quiet for me," he added, hoping he'd spoken with more conviction than he'd felt.

Then, realizing the hypocrisy of his words with Brook lying limp as a noodle on the floor, the right side of her jaw already turning ballet slipper pink, Dr. Wallis knelt next to her body and carefully—lovingly—moved her onto the air mattress, where you could almost imagine she was sleeping peacefully.

Dr. Wallis turned to Guru expectantly.

"Let's finish this, brother."

ΔΔΔ

They entered the sleep laboratory together.

"Chad, how you doing over there?" Wallis asked.

The Australian didn't react to his voice.

"You've been pretty quiet, buddy."

No response.

Dr. Wallis stopped when he was directly behind Chad, who reeked of body odor and something else that made Wallis think of rotting wood. He motioned Guru, who was pushing the metal cart with the EEG equipment, to join him. "So this is the deal, Chad," he said. "We're going to do one of the tests on you with the computer and the headband, and then we'll leave you alone after that. You can keep sitting how you are. You don't even have to turn around. But you're going to need to pull off the hoody." He retrieved the electrode gel from the cart. "You might not remember how this works, he continued, "but it doesn't hurt at all. The gel might be a little cold, but that's it. Ready?"

Dr. Wallis pulled back Chad's hoodie.

The Australian twisted about with a venomous hiss.

Wallis gagged and heard Guru retch behind him.

Chad had no face.

He'd peeled away every inch of visible skin to reveal the harvest-colored stew of fat, muscle, and connective tissue beneath. In some places along his jaw he'd gouged his flesh so deeply that his mandible, wet and white, peeked through.

Where his lively blue eyes had been were hollow pools of black and blood. Where his nose had been was a mucus-encrusted hole. Where his lips had been were bleeding gums and a hideous rictus grin.

None of the missing organs lay discarded on the ground before him, which meant they'd most likely been ingested.

"My God," Wallis breathed, and even as he stared in shock at the monster before him, he found himself wondering whether Chad had torn away his face to rid himself of the hallucinatory mushrooms he'd believed to be growing there, or whether he, like Sharon, had been trying to let whatever was inside of him out.

Guru was saying something quickly in Hindi, maybe a prayer.

Ignoring him, Dr. Wallis said, "It's okay, Chad. You're okay. We're not going to hurt you." He tossed the electrode gel back onto the cart, as there would no longer be a need for a liquid agent given Chad no longer had any skin on his forehead. He picked up the headband. "Remember, pal, this isn't going to hurt."

Bending forward, holding the headband before him with outstretched arms, Wallis lowered it over Chad's head as if crowning a mutilated monarch.

With amazing speed, the Australian's hands gripped Dr. Wallis' wrists, and in the next instant Wallis found himself corkscrewing through the air. He struck the floor with bone-jarring force and rolled several feet before coming to a rest.

A dazed assessment of his body confirmed it to be in working order, and he quickly sat up.

Guru was backing away from Chad the way you would from a German Shepherd foaming at the mouth. "How—how—how did he do that?" he stammered.

"Just keep moving to the fucking door," Wallis told him.

Getting to his feet, and never turning his back on the Australian, he followed.

△△△

"That was impossible!" Guru said. "He would need the strength of five men to throw you the way he did!"

"Not impossible, my good friend," Dr. Wallis said, his eyes alight with excitement now that they were safely back in the observation room. "It *happened*."

"But *how*?"

"An educated guess? Adrenaline."

"Adrenaline? Surely—"

"Adrenaline, enzymes, proteins, endorphins, our emotions. When the body's entire stress response is activated, most people are capable of lifting six or seven times their body weight. The young woman who heaves the car off her father after it slipped off the carjack onto him. The man who tears a caved-in door from his crashed vehicle to rescue his wife. Such cases of superhuman strength are not unheard of."

"But we were not threatening Chad. He—"

"He might not have known that. He no longer has eyes to see with."

"What are we to do then? He clearly will not let us hook him up to the EEG machine, let alone remain cooperative for the duration of the tests."

"No, not in his present state," Wallis agreed. "But I have an idea."

△△△

Dr. Roy Wallis explained his plan to Guru Rampal, who reluctantly acquiesced to help him carry it out. Then he transferred Brook to Sharon's bed in the sleep laboratory, so the Indian could keep her contained if she were to regain consciousness while Wallis was gone. "If she comes around," he instructed, "don't let her out of that room, no matter what she says."

"Just please hurry, professor," Guru said.

Nodding, Dr. Wallis left Tolman Hall. The week-long storm thrashing the Bay Area remained in full swing. Slanting rain fell in icy curtains, while the howling wind whipped the branches of the nearby trees into a frenzy of flapping leaves. Thunder cracked loudly, followed by a burst of forked lightning.

Wallis' colleagues in the English Department would call this pathetic fallacy; he called it a pain in the fucking ass.

Head bowed, he hurried along Bayard Rustin Way to his car, then drove with his windshield-wipers thumping to Lawrence Berkeley National Laboratory, which was nestled high in the hills above the campus.

At the summit he passed through the main gate and followed the snaking road among the cluster of buildings. On a pleasant day he would have had distant views of the San Francisco Bay, but right then he couldn't see anything outside the twin tunnels the Audi's headlights punched in the darkness.

He parked illegally out front of Building 33 and dashed through the rain to the entrance. He swiped his keycard and stepped inside the lobby, his presence activating the computer-controlled lighting system.

Supported by the US Department of Energy, and managed by the University of California, Berkeley Lab conducted unclassified research across a wide range of scientific disciplines. They studied everything from the infinitesimal scale of subatomic particles to the infinite expanse of the universe. Building 33, aka the General Purpose Lab, had been designed to facilitate research between scientists from every walk of life.

Dr. Wallis took the stairs to the third floor, then passed all sorts of customized wet and dry labs before coming to his lab. He swiped his keycard and entered the small space. Although he had euthanized all of his mice some time ago, he hadn't yet returned the vivarium in which he'd kept them, the freestanding biosafety cabinet he'd used while handling them, any of the expensive research equipment cluttering his workstations—or, most significantly, the small pharmacy of drugs he kept in a locked cabinet.

He went to the cabinet now, unlocked it, and stuffed his jacket pockets with several syringes and vials of Vecuronium, a neuromuscular blocking agent he'd used to keep his mice still during certain experiments or surgery. It was also part of the three-drug cocktail used to execute death-row convicts in Tennessee, Virginia, and other states yet to abolish the death penalty.

Dr. Wallis locked the cabinet again and was about to leave the lab when someone called out, "Hello?"

Wallis froze.

However, remaining put and hoping the person went away seemed like wishful thinking, so he stepped out of the lab, pulled closed the door, and said, "Hello?"

He heard the squawk of rubber soles on the polished flooring, and then a middle-aged woman dressed in a tracksuit not unlike his own appeared from around a corner. With her mop of rust-gray hair, doughy face, and rotund physique, you wouldn't be blamed for mistaking her for a school crossing guard on the cusp of retirement. However, like many in academia who prioritized mind over body, her eyes were sharp, clear, and inquisitive.

"Roy!" she said, throwing wide her stubby arms. "I was wondering who might be here at this hour!"

"I was wondering the same thing, June," Wallis said, forcing a smile. June Scarborough was a fellow psychologist completing a Ph.D. dissertation on the complexity of squirrel behavior. She and her undergraduate helpers had spent the better part of the last two years armed with nuts and stopwatches and camcorders while they stalked fox squirrels around the campus. Dr. Wallis had run into her often last semester as she'd zeroed in on a population of squirrels living near Berkeley Way West.

"I forgot my work laptop here yesterday," she explained, slapping her forehead. "Stupid me! Because I'm heading to Colorado tomorrow with the hubby and kids to spend a week at my brother-in-law's cabin. It's a perfect opportunity for me to study tassel-eared squirrels, which are native to the southern Rocky Mountains."

"Can't separate work and pleasure, huh?"

"My work *is* pleasure, Roy! I love the furry little critters more than anything else save my kids...and even that comparison is pretty darn close. Have you ever wondered why a squirrel rotates a nut between its front paws the way it does?"

"Can't say it's ever crossed my mind."

"It's considering several factors such as the nut's perishability and nutritional value, as well as the availability of food at that time in the presence or absence of competitors—all of this to make the critical decision of whether it eats the nut right then and there, or buries it for later. Isn't that just fascinating? Squirrels are solving complex problems right under our noses, and most people are never the wiser."

"Guess their behavior isn't so...nutty...after all."

"Oh, Roy!" June said, clapping her belly like jolly old St. Nick. "Anywho! Enough about squirrels. What brings you here at close to midnight?"

"Same reason as you." He shrugged. "I had to pick up some work notes."

"Were they written in invisible ink on invisible paper?"

Dr. Wallis realized what she meant; he was empty-handed. "May as well have been," he said, "because they weren't here. Must be over in my office. Guess I'm going a bit senile in my old age."

"I'll let you get to it then. I have to get home to bed myself."

"Enjoy Colorado."

An earsplitting clap of thunder erupted in the sky almost

directly overhead.

"Oh my, this storm is something, isn't it? Don't catch your death out there, Roy!"

"Toodles, June," he said, and headed for the stairs.

△△△

Brook sat up slowly, wondering where she was and why she hurt so much. She wrinkled her nose at a rude stench that reminded her of her septic tank, only she wasn't on her houseboat. She was in the basement of—

Roy hit me.

Brook touched her jaw and found it swollen and numb. A sharper pain needled her gums, and when she probed the location with her tongue, she discovered one of her teeth had been knocked loose.

"You bastard," she mumbled. "You *hit* me."

She forced herself to her feet. After a moment of unsteady lightheadedness, she looked around the room. It was like a hodgepodge of Ikea display rooms all merged into one: bedroom, dining room, living room, kitchen, gym.

At the back, the door to the bathroom was slightly ajar, and she could see part of a tanned leg resting in a whole lot of blood.

The girl.

Dead.

Swallowing tightly, Brook turned toward the front of the room. Next to the big window obscured with crap and paper was the door to the antechamber.

She went to it, gripped the handle, and pushed.

It barely moved.

She pushed again, got it open an inch, but then it slammed shut.

Someone was leaning against it.

"Let me out, Roy!" Brook shouted, banging on the door with her open hand.

"I am sorry! I cannot!" came the reply.

It wasn't Roy; it was his assistant, Guru.

She leaned her shoulder into the door, but the Indian remained firm in his resistance.

"Guru?" she said. "Is that you?"

"Yes," he said.

"Why are you blocking the door?"

"Dr. Wallis told me you cannot leave."

"Is Roy there?"

"Not at the moment."

A pocket of hope opened inside her. "You have to let me out, Guru! Please? Before he returns."

"I cannot. He told me—"

"This is kidnapping!"

"I am sorry, ma'am, but—"

"There's a dead girl in here with me, Guru!"

Suddenly wondering where the other test subject was, she scanned the room and spotted him in a far quadrant behind the weight equipment, seated on the floor, facing the corner.

What's he doing?

And how long until he comes after me?

Brook banged the door again.

"Let me out of here, Guru! Please!"

"I am sorry but Dr. Wallis—"

"Screw him!" she blurted. "He's lost it! Can't you see that? His experiment has warped his mind!"

Guru didn't reply, and she shrieked in frustration. Then she paced, cold fear and hot rage warring inside her. Roy had hit her —*hit her*— and now he was keeping her locked up like an animal. How could this be the same man she'd cared so deeply for? How could she have been so completely fooled by him?

△△△

Dr. Wallis didn't park in his typical spot along University

Drive, because while he usually enjoyed the five-minute walk to Tolman Hall, he was already wet and cold and didn't look forward to getting any wetter or colder. Instead he drove directly to Tolman Hall and pulled into one of three handicapped spaces directly out front of the suspended breezeway.

He was about to enter the building when he noticed a flashlight beam bobbing through the storm toward him.

"For fuck's sake," he mumbled, recognizing who it was.

"Hiya, Dr. Wallis!" Roger Henn greeted, holding a black umbrella in one hand, the flashlight in the other. He wore a loose black rain poncho over his uniform. POLICE was stenciled across his chest in white letters. His short hair was tousled, his Monopoly Man mustache waxed, and his cheeks as ruddy as ever. "Ain't this weather something?"

"It's not raining under here, Rodge."

"Ah, righty-o." He lowered the umbrella, collapsed the ribs, and stamped the metal ferrule on the ground to shake the water from the nylon canopy. His boyish eyes twinkled as they gave Dr. Wallis the up-and-down. "Lookit you, doctor," he said with a good-natured smile. "I ain't never seen you dressed so…normal. You're usually all spiffed up—in a good way. What you doing running around in this weather?"

"Had to get some notes from my office."

Unlike June Scarborough, Roger Henn didn't notice or question where the notes were. Instead he nodded generously and said, "I hear ya, I hear ya. So how's that experiment of yours going? I haven't seen you out and about in must be days now."

"I've been back and forth," Wallis said. "And the experiment is going just fine, thanks." Then, realizing he could make Roger Henn an unwitting witness in the story he and Guru would inevitably have to spin to the police, he added, "Actually, Rodge, the experiment is just about wrapped up, to be honest. We've had a breakthrough tonight. My assistant and I are about to go out to celebrate."

Henn grinned. "You and that cute little Chinese thing?"

"She's South Korean," Wallis corrected. "And no. Me and the

bald little Indian thing."

"Ah, shucks, that'd be too bad, doc. She's a real hottie, ain't she? I haven't seen her around lately either. She always used to say hi to me in that funny accent of hers."

"She...ah...parted ways with the experiment a few days ago."

Henn frowned. "Is that so? How come?"

A rumble of thunder climaxed with a resounding explosion, causing both men to duck their heads and eye the heavens warily. Lightning flashed, branching into jagged steps.

"Jee-zeus!" Roger Henn said. "And I gotta work in this shit. So the Chinese girl's gone, huh?"

"Unfortunately, yes," Wallis said. "Her mother is sick—in Seoul. Penny returned to Korea to be with her."

"Sick as in *dying* sick? That's a real shame. Real shame. Didya bang her?"

Dr. Wallis blinked. "Excuse me?"

"Didya bang her before she left?"

"No, I did not. She was one of my students."

"I'm just asking, 'cause, word is, you don't have any problem with the ladies."

"That's the word, huh?" Wallis said, wondering who the security guard was networking with to gather such information. "Anyway, Rodge, I have to get back to work. A few details to tidy up before Guru and I hit the town."

"Sure, no problem. Wish I wasn't stuck here working, else I'd join ya. You and me, we could clean up, you know what I'm saying? I've had some luck with the divorced crowd myself. Seems they're not so picky once they got kids and wrinkles."

"You'd be right up their alley, Rodge. Just don't take no for an answer."

"Don't take no, I hear ya. By the way, doc, what exactly *is* the experiment you're wrapping up anyway? You've never told me nothing about it."

"And so it must remain that way for now, my friend. But I'm sure you'll be hearing about it soon enough."

△△△

Brook eyed one of the tubular steel chairs at the kitchen table. She picked it up, carried it to the front of the room, and launched it through the viewing window amidst a shower of shattering glass.

The assistant, Guru, appeared on the other side of the now paneless window.

"What are you doing!" he cried. "You cannot do this! Stop!"

Brook went to the nearest bed, removed the neatly made (and likely unused) duvet, and wrapped it around her right arm. She returned to the window and used her now-padded arm to clear the jagged triangles of glass jutting up from the frame.

"Stop this!" Guru said, waving his hands above his head as if this act alone would dissuade her.

"Get out of the way!" she said, tossing the duvet over the horizontal strip along the bottom of the frame.

"Stop!" Guru said, seizing the duvet and trying to pull it clear.

"Don't!" she said, grabbing her side of the cover. "Let go of it!"

"You cannot do this!"

They played tug of war for a few seconds until she released her grip. With no counteracting force to offset his pulling, Guru flew onto his butt.

Go! she thought. *Now's your chance!*

Planting her hands on the windowsill—ignoring the sharp bites in her palms from small, unseen pieces of glass—Brook leaped over it as if it were a pommel horse and rushed toward the door.

△△△

Inside Tolman Hall, Dr. Wallis shook as much rainwater from his beard and clothes as he could, then he went to the basement. When he heard Guru yelling, he broke into a run. He threw open the door to the observation room—and collided with Brook.

She bounced off him, stumbling backward a few steps.

"What the hell's going on?" he demanded.

"You are back!" Guru exclaimed. He was sprawled on the floor several feet away, his expression one of immeasurable relief. "She was about to escape!"

Brook pointed her finger at Wallis. "Get out of my way, Roy," she said, her words sounding mushed and slow. The pink bruise on her right jaw had swollen and turned an angry red. Her expression resembled that of a cornered beast: wary yet dangerous.

"I can't do that right now, Brook."

"*Let me go!*" she screamed, spittle flying from her mouth.

"I will, Brook, of course, I will," he reassured her. "But not until the experiment has concluded."

Her body was stiff yet at the ready as if she were considering charging past him. Her breathing came in labored heaves. "You don't have to do this."

"Do what?"

She didn't answer, and he didn't like what that silence implied. If she believed he had it in him to kill her, she would never keep quiet for him, ever.

"Do what, Brook?" he repeated, smiling.

"Holding me here," she said, seeming to intuit his thinking and changing the narrative. "You don't have to hold me here. I'm not going to...tell anybody anything."

"You already mentioned going to the police."

"As an option. But if that's not...what you think should be done, then...let's talk."

"This isn't the time to talk, Brook." He lowered his voice. "I don't know if you've noticed our friend Chad in the other room, but he's not in the best of health. I'm not sure how much time he has left, and I need to get a look inside his head before he expires."

"Roy! Please!"

"After, Brook. We'll talk after. I need to help Chad right now.

Now go back into the sleep laboratory.

"No."

Dr. Wallis stepped toward her. "Let's not repeat what happened earlier," he said meaningfully.

Her eyes went to his clenched fists—and the fight seemed to leave her. Shoulders sagging, she turned and entered the sleep laboratory.

"Block the door," Wallis instructed Guru, then followed her into the room, closing the door behind him.

Brook stood in the kitchen.

"Back of the room," he told her.

"I'm not going to go anywhere—"

"Back of the fucking room, Brook. *Now.*"

She went to the back of the room, her stride sure if not defiant. He watched her until she reached the far wall. Then he crossed the room to where Chad was seated on the floor facing the same corner he'd been facing for the past twenty-four hours.

Dr. Wallis' pulse had quickened, and he could feel sweat slicking the palms of his hands. What he was about to attempt was anything but guaranteed to succeed. He had the advantage, certainly. Chad was blind. Nevertheless, as soon as the needle pierced the Australian's skin, the advantage would be lost. Which meant Wallis would have to inject him quickly, then put space between them until the paralytic drug took effect.

You screw this up, man, you're going to have someone with the strength of a gorilla bashing in your skull.

I won't screw it up.

Dr. Wallis stopped behind Chad. From his jacket pockets he produced the syringe and the vial of Vecuronium he'd collected from his lab. Both the metal band around the top of the vial and the over-seal read: "Warning: Paralyzing Agent."

Holding the syringe in his hand like a pencil, the needle pointing upward, he pulled back the plunger. He plugged the needle into the rubber top of the vial and depressed the plunger, filling the vial with air to prevent a vacuum from forming. He turned the vial upside-down, then pulled the plunger as far back as it would go, thinking, *Going to be one big dose, Chad, my man. One doozy of a dose.*

Under normal circumstances—say a doctor prepping a patient for surgery—he or she would inject the drug into the patient intravenously. Dr. Wallis clearly did not have the luxury of this option. Instead, he would inject the drug straight into Chad's spinal column. This would destroy the nerve cells along his spine and induce permanent paralysis—which, of course, was exactly what Wallis wanted.

Crouching, Wallis judged where Chad's spinal cord would be beneath the sweatshirt, counted to three in his head, then jabbed the needle and depressed the plunger.

Chad shot to his feet, caterwauling in an unholy rage.

Dr. Wallis scuttled away, preparing himself for any eventuality. Chad flared his arms blindly, lurching at unseen assailants, the hoodie slipping free of his head. Then, spinning in a circle like a dog trying to catch its tail, he unsuccessfully probed for the needle protruding from his back.

He soon slowed, then stumbled. He dropped to his knees, then his side. He stopped moving completely.

That's when Brook began to scream.

ΔΔΔ

"What did you do to him? Look at his face! *What did you do to him?*"

"I didn't do that!" Dr. Wallis told her. "He did it to himself!"

"He doesn't have a face!"

"Brook! Listen to me! I didn't do that—"

"It doesn't matter. It was your drugs that did that."

She sank to her butt, dropped her head into her lap, and sobbed.

Trying his best to ignore her, Wallis wheeled the cart with the EEG machine next to where Chad had fallen. He rolled the Australian onto his back and slid the electrode headband over the pulpy mess that was his forehead. He clicked on the amplifier, which boosted the electrical signals produced by the millions of nerve cells in Chad's brain, then pulled up a chair to study the wave patterns appearing on the monitor.

△△△

Guru was speaking via the intercom, asking if everything was all right. Dr. Wallis had no idea how long he had been staring unmoving at the monitor, but he was no longer seeing the data on the screen. He was thinking about all the wonderful ways in which his life was about to forever change.

"Professor, can you hear me?"

Dr. Wallis snapped back to the moment, feeling as giddy as a boy on Christmas morning. "Guru, my beautiful friend, get your butt in here!" he said with a huge smile.

Brook, he noticed, had raised her head from her lap in curiosity at the sudden commotion.

"It's over, Brook," he told her, his smile growing. "We did it."

"What are you talking about, Roy?"

The door opened and Guru entered.

"Get over here, brother."

Guru looked apprehensively at Brook.

"She's not going to go anywhere," Wallis told him. "She's going to want to hear what I have to say. I mean it. She's really going to want to hear what I have to say." He opened his arms wide. "So get on over here and give me a hug."

Guru frowned. "Professor?"

"Jesus Christ, man!" Wallis went to the Indian and lifted him off the ground in a bear hug, turning in a circle while laughing. When he set Guru down, he rubbed the Indian's bald head affectionately. "You stayed with me, man. You. Stayed. With. Me." He slapped Guru on the shoulder, perhaps with too much gusto, because Guru nearly fell over.

"What's going on, Roy?" Brook asked.

"Neuroscience 101," Dr. Wallis said, slipping easily into lecture mode. "Our brain cells—aka neurons—communicate with each other via electrical signals and are always active, even when we're asleep, and it's this communication that's at the root of all our thoughts, emotions, and behaviors. Essentially, what you think of as 'consciousness' is an ever-changing concert of electrical impulses. Brook's brain, mine, Guru's all have about one hundred billion of these neurons. An EEG"—he waved at the equipment on the cart—"tracks this neural activity. Picture yourself dropping a pebble into the middle of a still pond and the ripples it would make on the water. Now picture the pebble as a neuron and the pond as the surface of the brain and the ripples as brainwaves. You with me, Brook?"

She nodded.

"Good, now listen up, both of you, because this is the important stuff. Instead of dropping a single pebble into the pond, imagine yourself dropping an entire handful. You'd get a whole lot of overlapping ripples. This is similar to what happens when you have multiple neurons firing off synchronized electrical pulses: you get a whole lot of overlapping brainwaves. An EEG detects these brainwaves and divides them into different bandwidths measured in Hertz. Slow delta bands are less than 4 Hz. Theta bands are anywhere between 4 to 8 Hz. Alpha bands range from 8 to 12 Hz. Beta bands, the most abundant during our normal state of waking, are between 14 and 30 Hz, and gamma bands, the fastest, are between 30 and 80 Hz. Together the brainwaves, or bandwidths, create our continuous spectrum of consciousness, always reacting and changing according to what we're doing and feeling. When slower ones dominate, we feel tired and sluggish. When higher ones dominate, we feel hyper-alert. So all those funny lines that appeared on that computer screen during Chad's EEG? They're his brainwaves, his consciousness. And much as a fortune teller reads tea leaves to gain insight into the natural world, I read these bandwidths to gain insight into Chad's mind."

"And...?" Guru asked eagerly.

"After I filtered out all of the artifacts and extraneous information, I discovered an entire spectrum of...shadow... brainwaves, I suppose you might call them, although they all possessed different amplitudes and frequencies than the originals."

Guru and Brook stared at him like deer caught in headlights.

"*Shadow brainwaves!*" he repeated, doing his damnedest to keep his composure despite the high he was riding.

"I have no idea what that means," Brook said.

"It means, my lovely, lovely darling," Dr. Wallis said, grinning wider than ever, "that residing within Chad's brain are two distinct consciousnesses."

△△△

"Impossible!" Guru blurted immediately.

"No, it is not, my good man. The proof is in the pudding, right over there on that computer."

"Two consciousnesses?" Brook said. "You mean like Dr. Jekyll and Mr. Hyde?"

"Not at all," Wallis said. "I'm not talking about a common dissociative identity disorder. There are *two distinct consciousnesses* inside him. Two people in one. Or, given what I suspect to be at the root of our beings, one person and one demon."

Brook shot to her feet. "What are you talking about, Roy? This is ridiculous!"

"Don't be so quick to judge, my darling. There is still so much you have yet to understand."

Wallis explained.

△△△

He repeated to her everything he'd told Guru the day before. The mice with the mutated genes that led to the development of the stimulant gas. The significance of micro-sleep, or the lack thereof, and how absolute sleep deprivation turned the mice into murderous cannibals. And ultimately his theory that all biological lifeforms are born with madness inside them, kept in check only by instinct and sleep.

Brook interrupted him about a thousand times, but when he finally got it all out, her skepticism had been replaced with studious contemplation. Even better news, she no longer appeared as though she were in fear of her life. In fact, he began to wonder if he could win her over after all.

"Let me get this straight, Roy," she said now. "You mentioned *demon* earlier. That's the word you used. One person, one demon inside that young man. Are you suggesting this...madness... inside us is a *demon*?"

"A demon. The devil. Hell itself. Whatever tickles your fancy. They're all suitable metaphors for, yes, the madness within us, which I believe to be responsible for the evil we perform."

She looked at Chad, then quickly looked away again, the tone of her skin draining to the color of winter. "And it was this madness that caused him to do that to himself—"

Wallis' eyes bulged.

△△△

Chad was sitting up.

Which, given the dosage of Vecuronium that Dr. Wallis had injected into him—*into his spinal column no less*—should have been very much impossible.

Wallis withdrew another syringe and vial from his jacket pocket and filled the syringe even as he crossed the room. As he approached Chad, he slowed to a stealthy walk, knowing the Australian still had his hearing. Very quietly, he crouched in front of Chad, waving his hand before the young man's ruined face. The Australian didn't react.

Dr. Wallis wasn't going to take any chances this time.

He hovered the needle directly before the Australian's heart.

"No!" Brook cried—too late.

Wallis had already plunged the needle into Chad's heart. He inhaled sharply—a terrible dry and rattling sound—but did little else. Then he slumped backward and lay still.

"You said this was over, Roy!" Brook cried. "You said—"

"It should have been over, Brook. I gave him ten times the regular dose of that drug directly into his spine. It should have…" He didn't finish this sentence for fear of alienating her further, but he thought, *It should have paralyzed every muscle in his body, even those used for breathing, which in the absence of ventilatory support, would have led to asphyxiation.*

"It should have what, Roy?"

"Nothing."

"It should have killed him?"

"Look at him, Brook!" he snapped. "You think he was going to survive regardless? You think he would have *wanted* to survive?"

She turned her back to him, and to hell if she wasn't crying again.

Dr. Wallis stood and went to the door.

"Where are you going, professor?" Guru asked him.

"To turn off the gas."

ΔΔΔ

When Dr. Roy Wallis returned to the sleep laboratory after shutting off the stimulant gas, he said, "It's over now, Brook. For good."

She wiped tears from her eyes and took a deep breath. "Okay."

"Okay?" he said.

"Yes," she said.

"What does 'okay' mean?"

"It means…I'm okay with…everything."

Dr. Wallis studied her closely. He couldn't decide whether she was speaking honestly or only telling him what he wanted to hear. Probably the latter.

"So what do you think we should do now?" he asked her.

"I think… What do *you* want to do?"

"Guru and I had plans to go out and celebrate. Right, buddy?" Guru nodded with reticence.

"Celebrate," Brook repeated.

"I know what you're thinking, Brook. How could we celebrate when we have two dead bodies on our hands?"

"Your experiment has been a great success, Roy. It will no doubt change the world, or how we perceive the world. But, yes, you're right. There are two dead people down here." Her voice choked on the words *dead people*, yet she pressed on. "We can't ignore that fact. The police won't ignore that fact either, despite the experiment's success. But you and your assistant have plans to *celebrate*?"

"I hear what you're saying, Brook. Loud and clear. So let me explain. Less than twenty-four hours ago, Chad and Sharon were in fine health. They were experiencing hallucinations and such, but they were in fine *physical* health. Sharon took her life only this morning. I was sleeping. Guru woke me. I was too late to save her. And calling the police would not have saved Chad either. He had already done what he'd done to himself. I wasn't aware of this at the time because he had his hoodie on. But he'd already done it."

"You knew what you were going to find, didn't you, Roy?" she said. "You knew about the so-called shadow consciousness?"

"Yes."

"Was it present in your mice?"

"Yes."

"And that wasn't good enough for you? You had to try the gas on humans?"

"We're getting off-topic here, Brook," he said tersely. "What I'm trying to say is that if I'd shut down the experiment after Sharon's death, and called the police, we wouldn't be discussing this legal gray area right now. Sharon had signed a consent form. She knew there would be risks in participating in the experiment. Unfortunately, she succumbed to one of those risks."

"But she didn't know the extent of the risks, did she? She didn't know what happened to the mice, did she?"

"Just finish hearing me out, Brook. If I'd shut down the experiment, if I'd called the police, I wouldn't have recorded Chad's brainwaves, and the experiment would have been for nothing. Chad and Sharon would have died for nothing. So all I'm guilty of, if I'm guilty of anything, is not reporting Sharon's death right away. I'm not even sure that's a crime. But why wade through murky legal waters at all?" He held up a hand. "Imagine this scenario. Chad and Sharon are still alive. They've...crossed over, for lack of a better expression...but they're still alive and haven't harmed themselves. I conduct the EEG on Chad, the experiment concludes, I turn off the gas, and we all go out and celebrate, you, me, Guru. When I return in the morning, I find the Australians in their current state. They reacted badly to coming off the gas when I wasn't present. They tripped out and performed these horrific acts of self-harm when I wasn't present. I can't be held accountable for that. Nobody gets fucked over. End of story."

Brook was silent.

Guru was looking at his shoes.

"All we'd be doing, Brook," Dr. Wallis pressed, "is postponing calling the police. Considering the implications of the Sleep Experiment, don't you think postponing calling the police for a few hours is justifiable? I mean, I've just fucking proven that a second, repressed consciousness resides within every member of humankind—"

"Did you hear that?" Brook said.

Dr. Wallis looked at Chad.

"I swear," she added, "I heard him say something."

"I heard him too, professor," Guru said.

"Impossible!" Wallis crossed the room and stopped before Chad. The Australian looked just as dead as ever. True, Wallis had never checked his pulse after injecting the paralytic drug into his heart, but there was no way anybody could have survived that.

There was no way anybody could have survived the paralytic drug injected into their spine either.

With a cold ball of unease forming in his gut, Dr. Wallis checked Chad's wrist for a pulse. He couldn't find one—

"Ache."

Wallis sprang back in surprise.

"See!" Brook said.

"*How?*" Wallis hissed.

"What did he say, professor?" Guru asked.

"I—I don't know. 'Ache,' I think."

"*Ache?*" Brook said. "Oh God, he's in pain!"

Heart pounding, Dr. Wallis crept closer to Chad's body. "Chad?" he said. "Buddy?"

"Aaaaaaaache..." He spoke the word without moving the lipless, crusty hole that had once been his mouth.

"This is impossible," Wallis said. "It's simply impossible."

"*Aaaaaaaaaache...*"

"Help him, Roy!" Brook cried.

Wallis realized Chad was still wearing the electrode headband. He slapped the keyboard to wake the monitor. Chad's brainwaves appeared on the screen, only now...

"My God," he breathed.

Guru appeared next to him. "What is it, professor?"

"It can't be..."

"*What is it?*"

"It appears his shadow consciousness isn't a shadow anymore. It's his *only* consciousness."

Abruptly Chad began convulsing as if suffering a major seizure.

"Help him!" Brook cried.

"Don't touch him!" Wallis ordered.

Abruptly, Chad let loose a scream so loud and shrill it sounded utterly inhuman. His head flailed back and forth. The cords in his neck stood out like knotted ropes. His hands clenched and unclenched while his body spasmed. Thick, sludgy blood oozed from his eye sockets and nose cavity.

Then the seizure, if that's what it was, ceased. The Australian went still.

"Look!" Guru said, pointing to the monitor.

The fast scribbling patterns of Chad's shadow beta brainwaves, indicative of an active cortex and an intense state of attention, had transitioned to slower, low-frequency shadow theta waves.

In the next moment, the brainwaves flat-lined.

△△△

"He died!" Guru said.

"At the very moment he fell asleep," Dr. Wallis marveled. "Fascinating!"

"Is he dead for certain this time?"

Dr. Wallis toed Chad's body. "Seems like it."

"What did you mean, professor, when you said his shadow consciousness was his *only* consciousness?"

"Exactly that, Guru. The person Chad had once been had died, and all that remained was the demon within him."

"Could that be why the drugs did not have the anticipated effects on him?"

"I'd bet the farm on it. And I'd also bet he—or *it*—wasn't saying 'ache.' It was saying 'wake.'" It somehow knew we'd turned off the gas, and it knew it had to remain awake or else..."

They both looked at Chad's body again.

"So the demon *took him over*," Guru said, appearing appalled at this possibility. "It *possessed* him."

Wallis nodded. "It makes one wonder whether all those cases of demon possessions and exorcisms over the centuries weren't total bullshit. Perhaps the victims were suffering from severe cases of total sleep deprivation..."

"Oh my, professor," Guru said, shaking his head. "This is not good. This is not good at all. We have opened Pandora's Box! When others learn of this discovery, when they too begin to play God...what if these demons *get loose and take over*? Not only a few individuals but the entire human race?"

Dr. Wallis grinned. "Sort of sums up the Book of Revelations pretty nicely, doesn't it?"

"I do not joke, professor! *What have we done?*"

"Calm down, man! What are you freaking out about? We haven't opened the gates of hell. We've simply located where they are. Can you grasp that? We're not villains! *We're heroes!*"

The door connecting the sleep laboratory and observation room banged closed.

Brook had fled.

ΔΔΔ

Dr. Roy Wallis gave chase, stopping when the narrow hallway opened up before the inoperable elevator and the bathrooms. The primary staircase was tucked away out of sight to the left of the elevator, easy to miss. Conversely, the secondary staircase was around the corner to the right. The layout was disorienting, and during the early days of the Sleep Experiment, he had mistakenly taken the emergency staircase on several occasions —mistakenly because it brought you to the loading dock on the ground floor rather than the building's main entrance.

Dr. Wallis had no way of knowing which way Brook had gone, and so he randomly chose the primary staircase. He emerged in the peach- and avocado-colored lobby. It was deserted. A glance through one of the four glass entrance doors that gave to the breezeway didn't reveal Brook fleeing into the night, which meant she had likely become disoriented herself and had taken the secondary staircase.

Wallis went west down the dark hallways, and much to his relief, he discovered the silhouetted shape of Brook in one branching corridor, coming his way.

Spotting him, she cried out in surprise, put on the brakes, and reversed, slipping out of sight through a doorway that led back to the secondary staircase.

Wallis followed hot on her heels, ascending the steps two at a time, his eyes already adjusting to the gloom. Although he couldn't see her, he could hear her shoes slapping the cement steps above him, indicating she had bypassed the first floor. When he reached the second floor, he paused to listen. He made out her footsteps fleeing down a distant hallway. Knowing he could lose her amongst the maze of corridors, he resumed his pursuit, sprinting full speed, and he soon had her in his sights once more. She was fifty feet ahead of him, racing east down the long hallway that spanned the breezeway and connected the psychology and education departments.

She swung left and out of sight. He reached the same spot five seconds later and followed her into the library. Although the wooden cubicles and tables and chairs had all been removed, for whatever reason the demolition contractors had left behind the steel book stacks.

Through the empty shelving—the books had long ago been transferred to the Gardner Stacks and the Social Research Library—Dr. Wallis glimpsed Brook climbing the staircase to the mezzanine.

And he knew he had her, as those stairs were the only way up or down.

Slowing to catch his breath, he said, "Stop this, Brook! What the hell are you doing? I thought you *understood*. I thought you were going to play ball."

"Leave me alone!" she shouted from above him. "Go away!"

He ascended the stairs. "I haven't given up on you, Brook," he lied. "We can still work this out. Just come back to the basement with me."

"Go away, Roy! I've called the police! They're on their way!"

A jolt of fear shot through him before he told himself she was bluffing. Her phone hadn't been on her when he'd transferred her, unconscious, from the air mattress to Sharon's bed. Which meant it had likely been in her handbag on the table in the observation room. And unless she'd had the presence of mind to grab it when she'd fled the sleep laboratory—which he doubted, because why not simply take her entire handbag, which would have been easier and faster—he had nothing to worry about.

When he reached the top of the staircase, Wallis spotted Brook at the far end of the aisle dividing seven or eight rows of stacks, swinging her head left and right, knowing she had nowhere left to go.

He started down the aisle toward her.

"Why are you doing this, Roy?"

"Doing what, Brook? You're the one running around like a chicken with its head chopped off."

"Please let me go."

"Come back to the basement with me."

She dashed to her right, and by the time he reached where she had been standing, she had put the full length of the steel shelf between them.

He started down the row; she started up the parallel one.

They met in the middle of the stack with only the steel shelving separating them.

They were so close to one another he could see the perspiration beading her shadowed face and the fear swimming in her eyes.

"Where's your phone, Brook?"

She didn't say anything.

"Didn't you say you called the police?"

She stepped left. He stepped left also.

She stepped right. He stepped right.

"Nowhere to go, Brook."

"I loved you, Roy."

"Did you?"

"Why are you doing this?"

"All I'm doing, Brook, is preventing you from sabotaging my life's work."

"I haven't done anything!"

"It's not what you've done. It's what you're going to do. You're going to betray me."

"I'm not, Roy. I just want to go home."

"If I let you leave, you're going to go back to your little boathouse, snuggle up in bed, and forget you ever stopped by here this evening?"

"Yes!"

"Bullshit!"

He feinted left as if to sprint around the book stack. She stumbled right, yet when she realized he wasn't coming for her, she went no further.

Slowly, confidently, he walked back down his row so he stood opposite her once more.

"How long are you going to keep this up, Brook?"

"I was wrong, Roy. I shouldn't have questioned you. You couldn't have saved Chad. I understand that now. I'm on your side."

"Good," he said. "Come back to the basement with me then."

"Why?"

"So I can keep an eye on you."

"For how long?"

Dr. Wallis clenched his jaw. The charade was up. They both knew the other's real intentions. They were simply wasting time.

Wallis dashed to the left, deciding the only way to end this would be to chase her down, even it if took him a dozen loops around the shelving.

Brook ran right, but instead of rounding the end of the stack and coming up the other side, she scissor-stepped over the stanchion handrail that ran along the edge of the mezzanine.

"Brook!" he shouted, believing she would jump.

She didn't. She lowered herself so she hung by her hands from the edge of the balcony, reducing the distance between her feet and the floor below.

She let go as he lunged for her.

She landed with a pained grunt, and even as he was deciding

whether to do as she had done, or return to the staircase, she was scrambling to her feet and fleeing once more.

"Shit!" he said and ran to the stairs.

ΔΔΔ

Guru Rampal knew he had made a grave mistake.

He should have done the right thing after Sharon had killed herself and called the police. By going along with Dr. Wallis' plan to keep her death under wraps until the experiment concluded, he had committed himself to a path that, at every unexpected turn, had proved very difficult to leave no matter how much he'd wanted to.

And, ultimately, look where it had led him.

Sharon dead.

Chad dead.

Brook...

Yes, what of the pretty woman Brook?

If Dr. Wallis caught her, he wasn't going to sit her down for a stern talking to. He had punched her in the face. He had imprisoned her against her will.

If he caught her...he wasn't going to sit her down for a stern talking to, no...and he wasn't going to let her go either.

He was going to kill her.

Guru couldn't believe he was entertaining such a thought, but after everything that had happened over the last few hours, he knew it to be the truth.

You can't let him do this!

No, he couldn't.

Guru began racking his brain for options.

ΔΔΔ

When Brook reached the hallway spanning the breezeway, she knew she had two options: run or hide.

Her instinct was to run, but reason insisted Roy would catch her. He was faster than her; he knew the building better.

Besides, even if she managed to find her way outside, where would she go? Her car was parked a block away. Nobody was around to help her.

Her mind had processed all these thoughts in less than a second, and it offered up its counsel just as quickly:

Hide then.

She ducked into the second room on the left of the hallway.

It was empty but dark.

She went to the corner to the left of the door where the shadows seemed thickest.

She waited.

△△△

When Dr. Roy Wallis emerged from the library, he expected to see Brook sprinting down the long hallway, backtracking to the building's entrance.

Yet it was empty.

He listened. Didn't hear her footsteps.

Which wasn't right.

Sound carried in the old cement structure, almost as though it were a giant echo chamber. Given she hadn't gotten that much of a head start on him, he should still be able to hear her, whichever way she'd gone.

Unless she'd decided to hide.

Dr. Wallis started down the hallway, slowly, to mask his approach. Six classrooms lined each side of the corridor. He entered the first one on the left. Rain pelted the large windows that faced Hearst Avenue. Although his eyes had adjusted to the lack of light, they couldn't probe the thick shadows that had pooled in the far corners of the room. Only when he'd moved to the center of the room was he satisfied it was empty. He returned to the hallway and entered the first room on the right.

Empty too.

A greasy sensation built in his gut as he worried that Brook may have somehow given him the slip, that she was already outside, on her way to the police to blow the lid off the Sleep Experiment before he could tie up all the loose ends and hammer out a plausible story.

Bitch! he thought, spangles of red creeping into his vision. *Should have finished her off when I had the chance!*

He returned to the hallway and entered the second room on the left. A deafening clap of thunder shook the sky, and had Wallis not instinctively flinched and turned his head, he might not have seen Brook slinking out the door behind him.

He hurried quickly yet quietly after her, and he managed to close the distance between them to less than five feet before she either heard or sensed him.

Glancing over her shoulder, her eyes flashed wide and she issued a high-pitched yelp. She picked up her speed, no longer concerned about stealth—but it was too late.

His right hand snagged the back of her blouse, dragging her to a halt. She spun, swinging her arms. He got his arms around her. She yelled and twisted and kicked her feet so ferociously he could barely hold on to her.

"Stop it, Brook!"

"Let me go!"

"Stop it!"

He launched her sideways. She bounced off the cement wall and crumpled to her hands and knees. Towering over her, he gripped fistfuls of her blouse and hiked her to her feet.

"Two choices, Brook," he snarled, his face inches from hers. "You walk with me back to the basement, nice and civil, or I knock the sense out of you one more time and drag you by the hair. What's it going to be?"

△△△

Guru was in the sleep laboratory seated on Chad's bed with his head held in his hands when Dr. Wallis marched Brook through the door.

"Thanks for the help, buddy," Wallis remarked sardonically.

Guru looked up. "I was waiting for you to return, professor. I wanted to tell you—you cannot do this." His eyes flicked momentarily to Brook.

"Can't do what?" Wallis asked.

Suddenly and comically, Guru produced a steak knife that had been stuck in the waistband of his pants against the small of his back. He held it before him in a shaking hand.

"What the hell is that?" Wallis demanded.

"Do not harm her, professor!"

"Put the goddamn knife away."

"Let her go!"

Dr. Wallis considered the situation, then said, "You're fucking up, my man. But I'm going to offer you a way out."

Guru frowned. "What do you mean?"

"Kill her with that knife."

"*What?*"

"She's going to tell the police on us—"

"I am not—"

"Shut up, Brook!" Wallis shouted, glaring at her until she broke eye contact. To Guru: "She's going to tell the police on us. Try to pin Chad and Sharon's deaths on us."

"But we did nothing…"

"That's exactly it, buddy. We did *nothing* after Sharon died. We continued the experiment with Chad. The cops aren't going to look too favorably on that. But when you kill Brook, we no longer have that problem. We'll come back tomorrow and discover the three bodies."

"Three?"

"Just like I told you earlier. The experiment concluded. We turned off the gas. We went out to celebrate. Now—here's the new twist. Brook comes by to monitor the Australians for us while they sleep off the gas. They begin behaving oddly. She goes in to check on them and they kill her, then they kill themselves. It's even better than the original story!"

After this declaration, a momentous silence filled the sleep laboratory. Then Brook began to cry. Guru shook his head frantically.

"No, professor," he said, waving the knife. "We cannot! We cannot!"

"We have no choice!"

"That is murder!"

"Jesus, Guru, do you want to go to prison?"

"This cannot be happening. How did you talk me into any of this in the first place?"

"I'll hold her down. All you have to do is cover her face with a pillow. Then it'll be over—"

A bloodcurdling, filthy sound erupted from the other side of the sleep laboratory.

Chad was sitting up.

And laughing.

ΔΔΔ

Dr. Roy Wallis stared at the faceless abomination in disbelief.

It was impossible, utterly impossible, that Chad could be alive. *I watched him die! I witnessed his brainwaves flatline!*

But there he was, sitting up.

And laughing.

At us?

Chad pushed himself to his feet then, not in the lumbering manner of the rotting undead, but in the easy, graceful way of a virile twenty-two-year-old in perfect health.

"What are you?" Wallis demanded as reality seemed to fade around him in a hot wave of melting light. "*What are you?*"

"I. Think. You. Know."

Although Chad's lipless mouth didn't appear to move, the

slow, mushy words most definitely originated from within the permanent rictus.

Dr. Wallis shuffled backward a step. Guru and Brook seemed rooted to the floor in wide-eyed, slack-jawed shock.

"*What are you?*" Wallis demanded once more, ashamed by the naked fear in his voice.

"You," the thing that was Chad rasped. "The deepest animal part of you...that you hide from...in your beds." He stepped forward, sightless yet surefooted. "What you sedate into silence...every night." Another step. "We are *you*."

Issuing a low, fragile whimper, Guru bolted for the door.

The Chad-thing moved incredibly fast. It rushed across the room, crashing blindly into Sharon's bed. It fell to its knees atop the mattress but regained its feet with barely a second lost.

It reached Guru just as he opened the door, seizing the Indian from behind and throwing him back into the sleep laboratory as if he weighed little more than a rag doll.

Guru must have soared a good fifteen feet through the air before crashing into the refrigerator. The steak knife clattered away from him across the floor.

The Chad-thing cocked its head to one side.

Listening, Wallis thought.

Guru seemed to understand this too as he clamped his trembling mouth closed in a desperate effort to suppress any unwanted sounds.

The Chad-thing moved toward the kitchen.

It passed within a foot of Dr. Wallis, who summoned all his willpower to remain still and silent.

Brook, he noticed, was a bloodless white statute.

The Chad-thing continued moving toward the last sound it heard.

Eyes bulging, Guru raised his hands in the slow, cautious manner of a man who had a gun pointed at him, then pressed them over his mouth.

The Chad-thing cocked its head to the left, then to the right.

In the face of the approaching nightmare, Guru's bladder gave out. The groin area of his beige khaki trousers darkened, then the legs, and then urine was leaking out of his left cuff, spraying the floor.

The Chad-thing zeroed in on the noise.

It grabbed Guru by the head and lifted him high enough his feet dangled in the air.

Guru was screaming now, and Dr. Wallis thought it was in terror before realizing it was in pain, for the Chad-thing had dug its thumbs into Guru's eye sockets as if they were the finger holes of a ten-pin bowling ball.

Blood gushed down the Indian's cheeks like bright red tears.

Backing away from the gruesome scene as silently as possible, Wallis slipped unnoticed from the sleep laboratory.

ΔΔΔ

Brook had gotten her shit together enough to follow him, and together they hurried through the observation room. Yet as soon as Dr. Wallis opened the door to the hallway, he heard the Chad-thing wail, followed by a loud commotion.

It had heard the door open.

It was coming.

"Run!" Brook shouted from behind him, shoving him through the door.

Wallis ran for all he was worth. He didn't hesitate when he came to the defunct elevator. He blew straight past it and made a hard right to reach the main staircase. Moments later he reached the ground floor. He shoved open one of the glass doors and shot through it. In his haste and panic, however, he tripped over his own feet and toppled forward, his knees and palms skinning the wet pavement before his body rolled twice. But then he was back on his feet, bee-lining toward his car, thanking God he had parked in one of the disability spots right out front of the building.

Digging the remote key from his pocket, he jabbed the unlock button, whipped open the Audi's driver's side door, and slid inside. At the same time the passenger side door opened, and Brook jumped in next to him.

Both doors thudded closed moments before the Chad-thing burst through them into the storming night.

Dr. Wallis reached for the push-button ignition, but before he pressed it, Brook seized his wrist.

She was shaking her head: no.

Wallis looked past her to the Chad-thing.

It was moving in their direction, but it seemed aimless as if it had lost their scent.

Our sound, Wallis amended.

He nodded so Brook knew he understood the meaning of her head shake, though he kept his hand hovering near the push-button, ready to press it in a heartbeat.

ΔΔΔ

The Chad-thing banged blindly into the Audi. It raged against the roof with its fists, then began making its way around the trunk. It moved down Dr. Wallis' side of the car and stopped next to his window. It stood there for a dreadfully long moment, silent, no doubt listening for movement with its super-human hearing, which seemed matched only by its super-human strength. Wallis didn't understand the physiology behind these amazing feats, and he realized the Sleep Experiment had not reached its conclusion. It had only just begun.

There's so much to learn about these...demon souls.

So much to learn about...us.

The Demon Soul—for that was now how Dr. Wallis thought of the Chad-thing—turned quickly so it was facing Hearst Avenue.

Wallis saw a flashlight beam arcing through the dark some fifty feet away.

Brook saw it too and gasped.

Hearing her, the creature turned back to the car, bending over to peer into the driver's side window with its empty, bloody eye sockets.

Wallis didn't flex a muscle. Didn't dare to breathe. A bead of perspiration slid down his brow and into his left eye, stinging it.

He didn't blink.

"Roy?" the distant voice of Roger Henn called. "That you?"

The Demon Soul vanished from the window, reappearing a moment later moving in a quick gait on all fours toward the police officer.

"No!" Brook breathed, and tried to smack the car horn.

Wallis grabbed her hand and said, "*What the fuck are you doing?*"

"It's going to kill him!"

"Better him than us!"

"Roy, no! Enough!"

When she couldn't yank her hand free from his grip, she screamed.

The Demon Soul, Dr. Wallis saw in alarm, stopped to look back at the car.

"Hey, who's there?" Roger Henn called, picking up his pace. The curtain of rain and inky darkness clearly obscured his vision, and he didn't see the creature until he was nearly on top of it. Skidding to a stop, he said, "Whoa—oh boy! *What?*"

Brook slapped the horn.

The Demon Soul paid the sharp *honk!* no notice. It sprang toward Roger Henn. The big cop, nimble for his girth, dodged the attack, tearing his pistol free from its holster.

"Freeze!" he shouted, aiming the weapon at the creature. Then, almost as an afterthought: "Police!"

Thunder exploded. A detonation of lightning shredded the night sky, casting a stroboscopic effect over the unfolding action. The Demon Soul scrambled forward. Henn fired two shots at point-blank range, the twin rounds dropping the creature to the ground.

Brook threw open her door. Wallis reached in front of her and pulled the door shut again.

"Let me go!" she shrieked.

"*Quiet!*" he hissed.

"Roy?" Henn called, close enough to now recognize the Audi. "*Roy?*" he repeated, his voice several octaves higher than usual. "What the fuck is going on? *What happened to this guy?*"

"Help!" Brook yelled. "Help me!"

Wallis punched her in the mouth. She slumped against the door, blood leaking from her lips, but still holding onto consciousness. He punched her again, this time in the nose, and heard her nasal cartilage crunch. She went slack.

△△△

"Out of the car, Roy!" Police Officer Roger Henn shouted. "I can see you! Leave that woman alone!"

But all Roger Henn could think was, *I shot that man, I killed him, goddammit I killed him!* And in concert with this, *What happened to him? He had no face! It looked like it'd been chewed off!*

"Hear me, Roy? Come out of the car with your hands where I can—*Jesus!*"

Henn stared dumbfounded as the guy with no face and two .40 caliber rounds in his chest pushed himself to his knees, then his feet.

Henn raised the Glock 22, but the man's Lazarus act had filled his veins with ice and slowed his reflexes. Before he could squeeze off another round, the man was on him, tackling him to the ground, clawing and biting him with a strength and ferocity that defied comprehension.

△△△

Dr. Wallis jabbed the ignition button, put the Audi into reverse, and swung out of the parking spot. He shifted to first and stepped on the gas. His first thought was to speed away down Hearst Avenue. In the same instant, however, he changed his mind and swerved left toward the Demon Soul. Lit up in the stark white light of the LED headlights, it was hunched over Roger Henn's unmoving body, throwing fistfuls of the cop's innards into the air as one might throw rice or confetti at a wedding.

Dr. Wallis realized he was screaming uncontrollably as the Audi barreled down on the monstrosity.

Hearing the vehicle approach, it leaped to its feet.

Wallis shut his eyes as the three-thousand pounds of German engineering plowed into the Demon Soul, launching it up the hood and over the roof.

Slamming the brakes, he opened his eyes to find the windshield spider-webbed and bloodied.

He glanced in the rearview mirror and saw the creature lying on the pavement awash in the hellish red glow of the car's taillights.

It twitched.

Wallis shifted into reverse, floored the accelerator. The tires squealed.

The Audi jumped, once, twice.

Whud! Whud!

Wallis stamped the brakes.

Lying on the pavement in front of the car now, lit up once more in the headlights, the Demon Soul was a bloody lump of flesh and blood.

A bloody *unmoving* lump of flesh and blood.

△△△

Brook stirred, and maybe moaned, but the darkness remained impenetrable, cloaking her thoughts in a black fog. Dimly she knew she was in the passenger's seat of Roy's car. Understood her life was in danger, from both Roy and the poor Australian, or whatever it was that the poor Australian had become. Yet she couldn't seem to clear her mind or move her body...and then, from a place very far away, someone spoke her name.

She moved her mouth, formed a word, though what it was she wasn't sure.

"Brook?"

The voice was closer now.

"Roy...?" she managed.

"Brook?"

She forced open her eyes. This set off bright lances of agony inside her skull. She could see little more than dark shapes, though she could hear the steady, angry drone of the rain falling on the roof of the car.

Cool, wet air. Hands shaking her shoulder.

Someone had opened her door.

It was Roy, soaking wet, his hair plastered to his skull, rain streaking his face.

He hit me—again.

She touched her face. It felt numb like it belonged to a different person. Yet there was a sharp pain as well.

"Wherezhe...?" she asked, finding it extremely difficult to work her lips. She tasted slippery blood.

"It's dead," Roy said, holding out his hand for her.

"Dead...?"

"Come on," he said.

"Where...?"

She couldn't complete the sentence and simply took his hand. He all but lifted her from the car until she stood on jellied legs. She teetered against his chest and felt his arms encircle her body in an embrace. The rain hammered her head and splashed the ground at her feet.

You have to get away.

Yet she didn't know how to go about achieving this feat. She couldn't think clearly, could barely stand, let alone fight him off her. "The policeman...?" she said.

"It's going to be okay," Roy said soothingly and kissed her on the forehead.

His arms moved up her back and wrapped around her head, and she didn't like this, it wasn't right, wasn't how you hugged someone—

"*Roy...?*"

His arms flexed and twisted.

The next thing Brook knew she was flat on the ground, staring at Roy's cap-toe Oxfords. She tried to get up, couldn't. Her right arm was pinned beneath her, but it wouldn't move. She felt no pain, but she found it was becoming increasingly difficult to breathe, and this sent a wild panic through her.

Roy crouched. Although she couldn't see his face, she could hear his voice.

"It's okay, Brook. It won't be long now. Everything's okay."

What have you done to me, you bastard? What have you done to me? WHAT HAVE YOU DONE?

She was still screaming these silent questions inside her head when she died from asphyxiation two minutes later.

EPILOGUE

D r. Roy Wallis scavenged Sharon's bloody tension bandages from the floor of the sleep laboratory and dumped them, along with the used syringes and empty vials of Vecuronium, through the iron grates of a rainwater gutter on Shattuck Avenue. Next he went to Chad's body and wrapped his arms around it, to transfer the Australian's blood to his clothes.

Then he called the police.

Within minutes, three squad cars and an ambulance, gumballs flashing, screeched to a halt in front of Tolman Hall. Half a dozen officers secured the scene. Paramedics attended to the victims and confirmed there were no survivors. The senior cop grilled Dr. Wallis on what happened. When Wallis refused to make a statement without his attorney present, he was hauled off to the Berkeley Police Department Jail Facility, questioned some more by a pair of detectives, and eventually arrested and booked.

After being fingerprinted and photographed, Wallis said, "I have the right to one phone call."

The guard shrugged. "Make it quick."

Wallis used the telephone on the guard's desk to call his attorney.

"Don?" he said, turning away from the guard. "It's Roy Wallis."

"Roy," Don Finke said, a note of concern in his voice. "A call at this hour can't be good news."

"I've been arrested," he said. "They're holding me at the Berkeley Police Department Jail Facility, and I don't want to sit around here for any longer than I have to."

"Don't sweat it, Roy. Don't sweat it at all. I'll have you out of there in no time."

△△△

There was no longer a municipal courthouse in the City of Berkeley, so midmorning Dr. Wallis was driven to the Superior Court in Oakland for his arraignment. He pleaded not guilty. The district attorney, a fussy, gaunt man named Edward Prince, did his damnedest to fight Wallis' bail request, while Don Finke argued that Dr. Wallis was a reputable university professor and stalwart of the community and no flight risk. In the end, after more than twenty minutes of back-and-forth, the presiding judge ruled, "Bail is granted for five hundred thousand dollars."

△△△

Three days later district attorney Edward Prince charged Dr. Wallis with five counts of involuntary manslaughter, just as the Sleep Experiment was becoming a bona fide international phenomenon. On a purely criminal level, the experiment involved a mass murder that claimed the lives of five people. Given the self-mutilations and violent deaths involved, it rivaled the sensationalism of the 1969 Tate murders. Add to this Dr. Wallis' public claims that the killer, Chad Carter, had been possessed by madness that resided at the core of all of humanity, a madness largely kept in check only by the miraculous powers of sleep—well, you had a media blitzkrieg the likes of which had not been witnessed in recent history.

While the vast majority of the public believed Dr. Wallis to be running some sort of publicity hoax, this didn't stop his name from entering the daily lexicon of every major newscaster and talk show host in America, or the phrase "Demon Souls" from becoming one of the top trending hashtags across social media sites the world over.

Indeed, the buildup to what became dubbed the latest and greatest "Trial of the Century" could not be understated, and the criminal case against Dr. Roy Wallis commenced to global fanfare four months later on October 14, 2018. It was heard in the San Francisco Hall of Justice complex. The granite-clad building housed the Sheriff's Department, the County Jail, as well as various municipal courts, and until recently it served as the location of the Office of the Chief Medical Examiner. The courtroom selected for the trial featured paneled oak walls, a coffered ceiling, and linoleum flooring. Hanging on the wall at the front of the room, behind the imposing mahogany bench, was the seal of the jurisdiction, bookended by the flags of the federal and state governments. Adjacent to the bench was the currently empty witness stand, as well as desks behind which the court clerk and court reporter were seated. Against the left-hand wall was the jury box, occupied by the twelve jurors, six men and six women, all white.

For the last three weeks they had patiently listened to accusations and counter-accusations and expert testimony by more than two dozen witnesses, which included the chief of forensic pathology at the coroner's office, SFPD detectives in the robbery-homicide division, various doctors, a toxicologist, a narcotics expert, a computer forensics examiner, and a physician specializing in internal medicine. And today, the final day of the trial, they would hear the prosecution's and defense's closing arguments.

Dr. Wallis sat at the defense table, handsome, composed, and meticulously dressed in a black tailored suit and matching silk tie. Ever since he had become a household name, there had been nearly as much discussion in the media regarding his looks, his style—and even his beard—as there had been about his guilt or innocence, or his Demon Soul theory. He had amassed a legion of female fans from as far away as New Zealand and Japan who mailed him over a thousand letters a week, in which he often found racy photographs and propositions of marriage. On several occasions during the trial women had made catcalls from the packed gallery, prompting the presiding judge to twice clear the courtroom and once threaten to close it to the public for the remainder of the proceedings.

Nevertheless, not everybody who came to watch the criminal case against Dr. Wallis supported him. Some displayed neither adoration nor sympathy, but enmity and expectation. They despised him for his wealth and his attractiveness and the cult-like status he had garnered, and they wanted nothing more than to see him cut down to size.

At nine o'clock sharp, the uniformed bailiff called the court to order.

Everybody rose as Judge Amanda Callahan, clad in plain black robes, entered the courtroom and took her seat behind the bench. At her prompting, District Attorney Edward Prince went to the lectern between the two counsel tables and addressed the jury. He had proven himself to be a skilled and able prosecutor, and in simple, broad strokes, he outlined the State's case against Dr. Roy Wallis. He argued that Dr. Wallis was a dangerously ambitious man who had put the success of the Sleep Experiment above all else. When the two test subjects began to demonstrate severe mental and physical deterioration, far from ending the experiment, or even temporarily suspending it, he continued full steam ahead, consequences be damned.

Edward Prince concluded his address by saying, "The events set in motion four months ago are now at a close. On June 14 crimes of ghastly proportions were committed. On that day a young girl ripped her heart from her chest and a young man brutally murdered three other people before his own life was taken—five lives squandered and gone forever. The questions that had been on everybody's mind from coast to coast, and indeed across the world, were, *How could this have ever been allowed to happen? And who should be held accountable?* Well, those questions have come to rest right here in this courtroom, and it's fallen to you as members of this jury to answer them.

"Based on the evidence presented to you over these last three weeks, based on what you've heard and seen, the answers are clear. The tragedy should never have been allowed to happen, and the defendant, Dr. Roy Wallis, must be held accountable, for he is guilty of criminal gross negligence.

"Everyone in this courtroom agrees that Dr. Roy Wallis, as the person in charge of the notorious Sleep Experiment, is responsible for the deaths of the five unfortunate victims. This is not up for debate. The defense believes it. The State believes it. Sharon Nash's life didn't have to end on a bathroom floor with her heart clutched in her hand. Brook Foxley didn't have to die slowly and terrifyingly from asphyxiation due to a broken neck. Officer Roger Henn, a husband and father of two boys, didn't have to lose his life to Chad Carter, his intestines torn from his stomach.

"So this case isn't about whether Dr. Roy Wallis is responsible for the massacre or not. This case is about whether his conduct during the Sleep Experiment constitutes not just negligence but *criminal* negligence—and the State submits to you, ladies and gentlemen, that it most certainly does.

"You have heard several instructions from the judge throughout the trial. The State would like to refresh your memory on a couple of them.

"The first is the character instruction that stated you *may* consider the character of the defendant in assessing his guilt or innocence. The defense will have you believe Dr. Roy Wallis is an upstanding citizen, a respected university professor and scientist, and an all-around good guy. However, do not forget the witness testimonies that described him as an alcoholic, a serial womanizer, a playboy who lives in a multi-million-dollar penthouse, and a delusional megalomaniac whose ambition has no limit.

"Another instruction the State would like you to remember referred to callous disregard of human life. The judge put the definition of *callous* in parentheses because it was important for you to make the distinction as to whether the deaths of the five victims were the result of simple negligence, or negligence so gross, wanton, and culpable as to show a *callous disregard of human life*. The State would now like to remind you the definition of callous is "showing or having an insensitive and cruel disregard for others," and this would most certainly encompass the cruel disregard present in this case. Fourteen days of cruel disregard.

"In successfully tried cases of involuntary manslaughter against motorists under the influence of drugs or alcohol—the most common case of involuntary manslaughter heard by the courts—the killings happen in a flash." He snapped his fingers for emphasis. "It's momentary. In the case against Dr. Roy Wallis, on the other hand, the deaths of the five victims weren't momentary, nor did they occur in a momentary lapse. The defendant had fourteen days to end the experiment, *fourteen days*, which was the time it took for two young people to literally lose their minds while under his supervision. It was in his power all along to stop the Sleep Experiment when it began spiraling out of control, but he never did so. The defense would like you to believe that Dr. Roy Wallis had no forewarning that Chad Carter or Sharon Nash would become dangerous to themselves or others. But how can you possibly believe this claim? The day before the massacre they covered the viewing window into the sleep laboratory with their feces—*covered the window with their feces*. Now, I might not be an acclaimed psychology professor— but I don't need to be—to deduce that these people needed help. Help that Dr. Wallis denied them for fourteen long days."

Edward Prince walked toward the jury box.

"Everyone is entitled to what we refer to as self-evident truths: life, liberty, and the pursuit of happiness. Chad Carter, Sharon Nash, Guru Rampal, Brook Foxley, and Roger Henn had a right to life, to experience joy and love and disappointment that comes with life too, to grow old and die peacefully...but because of Dr. Roy Wallis' callous disregard of human life, because of his blind and reckless ambition, their lives, liberties, and pursuits of happiness were stolen from them.

"Don't be fooled into thinking the defendant should get a pass because his scientific research was special or noble, or because he shed new insight into the human condition. Even if his claims of so-called Demon Souls are ever independently verified, he still shouldn't get a pass. You must make the same decision about Dr. Roy Wallis' callous reckless actions as you would about anyone else's. It doesn't matter if you believe he had good intentions in undertaking his experiment. That's a sentencing issue. That's not a guilt/innocence issue."

Edward Prince spread his arms.

"So when it's all said and done, Chad, Sharon, Guru, Brook, and Roger didn't have to die how they died. They shouldn't have died how they died. Dr. Roy Wallis should have ended the notorious Sleep Experiment well before it reached its bloody conclusion. The fact that he didn't displays not only negligent conduct on his part but *criminally* negligent conduct that is gross, willful, wanton, and culpable.

"Thus the State asks you to find the defendant guilty of involuntary manslaughter based on all of the circumstances presented here. Ladies and gentlemen of the jury, the decision is in your hands. Thank you."

You could hear a pin drop in the courtroom as the scrawny Edward Prince returned to his seat behind the prosecution table. Dr. Wallis averted his eyes from the jurors, for the faces he had come to know so well the last three weeks now appeared cold and unfriendly.

Judge Amanda Callahan said, "Mr. Wilks, are you going to close for the defense?"

"I am, Your Honor, may it please the Court."

Stephen Wilks, a former judge himself, was a short, portly man with a receding hairline, out-of-fashion red muttonchops, and heavy eyeglasses that seemed to magnify the size of his eyeballs behind the lenses. Dressed in an unassuming tweed suit and scuffed loafers, he ambled to the lectern. He shuffled through his papers, then looked up, blinking, as if awed by his formal surroundings. At first glance he was the antithesis of the flashy defense attorneys usually retained by wealthy defendants accused of felonies, yet he was one of the most respected criminal lawyers in the country. He held the impressive record of never having lost a major case in his career, which was why Dr. Wallis had chosen him to lead his defense team.

"Five people are dead and somebody must pay," Stephen Wilks began, pushing his eyeglasses up the bridge of his nose. "You heard it from the witnesses, and you heard it from most of Mr. Prince's closing argument. Right to life. Right to grow old. Five people dead; someone must pay. Dr. Roy Wallis must pay. Well, on one level, the defendant will pay. He'll pay for the rest of his life, but that's not what this case is about. It's about whether you the jury can find beyond a reasonable doubt that the deaths of the five victims were the direct result of criminal negligence on the part of Dr. Wallis, criminal negligence that was so gross and wanton and culpable as to show callous disregard for human life.

"So let's look at what facts the State has used to argue that Dr. Wallis acted with callous disregard for the lives of the victims, what they think they have proven beyond a reasonable doubt. Their main argument is that Dr. Wallis did not stop the experiment early enough. However, the Court has instructed you time and time again that the fact the defendant did not end the experiment sooner, in and of itself, is not enough to justify a conviction of involuntary manslaughter. It doesn't show Dr. Wallis had a callous disregard for his test subjects' well-being. Thanks to the meticulous notes recorded by the defendant and his two assistants, we've had access and insight into the hour-by-hour functioning of his test subjects' minds. And, yes, while some of their symptoms might seem alarming to you, particularly as they approached the end of the Sleep Experiment, there were zero red flags indicating they posed dangers to themselves or others. Dr. Wallis didn't know they would snap to the extent they did. After all, he didn't expose them to torture. He simply deprived them of sleep. He didn't know what the full repercussions of this would entail—for that was the exact purpose of the experiment!"

Stephen Wilks scratched his head, and for a moment he seemed to have lost his train of thought. But then just as the jury members began fiddling uncomfortably in the silence, he said, "The act of not knowing, ladies and gentlemen, is involuntary. You don't intentionally not know something because then it isn't something you don't know. It's something you're ignoring. If you ignore something, that's different than not knowing it. Dr. Wallis didn't ignore any red flags in his test subjects. He simply didn't know what was going to happen. And although the act of not knowing is involuntary, it doesn't meet the standard of involuntary manslaughter because it doesn't prove criminal negligence.

"Now, when events *did* make a turn for the worse, and it was clear the test subjects *did* become a danger to themselves and others, if—*if*—Dr. Wallis had done nothing at this point, then I would not be arguing before you in his defense, because he most certainly would be guilty of criminal negligence. But this is not what happened at all. As soon as Guru Rampal informed him that he was concerned about Sharon Nash, Dr. Wallis attempted to help her. Unfortunately, by that time, there was nothing he could do. So he immediately terminated the experiment, shutting off the gas, and went to assess the other test subject, who suddenly and inexplicably attacked Guru Rampal. At this point did Dr. Wallis run? No, he did not. According to his testimony, he valiantly wrestled Chad off Guru, suffering a nasty gash to his head, and blacked out. When he came around a short time later, he found his assistant Guru Rampal dead, his girlfriend Brook Foxley dead, and Chad Carter savagely attacking Roger Henn. Again, did he run or hide? No, he did nothing of the sort, and although he was not able to save Mr. Henn, his actions could not be described as anything but heroic."

Stephen Wilks ambled from the lectern to the jury box and smiled timidly at the men and women seated there. "Please don't be swayed by the gruesome way in which the four victims perished," he said. "Their deaths are in every way a tragedy, but not every tragedy is a crime. Allow me a moment to read some of the judge's instructions to you." He produced a piece of paper from his pocket. *"If you find that the facts are susceptible to two different interpretations, one of which is consistent with the innocence of the defendant, you cannot arbitrarily adopt the interpretation which incriminates the defendant. Instead, the interpretation more favorable to the defendant should be adopted unless it is untenable, under all the circumstances. The evidence must not only be consistent with guilt, but it must be inconsistent with every reasonable hypothesis of innocence."*

Stephen Wilks tucked the paper away.

"So you see, ladies and gentlemen," he said, "the act of keeping two individuals awake with a stimulant gas is simply not enough to warrant a conviction of involuntary manslaughter. Yes, there are five dead individuals. Yes, Dr. Wallis, as their supervisor, is responsible for those deaths. He has never denied this. But the question at hand is whether a criminal, a felon, stands before you. If you are unsure of your position on this, even in the slightest bit, then the State has not proven beyond a reasonable doubt that Dr. Roy Wallis is guilty of the callous disregard of life, and you must rule in his favor. And he *is* innocent, ladies and gentlemen, for if the State had shown that he knew Chad Carter and Sharon Nash were a danger to themselves and others, and continued with the experiment, then that would have been involuntary manslaughter. Heck, I'd be happy to argue the case that it was *voluntary* manslaughter. Yet on the contrary, the State did *not* prove this at all, and so I ask you to understand that, despite whatever you think of the Sleep Experiment, or Dr. Wallis himself, he is not a criminal, and there is only one verdict you can reach. Not guilty."

△△△

The jury was out for four hours. Dr. Roy Wallis watched

as they filed back into the courtroom. Although he remained outwardly calm, he felt as though a nest of snakes was slithering inside his stomach. A guilty verdict, while not the end of his life, would be devastating. He could not afford to spend the next five years in prison. He had so much work yet to do!

Judge Amanda Callahan asked, "Has the jury reached a verdict?"

"We have, Your Honor." The jury foreman held up a piece of paper pinched between his fingers.

"Would the bailiff retrieve the verdict, please?"

The bailiff went to the juror, took the piece of paper, and passed it to the judge. She opened it, read the contents, then looked up. "The jury finds the defendant not guilty."

Pandemonium resulted. The spectators in the gallery shot to their feet, with everyone talking at once, many applauding and cheering, others shouting profanities.

△△△

Outside the Hall of Justice, Dr. Wallis stopped before a phalanx of television cameras for an impromptu and celebratory press conference. When the throng of journalists and reporters quieted down, he said into the two-dozen or so microphones thrust at him, "Walt Whitman once wrote that 'the fear of hell is little or nothing to me.' But he was Walt Whitman, so he can write whatever he damn well pleased." Wallis stroked his beard, reveling in the knowledge the world would be hanging onto his every word. "I'm guessing," he continued, "Walt most likely never believed that hell existed in the first place, hence his cavalier attitude." He shook a finger as if to scorn the father of free verse. "But I, my lovely friends, I now know hell exists, and let me tell you—it scares the utter shit out of me."

Resounding silence except for the *cluck-cluck-cluck* of photographs being snapped.

Then everyone began shouting questions at once.

"Will you perform another sleep experiment in the future, professor?"

"Do you plan to make your complete research available to the public?"

"What would you like to say to your doubters?"

"Are you going to apologize to the families of the deceased?"

"Do you know where Penny Park is?"

"Do you have plans to sell the stimulant gas to pharmaceutical companies?"

Ignoring the bedlam, Dr. Wallis followed the path his defense team cleaved through the crowd to a waiting black SUV. He climbed into the backseat, closed the door, and frowned at the driver in the front seat.

"Who are you?" he demanded.

"I'm your driver today, sir," the gray-haired man replied.

"Where's Raoul?"

"Sick."

"Sick?"

"He called in sick today, and I was given the gig."

"Do you know where my apartment building is?"

"The Clock Tower Building, sir. I live only a few blocks away from it."

Demonstrators were slapping the windows and roof of the SUV, so Dr. Wallis said, "Get a move on then."

The driver rolled away from the curb. Once the vehicle cleared the crowd, Wallis noticed a palpable quiet in the streets, and it wasn't until they passed a busy bar—at 11:45 in the morning—that he realized the quiet was because of him. The city—hell, the country, more like it—had ground to a halt as people in their living rooms and offices, at work and at play, had gathered to watch on their televisions and their phones as his verdict was read.

Dr. Wallis googled himself on his phone and read the headlines from a half dozen leading newspapers:

Jury Clears Dr. Roy Wallis of Involuntary Manslaughter

Spellbound Nation Divided on Sleep Doctor Verdict
No Justice!
Not Guilty!
Jury Stunner: Wallis Walks
Demon Soul Doctor Free!

As Dr. Wallis skimmed the lead story in *The New York Times*, however, his smile became a frown. The journalist was clearly a biased hack, as the piece was a hit job on Wallis. It labeled him a murderer who escaped justice while lambasting his Demon Soul theory as a "fantasy role-play of a delusional megalomaniac."

Scowling, Dr. Wallis shoved his phone back into his pocket. He shouldn't be surprised by the coverage. The press had been largely critical of him the entire trial, too close-minded—and frightened—to believe the evidence he'd put before them.

We'll see who has the last laugh, assholes, he thought, already anticipating his second sleep experiment, which he'd live stream to the masses. *Let them see with their own eyes what we are and what we become when sleep is banished and the gates of hell are thrown wide open.*

Wallis was so engrossed in his thoughts he didn't realize they'd arrived at the Clock Tower Building until a mob of reporters and journalists surrounded the SUV, cameras and microphones at the ready.

"Get me as close to the front door as possible," he grunted.

"Yes, sir," the driver said.

Inching through the excited crowd, the SUV eventually stopped directly before the building's front entrance. As soon as Dr. Wallis stepped out of the vehicle, microphones were shoved in his face, everyone shouting questions over everyone else.

Ignoring the bedlam, he quickly entered the building, closing the glass door securely behind him so none of the jackasses could follow him inside.

Straightening his blazer and smoothing his tie, he studied himself in the annualized steel elevator doors, deciding he looked damned good.

When the doors opened, he took the cab to the top floor

and let himself into his penthouse apartment. The first thing he did was put CNN on the large TV in the living room. With the news anchor talking about Wallis and the Sleep Experiment in the background, he went to the bar and made a Dark 'n' Stormy. He watched a bit of the coverage, but when the white-haired nerd continued to belittle his life's work, he decided to go to the wraparound deck for a cigarette.

He froze when he noticed the glass in the door to the deck had been broken.

"That was me," a male voice said from behind him.

Dr. Wallis spun around as a man emerged from the clock tower room. With slicked-back black hair and a haggard face, he looked like someone who had spent more than his fair share of time in smoky bars. He wore blue jeans and a black leather jacket over a denim shirt a slightly lighter shade than his pants. He was thin yet clearly not weak as cords of muscle stood out like knotted ropes in his neck.

"Who the fuck are you?" Wallis demanded, his voice brash and unafraid even as his pulse spiked and his insides hollowed. Nobody was okay with finding a stranger in their home—let alone an armed stranger, as the man gripped a baseball bat in his right hand.

"Bill," the man said. "I'm Bill."

"What are you doing in my house, Bill?"

"I'm here to kill you, Roy."

Wallis' throat tightened to the size of a straw. He swallowed hard. "Why would you want to do that?"

"Let me introduce myself properly, Roy. I'm Bill *Foxley*."

Dr. Wallis' eyes widened, and that hollow feeling inside him intensified tenfold.

"Hey look," he said, holding up his hands, "I didn't kill Brook. That was Chad Carter—"

"I don't care if it was you who broke my sister's neck, or that psycho patient of yours. The fact is she's dead, and she wouldn't be if it wasn't for you and your fucked-up experiment—"

Wallis threw his Dark 'n' Stormy at Bill and bolted toward

the front door. He heard the man coming after him, knew he wouldn't get the door open before the baseball bat hit a home run with the back of his head, so he whirled about midstride.

Deflecting a blow from the bat with his forearms, Wallis threw a punch, striking Bill in the jaw, staggering him. Even so, he knew he was outmatched unless he found a weapon. He turned, intending to make a break for the first level of the clock tower, where he could grab a pool cue—but came face to face with a second assailant.

He immediately knew the person was Bill Foxley's brother—the resemblance was reflected in their smarmy faces and their wiry physiologies—but even as he processed this, the man was swinging a bat.

The polished wood cracked Dr. Wallis squarely on the forehead. Pain exploded behind his eyes in fireworks of chaotic light. He was unconscious before he hit the floor.

ΔΔΔ

Dr. Wallis came around to trumpets of pain blasting from ear to ear. Despite the white haze that engulfed his thoughts and vision, he realized he was seated in a chair, his hands secured with rope behind his back.

Blinking salty tears from his eyes, he saw Bill pacing before him in the kitchen, a glass of whiskey in his hand.

Bill noticed him rousing and said, "About fucking time."

"I have money," Dr. Wallis mumbled, his thoughts still muddled but quickened with fear. "Look around. I have a lot of money. How much do you want?"

"Money?" Bill laughed mirthlessly. "I don't want your money, hotshot. I want my sister back. But since I can't have that, I want revenge."

And Wallis knew Bill could not be bought; the man was going to murder him.

"Please!" he said, straining violently at his restraints. "Brook's death wasn't my fault. I was just acquitted of—"

Arms slipped around his head from behind.

The second brother.

Bill nodded slowly, and before Dr. Wallis could protest, his head snapped violently to the left. He slumped forward in the chair, the rope around his wrists preventing him from falling forward onto his face. His breathing came in sharp, ragged gasps. He knew his upper cervical spine had been fractured, and he would die shortly from asphyxiation, just as Brook had died on the asphalt of the breezeway. Even as this morbid irony registered, he thought with indignant fury, YOU CAN'T DO THIS TO ME! I'M DOCTOR ROY WALLIS! *I'M FAMOUS NOW!*

The last thing the famous Dr. Roy Wallis heard in his life was Brook's brother telling him in a sanctimonious voice, "Good night, doctor. Sleep tight."

ABOUT THE AUTHOR

Jeremy Bates

USA TODAY and #1 AMAZON bestselling author Jeremy Bates has published more than twenty novels and novellas. They have sold more than one million copies, been translated into several languages, and been optioned for film and TV by major studios. Midwest Book Review compares his work to "Stephen King, Joe Lansdale, and other masters of the art." He has won both an Australian Shadows Award and a Canadian Arthur Ellis Award. He was also a finalist in the Goodreads Choice Awards, the only major book awards decided by readers.